THE BLUE
HOUR

ALSO BY PAULA HAWKINS

The Girl on the Train
Into the Water
A Slow Fire Burning

PAULA HAWKINS

A Novel

THE BLUE HOUR

MARINER BOOKS

New York Boston

FIRST EDITION

Designed by Leah Carlson-Stanisic
Art by korkeng/Shutterstock, Inc.

Library of Congress Cataloging-in-Publication Data has been applied for.

ISBN 978-0-06-339652-4

24 25 26 27 28 LBC 5 4 3 2 1

For Mum and Dad, with love

And death shall have no dominion.
Dead men naked they shall be one
With the man in the wind and the west moon;
When their bones are picked clean and the clean bones gone,
They shall have stars at elbow and foot;
Though they go mad they shall be sane,
Though they sink through the sea they shall rise again;
Though lovers be lost love shall not;
And death shall have no dominion.

DYLAN THOMAS

Life is short, the art long.

HIPPOCRATES

The moon woke me, bright and close. It shed such a strange light over the sea, a dark kind of daylight, like looking at the negative of a photograph. I couldn't go back to sleep. I haven't been able to work for weeks, so I went down to the beach. I was barefoot and the sand was cold under my feet; it made me want to run.

There was a wind. Strangely warm, it made the sands shift, and the clouds passing over the moon threw shadows to chase me. I kept thinking of the song Grace taught me, the one about the wolves digging the newly dead from the sod, strewing their poor bones over the earth.

Lately, I've been feeling a bit savage myself.

I ran and ran until I had my feet in the water, and when I turned, I looked back at the island, at the house, at my bedroom window with the light still on, and I saw something move. The curtain, probably, but I felt chilled through. I watched and waited, willing him to appear again, but there was nothing, nothing and no one, only suddenly the water lapping at my calves, at my knees.

The sands weren't shifting any longer, I couldn't see the sand at all, everything was underwater, and I had so far to go. I tried to wade, as fast as I could, but the wind was against me and the tide was like a river. I kept stumbling, falling to my knees; the cold felt like a slap, like being hit, over and over.

I don't think I've ever felt terror like it.

By the time I got back to the steps I was so exhausted I could barely move. I lay there, shivering so violently it felt as though I were convulsing. Eventually I managed to get up, to climb to the house. I showered and dressed and went up to the studio and started to paint.

Division II (circa 2005)

Vanessa Chapman

Ceramic, urushi lacquer, gold leaf, gold filament, artiodactyl rib, wood, and glass

On loan from the Fairburn Foundation.

One of just seven sculptures Chapman made combining ceramic pieces with found objects, Division II *is a deceptively simple spatial device: a group of objects are arranged in relation to each other, suspended by wires, enclosed in a glass box.*

In presenting these objects in this way, Chapman poses questions about inclusion and exclusion, about what we hide and what we reveal, where we are generous and where we are withholding, about what we make and what we leave behind.

From: bjefferies@gmail.com
To: info@tatemodern.co.uk
Subject: Chapman—Sculpture and Nature exhibition

Dear Sir/Madam,

I very much enjoyed my visit to Tate Modern this weekend, in particular the *Sculpture and Nature* exhibition, which contained some wonderful pieces. I did, however, spot an error on the exhibit label of Vanessa Chapman's 2005 work, *Division II*, which listed artiodactyl rib among the materials. As a forensic anthropologist of many years' standing, I can assure you that the rib in the piece is not artiodactyl; it is in fact human.

I suspect that it is quite possible that Ms. Chapman herself made the error: to the untrained eye, the rib of a deer looks very similar to a human one.

I thought perhaps you ought to be made aware.

Yours sincerely,
Benjamin Jefferies

ONE

In the chastening chill of a dazzling October morning, James Becker stands on a footbridge, hip hitched against the handrail, rolling a cigarette. Beneath him, the stream runs black and slow, the water close to freezing, oozing like treacle over rusty orange stone. This is the midpoint of his daily commute, which takes a full twelve minutes from the Gamekeeper's Lodge, where he lives, to Fairburn House, where he works. Fifteen minutes if he stops for a smoke.

Coat collar up, glancing quickly over one shoulder, he might appear furtive to an outsider, though he's no need to be. He belongs here, astonishing as that may be; even he can barely credit it. How can he— fatherless bastard of a supermarket checkout girl, state-school boy in a cheap suit—be living and working here, at Fairburn, among the blue bloods? He doesn't *fit*. And yet somehow, through hard work and dumb luck and only a minor bit of treachery, here he is.

He lights his cigarette and checks over his shoulder one more time, looking back at the lodge, warm light spilling from the kitchen window, turning the beech hedge golden. No one is watching him— Helena will still be in bed, pillow clamped between her knees—no one will see him breaking the promise he made to quit. He *has* cut down—to just three a day now—and by the time the water freezes, he thinks, he'll pack them in altogether.

Leaning back on the rail, he draws hard on his cigarette, looking up at the hills to the north, their peaks already dusted with snow. Somewhere between here and there a siren wails; Becker thinks he glimpses a flash of blue light on the road, an ambulance or a police car. His blood rushes and his head swims with nicotine; in his stomach he feels the faint but undeniable tug of fear. Smoking quickly, as though it might do less damage that way, he flicks the dog end over the rail and into the water. He crosses the bridge and crunches his way across the frosted lawn toward the house.

THE LANDLINE IN his office is ringing when he opens the door.

"'Lo?" Becker jams the handset between his shoulder and chin, turns on his computer, and pivots, reaching across to flick the switch on the coffee maker on the side table.

There's a pause before a clear, clipped voice says, "Good morning. Am I speaking with James Becker?"

"You are." Becker types in his password, shrugs off his coat.

"Right, well." Another pause. "This is Goodwin, Tate Modern."

The phone slips from Becker's shoulder; he catches it and presses it to his ear once more. "Sorry, who?"

The man on the other end of the phone exhales audibly. "Will Goodwin," he says, his cut-glass vowels exaggerated by enunciation. "From Tate Modern in London. I'm calling because we have a problem with one of the pieces on loan from Fairburn."

Becker stands to attention, his fist tightening around the handset. "Oh, *Christ*, you haven't damaged it, have you?"

"No, Mr. Becker." Goodwin's tone drips restraint. "We have taken *perfectly good* care of all three of Fairburn's pieces. However, we have had cause to withdraw one of the sculptures, *Division II*, from the exhibition."

Becker frowns, sitting down. "What do you mean?"

"According to an email we received from a very distinguished forensic anthropologist who visited our exhibition this weekend, *Division II* includes a human bone."

Becker's burst of laughter is met with bottomless silence. "I'm sorry," Becker says, still chuckling, "but that is just—"

"Well might you apologize!" Goodwin sounds murderous. "I'm afraid I do not share your amusement. Thanks entirely to your curatorial incompetence, in my very first exhibition as director and the museum's very first post-pandemic show, we find ourselves in the position of having inadvertently displayed human remains. Do you have any idea how damaging this could be for us as an institution? It's this sort of thing that gets people *canceled*."

When finally Becker gets off the phone he stares at the computer screen in front of him, waiting for Goodwin to forward him the email. This complaint—if you can call it that—is obvious nonsense. A joke, perhaps? Or possibly a genuine mistake?

The message appears at the top of his inbox, and Becker clicks. He reads the message twice, Googles its sender (a well-respected academic at a major British university—an unlikely joker), and then clicks on ArtPro, Fairburn's cataloging software, to search for the piece in question. There it is. *Division II*, circa 2005, by Vanessa Chapman. Color photographs, taken by Becker himself, illustrate the listing. Ceramic, wood, and bone, suspended by filament, float around each other in a glass case fashioned by Chapman herself. The ceramic and bone are identical twins: fragile spindles of pure white, fractured at their centers and bonded together with lacquer and gold.

The first time he saw it, he thought it must have been sent by mistake. Sculpture? Vanessa Chapman wasn't a sculptor; she was a painter, a ceramicist. But there it was, beautiful and strange, a delicate enigma, the perfect puzzle. No explanatory note, only the briefest mention in a notebook, where Chapman talked about the difficulties she'd had putting together its *skin*, the glass box encasing the other components. Indubitably hers then, and now his. His to research, to catalog, to describe and display, to introduce to the world. It was shown, briefly, at Fairburn House and since then has been viewed by thousands of people—tens of thousands!—on loan at galleries in Berlin and Paris and, most recently, London.

A human bone! It's *absurd*. Pushing his chair back from his desk, Becker gets to his feet, turning to face the window.

His office is in the public wing of the house, looking out over the east quad. At the center of a lawn as neat and green as baize stands a

Hepworth bronze, its curves burnished by morning light, the sloping convex walls of the hollow at its heart shimmering green. Through that oval space, Becker spies Sebastian striding quickly across the grass, his phone pressed to his ear.

Sebastian Lennox is the heir to Fairburn—once his mother shuffles off, Sebastian will own this house, the lodge Becker lives in, the quad, the Hepworth, and the fields beyond. He is also director of the foundation, so not only Becker's landlord but his boss, too.

(And his friend. Don't forget that.)

Becker watches as Sebastian skirts the bronze, his smile a little *too* wide, his laugh audible even at this distance. Becker turns slightly, and the movement catches Sebastian's eye; he squints, raising one hand in salute, and spreads his fingers wide, indicating *five*. Five minutes. Becker steps away from the window and sits back down at his desk.

Ten, fifteen minutes later, he hears Sebastian's footsteps in the hall, and a moment after that Sebastian bounds into the office, a golden retriever in human form.

"You're not going to *believe* the call I just had," he says, pushing a hank of blond fringe from his eyes.

"It wasn't from Will Goodwin, was it?"

"God, yes!" Sebastian laughs, collapsing into the armchair in the corner of Becker's office. "Wetting himself about getting canceled. He called you, too, then?"

Becker nods. "They're withdrawing the piece from the exhibition," he says. "It's . . . it's a total overreaction—"

"Is it?"

Becker spreads his palms wide. "Of course it is! It has to be. The piece has been viewed by God knows how many people, including experts. If the bone were human, I think someone would have spotted it by now."

Sebastian nods, his mouth turning down at the corners.

"You're *disappointed*?" Becker asks, incredulous.

Sebastian shrugs. "It might have escaped your notice, Beck, but the great British public haven't exactly been beating down our doors since we reopened . . . I thought maybe the suggestion of a mystery, a whiff of scandal . . ."

"Scandal? Oh, I like the sound of that." The two men turn to see Helena standing in the doorway. She is clad from her chin to her ankles in black cashmere, a ribbed dress that hugs her neat bump. Wisps of chestnut hair have escaped her ponytail, and there are bright spots of color across her cheekbones. She's slightly out of breath.

"Hels!" Sebastian leaps to his feet, embracing her, kissing her gently on both cheeks. "Radiant one. Did you walk over? Come in, sit!"

Helena allows herself to be guided to the armchair Sebastian has just vacated. "I fancied a little walk," she says, smiling at Becker, who's regarding her quizzically. "It's so beautiful out, what I'd really love is to go for a ride, but"—she wafts a hand in the air, preempting Becker's objections—"I'm obviously not going to do *that*. So tell me, what's all this about a scandal?"

She listens attentively as Becker explains, interrupting when he gets to the punch line. "But that piece was on display at the Berlinische Galerie! It was in the *Twenty-One* show at the Musée d'Art Moderne in Paris!"

Becker nods. "That's exactly what I said."

"So . . . what are you going to do?"

Sebastian perches on the edge of Becker's desk. "No idea," he says. "To be honest, I'm not entirely sure I see what the fuss is about. Say the bone *is* human. It's not likely she robbed a grave, is it? Does it *really* matter?"

Becker bites the inside of his cheek. "You can't just display human remains, Seb."

"The British Museum is full of them!"

"Well, yes." A smile breaks across Becker's face. "But I think this is a bit different."

Sebastian turns to him and scowls. "Well, Goodwin agrees. He's having kittens; he wants to send the piece to a private lab for testing, on the QT, you know—"

"Absolutely *not*!" Becker leaps to his feet, jolting the desk as he does so, knocking coffee onto its fine green leather surface. Sebastian and Helena watch as he frantically mops up the spill with a handful of tissues. "To test the bone, they have to break the glass case and the case is part of the piece. She made it herself. If you break the glass you . . . well, I should think you invalidate the insurance at the very least, but more than that you damage the work. They're not sending it off to some . . . *random laboratory* with no knowledge of its history and no expertise in this area."

"OK," Sebastian says, shrugging extravagantly. "Well. What, then?"

"We could start by asking someone else, some other expert, perhaps even a couple of experts, to take a look at it. Just a *look*, through the glass. And while that's going on, we could talk to our insurers, explain the situation, explain that there might be need for . . ." He doesn't want to say *testing*, doesn't want to concede that point. "For further *investigation* somewhere down the line."

"And in the meantime," Helena says, crossing and uncrossing her legs, "you could go and talk to Grace Haswell."

"No," Becker says, stifling a thrill of excitement, "I can't. I don't want to leave you . . ."

"In my enfeebled condition?" Helena laughs. "Yes, you can. Come on, Beck, you've been dying to get out to Eris; you talked of nothing else during lockdown. And now here's the perfect opportunity. The perfect excuse."

"I suppose," Becker says carefully, "I could leave early, nip up, and get back in a day . . ."

He glances at Sebastian, who shrugs. "I don't mind. Go if you think it'll be helpful. Not sure how the Wicked Witch of Eris Island is going to help with this, though? Unless you think she'll know something? Perhaps the bone's the last remains of one of the children she's lured to her gingerbread house?" Sebastian laughs at his own joke. Helena winks at Becker. *Idiot.* "No, it's a good idea. It is. You could kill two birds with one stone—clear up this bone business and let her know in person that we're sick of her foot-dragging. It's time she handed over Chapman's papers, along with anything else that belongs to us. You can remind her that the artistic estate was left to Fairburn and that she doesn't get to decide what to give us and what to withhold—"

"Well, technically," Becker cuts in, leaning back in his chair, "she does. She's the executor."

"Don't try to be fucking clever." Sebastian's playfulness evaporates like spit on a hot plate. Becker does his best not to flinch. Helena looks down at the carpet. "She's been holding things back, hasn't she? Papers, letters, and quite possibly some works of art. It belongs to us. *All of it.* Every canvas, every sketch, every porcelain bowl she threw on her wheel, every fucking pebble she picked up on the beach and arranged *just so.* It's ours. Anything related to the artistic estate is ours."

Becker bites his tongue. He is *desperate* to get his hands on Chapman's papers; a couple of notebooks found their way to Fairburn along with the main consignments of art, but there is a great deal more material that no one has ever seen. Becker knows from interviews that she kept process journals, that she corresponded with other artists about her work—if and when Grace hands these over, he will be the first to read them. He will have the power to shape how the world sees Vanessa Chapman, how it sees her work, how that work is valued. The thought of it is enough to make him lightheaded.

But Becker is cautious by nature, and kind, too. If there is a way of accessing those papers without threatening and bullying Chapman's executor—and dear friend—he would rather take that route.

"I'm not *trying to be clever*," he says eventually. "You know as well as I do that it has not yet been determined what constitutes artistic estate and what makes up the rest—"

"Boys." Helena gets to her feet, waving away Sebastian's offer of help. "This is all fascinating, but I think you might be missing the bigger picture. Say this bone does turn out to be human—then what? What are you going to do? How are you going to play this?"

"*Play?*" Becker repeats.

"Beck, Fairburn could end up on the front page of every newspaper in the country, on *The One Show*, on . . ."

Sebastian's face has lit up, but Becker is skeptical. "I'm not sure it's *that* much of a big deal, Hels," he says. "It'll be an oddity, sure, but—"

"Beck." Helena smiles at him, shakes her head. "Sweetheart, be serious. You don't think the press might be interested in the fact that a *human bone* has been found to form part of a sculpture made by the late, great, reclusive, enigmatic Vanessa Chapman? The same Vanessa Chapman whose notoriously unfaithful husband went missing twenty years ago? His body never found?"

TWO

Sometimes when he looks at his wife, Becker's heart feels too full for his chest, so brimming with blood that it aches. He has everything his heart desires, and that terrifies him, because it means (it must mean, surely) that he has everything to lose. This is why he's so anxious these days, so high-strung. He's been too lucky, he knows. He doesn't deserve all this.

Helena has just about bypassed the bronze when she comes to an abrupt halt, turning her head to the left, raising her hand to shield her eyes from the sun. Something has caught her attention. Into this tableau sprint a pair of liver-and-white pointers, heralding the arrival of Lady Emmeline Lennox, brisk and determined, her carapace of silver hair turned platinum by the sun. Helena turns her body so that she is facing the older woman, and from Becker's standpoint the silhouette of his wife's belly is echoed by Emmeline's pronounced dowager's hump.

He cannot hear what they are saying, of course, nor can he see clearly the expressions on their faces, but there is no mistaking the viciousness with which Emmeline takes hold of Helena's wrist, wrenching her unnaturally close. Becker raps sharply on the window: both women turn their heads in his direction. Hesitantly, Helena raises her free hand. Emmeline drops her other wrist and turns away.

"Evil hag," Becker mutters. He glances over his shoulder to ensure no one has heard. That there is no love lost between himself and Sebastian's mother is no secret, but it wouldn't do to be caught badmouthing her. He considers running after Helena, to ask what's been said, to make sure she's all right, but he knows she won't thank him for it. She can't bear to be fussed over. And in any case, his phone is ringing again.

While he listens to a deliveryman confirm details of a consignment of two acquisitions Sebastian has made for the foundation without so much as consulting him, Becker searches the internet, not for the first time, for articles about Vanessa Chapman's husband, Julian Chapman.

No one's had much to say about him for quite some time. The most recent substantial piece Becker can find was published in *Tatler* way back in 2009, a profile of Chapman's younger sister, Isobel, the interview ostensibly granted with the aim of "putting Julian back in the public eye," although Becker can't help but notice that quite a bit of the article is taken up with the launch of Isobel's interior design business. Still, there's plenty of Julian in the first few paragraphs.

Talk to people about Julian Chapman and you'll find the word *devil* crops up a lot. He was a handsome devil, he had a devil-may-care approach to life, he was in thrall to the devil on his shoulder. When I put this to Isobel Birch, she laughs. "Oh, that sounds about right," she says. "He could certainly be wicked." She pauses a moment. "But he was a devil who was loved. Everyone adored him."

The grand piano in Birch's immaculately restored Cotswolds pile is crowded with framed photographs, many of which feature Birch's beloved big brother: there he is, kayaking off the coast of Cornwall, here he's sharp-suited and Hollywood-handsome at Royal Ascot; in another he's deeply tanned and laughing on horseback against a glorious savannah sunset.

Kenya, Isobel tells me. "Julian loved Africa. It appealed to his wild side. He and Celia [Gray, his lover] were making plans to move there, they'd found a plot where they wanted to build a house, they were so excited." Birch blinks away tears. "And then, in the space of less than a year, they were both gone."

Gray was killed in a car accident in France on New Year's Eve in 2001. Six months later, Chapman drove to the Scottish island of Eris to visit his estranged wife, the artist Vanessa Chapman. He never returned from the trip. Neither he nor his red Duetto Spider 1600 were ever found.

Seven years have passed since that fateful trip, sufficient time for Julian to be "presumed dead." But Isobel has not lost hope. "I still get messages from people who say they've seen him; I've traveled all over the world—to France and Bulgaria and South Africa and Argentina—to follow up on leads." She shakes her head sadly. "I know it's not likely. He loved us, and though he could be wicked, he wasn't cruel. But I can't give up hope. Until I have a body to bury, I won't give up hope."

When I ask about what she believes might have happened to Julian, Birch's expression darkens. "We have no clear picture of his last movements. Vanessa claimed not to know anything— she supposedly wasn't on the island when Julian left." Supposedly? Isobel shakes her head. "I can't say anything more. What I do know is this: Vanessa never once called or wrote to find out how we—Julian's family—were feeling in the weeks after he went missing. She didn't seem to care about where he was." When I suggest that perhaps Vanessa was in shock or grieving herself, she gives me a rueful smile. "Vanessa was never emotionally expressive. I don't know what she felt, but I'd be surprised if it was grief. If anything, I think she was relieved to be rid of him."

In the paragraphs that follow, the journalist speaks to various friends of Julian's about him and about Vanessa. These unnamed sources talk about Julian's devilish sense of humor, his magnetism, his joie de vivre. They offer up anecdotes about running the bulls, climbing Ben Nevis, jumping off Magdalen Bridge one May morning. Vanessa is background noise: the beautiful wife. Talented, serious-minded, ambitious.

When the journalist raises Julian's financial difficulties and (frequent) infidelities, his sister is dismissive.

"I said he could be wicked, didn't I? He wasn't perfect. But he was the ultimate free spirit—he was funny and outrageous and never, ever boring. Everyone loved Julian. Everyone wanted to be around him." She pauses for a moment and then smiles, tears shining in her huge brown eyes. "Sorry, that's not quite right—not everyone. Everyone except her."

Vanessa Chapman's diary

[undated]

My black painting disturbs me. I found yesterday that I couldn't work with it there in front of me, leaning against the studio wall. I moved it down to the priest hole, but even then it was like I could feel its presence, so I left the house to get away from it, but that still didn't seem like enough, so I left the island, too.

I drove over to the mainland and called Julian from the box in the car park (landline at home out again <u>for two weeks</u> and I keep forgetting to get someone to fix it). I told him he must not come. I told him I <u>do not want</u> him here.

Afterward I went to the pub at the other end of the village. I sat by myself in the corner. About ten minutes after I got there, a man came to talk to me—an American, looking for gravestones. Something to do with his ancestors. He offered to buy me a drink; I knew that if I accepted I would miss the tide. I told him I was a married schoolteacher from Edinburgh and that I'd had a row with my husband.

The sex was vanilla but still very welcome.

———

This freedom is intoxicating
I eat when I please
work when I please
come and go when I please.
I answer to no one, only the tide.

THREE

It stirs her blood, the pull of the tide; it wakes her in the dead of night. All the years on Eris Island—more than twenty of them now—have made Grace tidal. A lunatic. An actual lunatic! Governed by the moon. She no longer sleeps when the tide is out; she only rests when the sea separates her from the land.

When she knows no one can sneak up on her.

Eris Island is not in fact an island. Like Grace, Eris is tidal. An almost-island, fused to the mainland by a slender spit of land roughly a mile in length. For twelve hours of the day, in two six-hour chunks, this causeway is passable on foot or by vehicle. When the tide comes in, Eris is unreachable. If, like today, low tide is at 6:30 in the morning, then the causeway is safely traversable from around 3:30 until 9:30.

In the dead of night, then, Grace wakes.

She lights a fire in the wood burner in the kitchen and puts the coffeepot on the Aga. She stands at the stove making porridge, stirring the oats gently, adding a pinch of salt, a slug of cream to finish. Breakfast is taken at the kitchen window; she can't see the sea, but she can hear it: a shiftless beast dragging its claws across the sand as it draws back from the coast.

Afterward, she sits at the kitchen table with her laptop. Rereading the email that arrived yesterday afternoon, she feels a flutter of panic behind her ribs, a nag of unease like the Sunday-evening dread of homework left unfinished. Five years Vanessa has been gone, five long years and still her affairs are not settled, still Grace is harangued, in letters and emails, by men she has never met. It's her own fault, and that doesn't make the feeling any better. Makes it worse, in fact. Five years! Five years of grief, of work. Of procrastination. Of hiding. She gets abruptly to her feet, the scrape of her chair on the tiles jarringly loud. It seems she can hide no longer.

Later, showered and dressed in warm clothing, she returns to the kitchen to fetch her spectacles. The day is yet struggling to dawn, a concrete sky pressing on the hills across the channel. Grace empties the coffeepot into a flask, grabs her mac, and picks up the studio key from the rack in the hall, weighing it briefly in her hand before slipping it into her pocket.

She steps out of the front door and pulls it closed behind her, inhaling a lungful of cold, salty air, looking over to her right, where the island falls away into the bay. A light is on in the cottage at the harbor. Marguerite is up. Another lunatic.

Grace turns to her left and walks away from the sea, up the path that leads to the studio and, if she chose to follow it, beyond: to the wood, to Eris Rock, to the Irish Sea.

Halfway up the hill, she hesitates. From the front door to the studio is a few hundred feet, but it might as well be a thousand miles; it has been more than a year since she last unlocked its door. She has found every excuse—work, exhaustion, her broken heart—to put off this reckoning. But the emails and the phone calls and the threats are not going to go away. She needs to face this, because what is the alternative? To hand over the key in her pocket and be done with it? To let some stranger sift through Vanessa's papers, to let some outsider decide which parts of their lives should remain private and which parts should be laid bare for all to see?

She takes a deep breath.

Up she goes.

The key turns surprisingly easily, and the huge metal door rolls back with a groan, releasing a gust of cold clay and dust, paint and turpentine. Grace stands in the doorway, her eye fixed on the three-legged stool in front of the potter's wheel. For a moment she finds herself unable to move, assailed by a memory of Vanessa sitting there, her foot on the flywheel, oblivious to the wind and the weather, oblivious to Grace, to the whole world but the clay moving beneath her fingertips.

Grace blinks Vanessa away, and the rest of the studio comes into focus: the workbench in front of the window, stacked with boxes; the kiln at the back of the room; the trestle in its center, thick with dust and strewn with papers and notebooks and yet more boxes. The shelves toward the back of the room are loaded with pots and brushes stiff with paint, palette knives, nubs of hardened clay, a perfect sphere of rose quartz, and birds' skulls, a kittiwake and a curlew with a long, curved beak, like a plague mask. There are clay harps and cutters, needles and rusted pliers, a whittling knife and a set of beautiful beech-handled mason's hammers in various sizes, lined up like Matryoshka dolls.

The hammers were a gift, Grace thinks. From Douglas, perhaps, or one of her other men. They were rarely used, in any case. Vanessa loved the *idea* of stone carving, but she grew frustrated with the practice. Too hard, too loud, too violent. She returned, as she always did after a period of infidelity, to the materials she loved, the ones she mastered: clay, paint.

Vanessa's canvases are long gone, her pots and vases, too. Three years ago, once probate had finally been granted, Grace had the artworks shipped south to Fairburn, the foundation that was named in Vanessa's will as the benefactor of her artistic estate.

Grace, who is the executor of Vanessa's will and her only other heir, had every intention of sorting through her papers—her letters and notebooks and photographs—before sending on anything she deemed part of the artistic estate, but there was just so much of it, and the Fairburn people proved impatient, demanding everything and all at once. Grace dug her heels in. Relations quickly deteriorated. It was suggested that Grace wasn't up to the job of executor. Accusations were flung about, claims that there were pieces missing, that Grace was holding things back, going against Vanessa's wishes. Grace used what power she had: she stopped engaging, let the phone go to voicemail, ignored their emails. For a while, everything went quiet.

Lately, though, it's been getting noisy again, with two solicitors' letters arriving last month—one demanding a comprehensive catalog of

Vanessa's papers and the other demanding a catalog of her ceramics—
and then, yesterday, an email. Which came not from a lawyer but from
a Mr. Becker, the curator at Fairburn. Grace has become accustomed
to deleting all email correspondence on the subject, but this message
stood out, its tone rather different from the legalistic belligerence
she's gotten used to from those people. *There is a matter of some urgency
I would like to discuss with you*, Mr. Becker wrote. *Please, do contact
me*— There was something imploring about the tone; it was almost
touching.

And so, here she is—in the studio. She walks around the room one
more time; she runs her fingers through the dust on the trestle table,
picks up a small, sharp scoring tool, weighs in one hand the largest of
the mason's hammers, in the other the featherlight kittiwake skull.

She picks up the nearest box of papers and starts down toward the
house.

Vanessa Chapman's diary

Sweltering.

The Whitewall exhibition closed on Saturday—unqualified success from a commercial point of view—every piece sold. One line in <u>Modern Painting</u>'s What's On roundup—"Chapman just about manages to stay on the right side of cliché."

Apparently I have beauty but no substance.

After the show closed we went to Izzy's, ostensibly for dinner, though no food ever materialized. Awful people—Bullingdon bores, dullards who come from money and who look down on me because I don't—all talking incessantly about holidays and property prices. The energy it takes to disguise my contempt could power a city.

All the while, Julian kept looking at me and smiling and telling me how proud he was. He's already spending the money.

FOUR

Becker is listening to the radio in the car; they're talking about Daphne du Maurier.

Three people, a presenter and two panelists, one of whom is a woman and the other a man, are discussing a *lurid* new biography of the writer that hints at an *inappropriate* relationship with her father.

An *abusive* relationship, the woman says.

An *incestuous* one, the man says. We don't know for certain there was coercion.

This relationship is alleged to have happened before du Maurier reached the age of sixteen, so *necessarily* it was abusive, the woman replies hotly. Children cannot consent.

Indeed, the presenter says. Why is it, he rushes on, trying to move the discussion to safer ground, that we are so interested in the private lives of artists, do you think? People seem to cleave to this idea that what a writer puts on the page must be drawn from experience, so the suggestion here, then, is that this . . . *relationship*, this situation between du Maurier and her father, somehow informed her books, most notably *Rebecca*.

This particularly happens with female writers, the woman says. Critics seem incapable of attributing to a woman a capacity for invention, they—

Oh come on, the man says. Not everything is about sexism, Marjorie.

Not *everything*, no, I didn't say everything, and if you'd let me finish my sentence you—

Becker turns the radio off.

The road has been climbing for a while; he has reached the top of the pass. He rounds one final bend and before him unfurls a valley painted in shades of green and bronze and copper, steep-sided. To his left the land falls away, down to flashes of steel where water cuts through the bracken. On the right there is a deer fence, and on three fence posts in a row sit crows, onyx and menacing, watching him pass.

"The Birds," he thinks, might have come out of a landscape like this. Not the film, warmed up by Northern California light and the luminous beauty of Tippi Hedren, but the original du Maurier story, bleak and terrifying and tragic. A prickle inches up his spine. He opens and closes his hands a few times, trying to relax his grip on the steering wheel.

He keeps thinking about that scene with Emmeline, out in the garden. Helena wouldn't talk to him about it. *Nothing*, she said, *it was nothing*. It didn't look like nothing, Becker said, and Helena shook her head and smiled and said, OK, well, it's the same old thing. "Just forget about it," she said. "I have. She's old, she's grieving, she's not all that well. She's nothing to worry about."

He keeps replaying that conversation in the office, too—Sebastian slapping him down—*Don't try to be fucking clever.* Sebastian! That prep school, Eton and Oxford *dimwit* treating him like an idiot! Sebastian, who knows nothing about anything, who has the attention span of a gnat, who chases after Hirsts and Banksys and whatever else happens to be fashionable and expensive. Who is tall and handsome and rich. Who had Helena first.

Becker despises himself for letting the thought cross his mind; he despises himself for badmouthing Sebastian, even if it is just in his imagination. Sebastian has been good to him—very good, under the circumstances.

He's unnerved, that's all it is; he doesn't like leaving Helena alone. Not because he's jealous, not because he doesn't trust her. He's just anxious, he can't help himself. He's been anxious ever since she told him she was pregnant, and she's seven months gone now.

It doesn't help that she's so disarmingly relaxed. She drinks wine (*I'm half-French, you know*) and dances at parties in four-inch heels; the other day he caught her loading a slab of blue cheese onto a cracker and almost had to slap it out of her hand. Helena has not read a single book about pregnancy; she has not watched any YouTube videos featuring women in labor. She has no birthing plan.

He, on the other hand, has driven from their house on the estate to the nearest hospital half a dozen times. He has experimented with different routes, he has even investigated the *next* closest hospital, a further sixty miles south. Just in case. "In case of what?" Helena asked when he told her. "In case the hospital is *closed*?"

He's tense because he's worried about her, that's all. And because he isn't sleeping. He can't: she snores now, and radiates heat. He lies at her side, helpless, his skin itching, lovelorn, terrified. What if something goes wrong? What if she changes her mind? What if she realizes this is all a terrible mistake?

What if he gets what he deserves?

Vanessa Chapman's diary

I'm so restless here. The Cotswolds is supposed to be countryside, but nowhere feels wild, everywhere feels like the suburbs, full of Range Rovers driven by fund managers' wives. And the heat has been unrelenting—all the hedgerows are dying and the sky has been stubbornly white for weeks, the meadows are scorched, the earth parched. I long for water, for green and blue and violet.

———

Have not written anything for a week. Just back from Cornwall. Left J behind in Oxfordshire—I hardly ever see him anyway—and stayed ten days. Swam and worked and talked and talked and talked. Frances is making the most amazing ceramic sculptures—sea creatures, glazed in heavenly blues and purples, mysterious and forbidding.

———

Struggling to paint.

———

I yearn for solitude, and yet I am so lonely. How does that work? Lonely when I am alone, lonelier still when Julian is here. We never talk, only fight and fuck.

Latest fight, boringly enough, about Christmas plans—I want to go back to Cornwall, he insists on being with family. Then Courchevel for New Year with Izzy's lot. (There I draw the line—he can go without me.)

Trying to finish final piece for Cube show in London but the sky is so dull and the light so flat—I feel hemmed in by cars and people and hedges.

———

Nothing sold at Cube. Julian says I'm wasting my time.

But! A piece in Art Review that called me one to watch. "Everything the YBAs are, Vanessa Chapman is not." So—old-fashioned? Fair enough, I do not deal in unmade beds. But also: "intense, moving."

That's not so bad, is it?

I haven't painted at all since the beginning of the year, though I have been throwing a little—I found a studio in Oxford that I can use. I go almost every day, even when I am not working—anything to get out of the house.

I will be alone soon—Julian is going to Nairobi next week for some "travel venture" he and Izzy are planning, then they go to Lamu. Celia Gray has rented a house there. Izzy tells me it is "just a fling."

I'm not sure I care. No, I do care. Sometimes I care. Part of me wants him to go and never come back. Part of me wants to lock him in a room and never let him out.

FIVE

At the end of the valley, Becker turns right, driving northwest toward the coast. The speedometer has barely touched sixty when an ambulance shrieks past, blue light flashing, and within a mile the road is blocked. It's a bad one, the young policeman manning the roadblock says with a grimace. Motorcyclist. It's going to be a while. You're probably better off going the long way round.

Becker turns back, racing through the valley, his eyes drawn to the clock on the dash. If he doesn't get to Eris before 10:45 he'll miss the tide, and it's 9:12 now, so that means, hang on, what does that mean? He fiddles with the GPS—*Reroute, reroute, you stupid bloody thing*—his foot heavy on the accelerator. As he takes the final, sharp corner at the head of the valley, he feels the back end of the car start to slide. He slams his foot on the brake, stomach lurching and heart pounding as the vehicle swings wildly across the double white line. In his mind he sees Grant Wood's *Death on the Ridge Road*, the black sedan seeming to cower in terror before the onrushing red lorry, he sees his own body, crushed between seat and wheel; he imagines Helena's voice as she answers the call, wavering before it breaks.

Lightheaded with adrenaline, he drives on, back down to forty miles an hour now, trying to lower his heart rate by focusing on the matter at hand. There's an opportunity here, he needs to seize it, he needs to handle this business with Grace Haswell just right.

He'll start with *Division II*. This disputed rib—that's his way in. He's assuming that Haswell won't know anything—nothing *definitive*, in any case—about the origins of that bone, so he can then ask whether there were preparatory sketches or other notes about the piece, and from there, he can segue neatly to the subject of Vanessa's journals.

He has read a couple—they were sent along with the second shipment of paintings—but knows from interviews that she wrote in
notebooks throughout her working life, so there should be dozens.
Letters, too, and photographs—all manner of invaluable material.
But he's going to have to handle things delicately if he's going to get
anywhere, to undo the damage that was done by Sebastian's father
and his lawyers.

The fact is—the fact no one acknowledges because of the
circumstances—this entire affair has been mishandled. That was partly
understandable—the contents of Chapman's will came as a shock
to everyone in the art world. No one imagined that she would leave
her entire artistic estate to Fairburn, the foundation established by
Sebastian's father, Douglas Lennox, Vanessa's former gallerist and,
for the last part of her life, her bitter enemy.

When the news became public, Douglas crowed. Vanessa Chapman
had seen sense at last! The bequest represented, he claimed in interviews, a posthumous apology. It was an admission of the terrible wrong
she had done him all those years ago; evidence that even after more
than a decade of estrangement, Vanessa had not forgotten him or all
that he had done for her. Their connection, deep and intimate as it was,
had never been broken after all.

It took more than a year for probate to come through, but once it
had, the shipment of pieces to Fairburn began. That was when things
began to go awry. Without providing evidence, Douglas claimed that
paintings were missing. He wrote to Grace Haswell, Vanessa's executor, accusing her of incompetence. Later, he all but accused her of
theft. Lawyers were engaged on both sides.

It was into this mess that Becker arrived. Sebastian's old college pal
and a Vanessa Chapman expert, he was initially under strict instruc-
tions not to meddle in the Haswell affair—it was being handled by the
lawyers. But then suddenly—tragically—Douglas died. Accidentally
shot during a deer cull on the estate.

All bets were off. The lawyers were stood down while Sebastian
and his mother grieved. Sebastian's forthcoming wedding to Helena

Fitzgerald was postponed. The family's business interests were restructured, the Highlands estate sold. Sebastian took over the running of the business. Then the pandemic hit, muddying the waters further, delaying any possibility of direct action.

This new development, however—this thing about the bone used in *Division II*—has presented Becker with an opportunity to take a fresh approach to the situation.

The mistake that Douglas and Sebastian and their lawyers have made all along, Becker believes, has been to treat Grace Haswell as Chapman's executor. She *is*, of course, but she was also Chapman's friend, her companion for almost twenty years, her carer toward the end of her life. There are rumors that they might have been lovers.

For Becker, the opportunity to meet this woman is tantalizing: there can be no one better placed to offer an insight into the real Vanessa Chapman. She is a contact to be cultivated, not ostracized, surely?

Who knows what she might have to give them? What insights she could offer? What stories she has to tell?

Vanessa Chapman's diary

In the post today, I received a clipping—no note, just a clipping—from the property section of *The Times*.

An island for sale. An entire island! Containing a house—small, dilapidated, an old farm, I think, or a fisherman's cottage—plus outbuildings. Two barns. One ruined, probably beyond repair. The other with "potential for conversion." There is an auction at the end of the month.

If I can't have it, I'm not sure my heart will take it.

SIX

Above Eris harbor sits a little row of whitewashed cottages and, in front of them, a small car park into which Becker's Prius gently rolls at 11:23. The pale stone of the causeway is visible beneath a limewash of shallow sea; the water looks to be wading depth, but the noticeboard to the left of his car bonnet warns of dire consequences for the poor fool who tries his luck against an incoming tide.

Becker sits, hunched over the wheel, glowering across the narrow channel to the dark wedge of gray and green that is Eris Island. On its southeastern tip he can make out a splodge of white: Vanessa's house, so close and yet unreachable. The next low tide is at eight o'clock this evening; he will not be able to cross before five. He is tempted to turn around and drive home, but Sebastian will be annoyed and he will feel an idiot. And it's not as though he has nothing to do: he has his laptop—he can work, and he has plenty to read. He'll find somewhere for lunch, go over his notes.

First, though, he decides to stretch his legs. He climbs out of the car, kicking out his limbs to loosen them after the drive. Buffeted by a chilly wind blowing in off the sea, he shrugs on his coat and pockets his phone, heading north through the car park, past the cottages and along a well-trodden coastal path. About a quarter of a mile from the village, the path begins to climb, marking a perilous border between emerald grazing land and a sheer drop into the sea.

The sky up ahead is a soft, washed-out blue, so it is not until Becker turns his face into the wind that he sees the massed ranks of anthracite clouds closing in from the west. He hesitates. Perhaps the storm will pass overhead? He strides on hopefully, but he's not walked more than a hundred feet when the first drops of rain ping, pellet-like, against his shoulders. He turns back, moving as quickly as he can, eyes narrowed and shoulders hunched against the downpour. As soon as he reaches safer ground he starts to run, sprinting back toward the car park, skidding in the mud. As he reaches the row of cottages he slows, ducking his head to the left and wiping the water from his face. In the window of the house at the end of the row he glimpses a face—anguished, pressed against the glass. He starts, stumbles, comes to a sliding halt. When he looks back, there is no one there, just a pot on the sill.

Back in the car, heart pounding, he turns the heat up full blast. He wriggles out of his damp coat and tosses it onto the back seat. Casts about for his phone, which is, of course, still in the pocket of the coat. He twists around to retrieve it and, wiping condensation from his glasses with the hem of his shirt, is relieved to discover a bar or two's worth of signal. Enough to access the articles he's saved to Dropbox, his virtual clippings file of press articles. Profiles of Vanessa, reviews of exhibitions, obituaries, and a few news pieces published once the estate had been settled and the contents of Vanessa's will made public.

The Times

March 4, 2017

RENOWNED ARTIST LEAVES MULTIMILLION-POUND ESTATE TO BITTER ENEMY

Vanessa Chapman, the reclusive artist who died of cancer in October last year, has left her entire artistic estate to a man who hounded her through the courts, it was revealed yesterday.

Chapman's artistic estate, estimated to be worth several million pounds, was bequeathed to the Fairburn Foundation, a charitable trust set up by Douglas Lennox, a philanthropist and art dealer.

Lennox and Chapman were embroiled in an acrimonious legal battle from 2002 until 2004, after Chapman withdrew from her solo show at Lennox's Glasgow Modern Gallery at the eleventh hour, incurring costs to the gallery of tens of thousands of pounds. The dispute was eventually settled out of court. Lennox claimed at the time that Chapman's actions had "come close to ruining [him]" and that the stress of the court case had damaged his health and his marriage.

The reviews date back to the very first exhibitions of her work in the early 1990s, when she was a more traditional landscape painter. The critic at *ArtFuture* magazine praised her exuberant use of color and her expressive brushwork but saw her paintings as nostalgic to the point of futility: "Chapman bravely swims against a sea of conceptualism, raging hopelessly against the dying of the paint."

The more abstract Vanessa's work became, the more the critics warmed to it. *The Independent* wrote of her contribution to the 1995 *Painting Today* exhibition at the Southbank: "Chapman's colour-saturated canvases inhabit an intriguing space between abstraction and figuration and are all the more thrilling for that . . ."

But if the press was beginning to like her work, they did not appear to like *her*. "Where Chapman's paintings are bold," one review stated, "her ceramics are delicate and restrained, as undemonstrative and chilly as the artist herself."

This became a theme: Chapman's work received accolades, and her looks—dark-eyed, dewy-skinned, graceful, slender—were praised effusively, while her character was not. She was described by a series of critics and interviewers as tricky, disagreeable, impatient, sullen, strident, and single-minded.

Rereading these pieces, Becker shifts in his seat, discomforted. He has never been able to reconcile the image of Chapman portrayed in the press with the sensitivity of the artist he loves. He scans the pages for references to her sculpture and ceramics, but little seems to have been written about her interest in media other than painting. He reads on and on, and eventually, lulled by the sound of the waves breaking against the harbor, he drifts off.

HE JERKS AWAKE, his mind grasping at the vestiges of some disturbing dream, to find someone—a child, he thinks at first—banging on the front of the car. This person, wearing a yellow high-vis jacket over an outsize gray sweatshirt with the hood pulled down so far it almost covers their eyes, gesticulates toward a sign across the car park that reads NO CAMPING.

"Do I look like I'm fucking camping?" Becker mutters as he opens the door, clambering out of the car into the mizzle. He beams graciously at the tiny figure. "I'm here to visit Grace Haswell," he says, "over on the island. I'm waiting for the tide to go out. Do you know what time it'll be safe to cross?"

The person's head jerks up and Becker starts: it is the face from the window—a woman, her skin weathered and wizened, her mouth twisted, her lips moving.

"I'm sorry?" Becker calls out after her, but she has turned away, walking toward the direction of the cottages.

After a few paces she stops and looks back at him briefly before turning away once more. As she walks slowly away, he sees that her hands, ungloved and pale at her sides, clutch themselves into fists and release, over and over, as she goes.

A wave hits the harbor wall, making a low, threatening sound, like a muffled explosion. Becker climbs back into the car, remembering as he does that he was in the car in the dream. He was in the car and there was water coming in, pouring in through the fan vents and around the doors; there was a baby in the back seat, and it was screaming.

SEVEN

Someone is coming. Someone new. They're coming across the cause-way, puttering along in a blue car. Grace can tell it's a new person by the way they're driving, slowly and tentatively. Taking their time.

She checks that the front door is locked before returning to her lookout spot at the large kitchen window. With the fraying sleeve of her cardigan she wipes condensation from the glass, but the car has disappeared; it will have reached the near side of the causeway, it will be idling at the bottom of the hill. Its driver will be looking at the chain slung across the track and at the PRIVATE PROPERTY sign dangling from it.

Grace moves from the large window overlooking the sea to the smaller one on the north side of the house. From here, she can monitor the top of the steps leading up from the track. A minute or two passes. Just as she starts to imagine that the person must have turned back, a tall, thin man reaches the top of the stairs. He is pale, with hair the color of damp straw, wearing a dark coat and thick-framed glasses. She starts—for a moment she thinks she recognizes him—but no. Just one of those faces. The man pauses at the top of the steps, catching his breath; he looks up at the house, rain falling on his face. She's not sure, but she thinks she sees him smile.

He doesn't *look* threatening, but Grace knows better than to imagine she can deduce the level of threat from a glance. You cannot infer a man's propensity for violence from how he looks. She has set bones broken by soft hands, stitched cuts inflicted by men with easy smiles and white collars; she's met brutes with angel faces.

She steps away from the window. From the rack on the wall in the living room she fetches the shotgun and carries it to the hall, propping it up against the bench—in full view of anyone standing on the door-step. At the third or fourth knock, she opens the door.

"Mrs. Haswell?" the man says, smiling nervously, holding out a damp hand.

Grace neither returns the smile nor takes his hand. "*Doctor* Haswell," she corrects him.

"Dr. Haswell, I'm sorry. Forgive me for turning up like this, I—"

"What do you want?"

"My name is Becker, James Becker, from the Fairburn Foundation? I've been trying to contact—"

At *Fairburn*, Grace starts to close the door. "I don't have anything more for you," she says, mortified by the tears in her own voice. "You've already taken everything."

Vanessa Chapman's diary

This place! No matter which way I turn, the landscape speaks to me. Look east, to those soft, rounded hills, so comforting, so female! Or up to the wood, green and black and mysterious, or, if you want real terror, climb to the rock and look down at the chaos of the sea. Right now I am captivated by the south, by the islands, by Sheepshead. So unsheep-like! To me, she is a wolf.

EIGHT

Grace Haswell is ugly. Becker is surprised by how ugly she is, and ashamed of the thought even as it occurs to him. She's afraid, too. He has frightened her.

For a minute, perhaps longer, he stands in front of the slammed door, thinking less of the frightened woman cowering behind it than of the humiliation he will feel when he is forced to relate the day's events to Sebastian. Perhaps he should simply lie? It wouldn't be the first time.

He's on the point of turning away when the door flies open, its edge almost catching the side of his head. He lurches back. "Did you not hear me?" Grace Haswell is glaring at him. Her eyes are iced water, her thin lips drawn back from her teeth in a snarl. Not cowering after all.

Becker retreats a little further. "Dr. Haswell, I should explain, it's not about . . . It's about *Division II*. The sculpture? That's what I want to talk to you about."

Grace shakes her head, frowning. "You have that, it was in the second shipment, or perhaps the third. I have the paperwork . . . Are you telling me it never arrived?"

"No, no, it arrived. The thing is, we lent the piece to the Tate for an exhibition, you see, and—"

"And they damaged it."

"No . . . at least not yet." Grace's frown deepens. Becker draws a deep breath, exhaling slowly, cowering a little as a fresh cloudburst opens upon his head. "It's a bit complicated," he says weakly. Her lip twitches, just slightly, and for a moment he thinks she's about to smile. She doesn't, but she does pull the door a little further open and steps backward to allow him in.

He crosses the threshold. His heart is pounding, he feels light-headed, he's holding his breath: he's waited so long for this, to be here, in her home—Vanessa Chapman's home!—and it's . . . dark. It's dingy, full of clutter—he wants so much to revel in this moment, but he's disappointed.

"In here!" Grace barks at him, and he turns, closing the front door behind him. He follows her along the hallway to her left and—oh!

Now there are yellows and blues and light; there's a view. He knows this view. It's the causeway, the sands, a trio of peaks in the distance, capped in pure white.

"It's *Eris Sands*," he says, a smile spreading over his face. He looks at Grace Haswell and beams. "*Eris Sands*!"

Grace is leaning against the Aga on the right-hand side of the room, her hands tucked behind her back, expression inscrutable.

Becker can't contain his excitement, can't suppress his smile. "She must have been standing right here, right on this spot, when she painted it! The perspective, the way the light falls . . . I suppose I'd always thought she painted it outside, but it was here, wasn't it?" He looks down at his feet and sees spatters of paint on the floor and on the walls where Vanessa once flicked her brushes; he feels all the hair on the back of his neck stand up. "Right here!"

When he looks at Grace, he thinks he catches the edge of a smile just before she turns her back on him. She picks up a kettle and takes it over to the sink to fill. "She preferred to work outside, of course," she says, "but it wasn't always possible. She braved most weathers, but sometimes the wind got the better of her." She places the kettle on the Aga. When she turns back to face him, her expression has softened. "When she was unwell, toward the end, she worked more and more in here . . ."

Becker nods. "Of course," he says, forcing his features into a more solemn arrangement. "I'm sorry, I'm . . . *excited*. I've wanted to visit this place for so long." Grace tilts her head back, lifting her chin just a little, her expression shifting again. He can't quite read it, but it looks almost like distaste. He's being insensitive; he ought to be more respectful.

This is Grace's home; it's not a tourist attraction. Chastened, he falls silent.

Grace waves a hand at him, indicating a seat at the kitchen table, and goes back to making the tea.

Becker sits. He looks around the room, at the dark beams running across the ceiling, the wood burner tucked into the alcove on the back wall. It is cozy—sun-drenched, he imagines, when the weather is good—but worn. The painting on the wood trim has faded, some of the cupboard doors hang on their hinges, and the walls, which once might have been primrose, have turned the color of nicotine. Here and there bear the ghostly outlines of pictures long hanged and then removed.

Becker tries to imagine what it was like when Vanessa was here—did she display her own pieces on the walls? Was the sea view once mirrored by its likeness in oil? Or did she hang something completely different? Grace catches him staring at the grimy outline above the alcove and scowls.

Grace really is not at all what he expected. Strangely, given the number of articles he has read about Vanessa Chapman and her life here on Eris, Becker has never seen a photograph of Grace Haswell, so the person he has been holding—until today—in his mind's eye comes from pure imagination. He pictured an aging pre-Raphaelite, tall and rawboned, with wide green eyes and long, auburn hair streaked with gray. In fact, Grace is short—no more than five feet—and stocky. He's not good at guessing the ages of older women, but if pushed, he'd put her at around sixty-five. Her face is soft, cheeks relaxing gently into jowls, and her colors are muddied: from her bowl of hair to her slightly protuberant eyes, her long cardigan and the trousers puddling at her ankles, she is painted in varying shades of brown.

Why, he wonders now, had he thought she would be beautiful? Partly it's about her name, which conjures up the image of a sylph, long-limbed and lovely, but more than that, it's by virtue of association, the echo of a lesson learned at school: the pretty girls hang out together. Because Vanessa Chapman was a beauty, he assumed her companion would be, too.

Grace thumps a mug of tea down in front of him, sloshing a little onto the table surface. It is strong and, when he tastes it, sugary.

"Is there a question about authenticity?" Grace asks, sitting down opposite him. "Because if there is, it's unfounded. *Division II* is unquestionably Vanessa's work." Becker puts down the mug, sits up straight in his seat, surprised. It has never crossed his mind that the sculpture might not have been made by Vanessa. "It *is* unusual," Grace continues, "because sculpture isn't what she was known for. I think in the end she only completed seven in the series. They were done during a period of her life when she was struggling to paint." She sips her tea. "There are notes, there are sketches," she says. Becker feels the inside of his mouth go dry, but before he can speak, she holds up her hand. "*Don't* ask to see them right now *this instant* because I won't be able to lay my hands on them immediately. Though I'm well aware how impatient you people are."

Becker takes another sip of tea, wincing at its sweetness, wondering whether perhaps he should tell her that he's only a recent employee at Fairburn, that he's an outsider, that he's not exactly part of the family.

"So?" Grace snaps. "Is that it? A question about authenticity?"

"No, no." Becker shakes his head vehemently, launching straight into the story he came to tell: about the visitor to Tate Modern, the forensic anthropologist; he tells her about the email, about the bone. When finally he gets to the point, Grace starts to laugh.

"Human?" she repeats, and he nods. She laughs again and the laughter lightens her features, rounding her cheeks into apples, transforming her face. Is she early sixties, perhaps, or maybe even late fifties? "You do know, don't you, that I'm a doctor?" she says. "If Vanessa had been using human bones in her sculptures, do you not think I might have noticed?"

Becker can feel his face reddening. "Well, I did say I thought someone would have noticed before now, but I'm told it's not uncommon to mistake a deer rib for a human one." Grace purses her lips, cocks her head to one side, as if considering this. "When I heard," he carries on, "I reacted exactly as you just did—I laughed. I pointed out to my boss that that particular sculpture has been displayed not just at Fairburn but at other galleries, too. But the fact is that the people at the Tate are nervous. They've withdrawn the sculpture from the exhibition, and they've been trying to persuade Sebastian—that's Sebastian Lennox, my boss—to *test* the bone, to establish whether—"

"You can't test it!" Grace interjects. "You can't open the case! It's—"

"Part of the piece," Becker says, finishing her objection. "That's what I said. That's *exactly* what I said."

Their eyes meet. "She made it herself," Grace says, her voice a little strained. "The case, she put it together herself; her fingerprints are on the inside of the glass. There are . . . *traces* of her inside that case. Her fingerprints, her DNA. Her breath."

Becker looks down at the table, swallowing his shame. Five years might have passed, but it's clear this woman is still grieving. Her house has been stripped, paintings pulled from her walls; it doesn't look as though she has much money. Meanwhile, she's been met with accusations of incompetence, and worse, she's been hounded by lawyers. And now he's shown up at her house at dusk, unannounced.

"I'm so sorry to have had to bother you with this, Dr. Haswell," he says, as gently as he can. "I thought that . . . in order to avoid any question of opening the case, I might be able to take a look at any sketches or notes that relate to the sculpture; at least if I could get some idea of where the bone was found, and when, then perhaps I—"

"Well, I can tell you *where* she found it," Grace replies flatly. "Not *exactly* where, but it'll have been in the wood up on the hill behind the house; that's where she went scavenging. There, or on the beach. There's bones all over the place here, deer and sheep and cattle. Seal, too." She tips her head to one side, looking at him through narrowed eyes. "But even if you could say where she found it, or when, I don't see how that helps. What does that really tell you?"

"Not a great deal," Becker concedes, "but if she mentioned the bone in her journals, if she mentioned finding it, she might say what *she* thought it was, and that would be something, I think, to demonstrate that the artist had no intention of using—"

"Of using what? Of using human remains in her sculpture?" Grace lets out another bark of laughter. "Why would anyone imagine—" She breaks off then, getting abruptly to her feet, her expression quite changed. That look of distaste is back, and then some. "Oh, *God*. I've only just realized what this is. You think it's *him*, don't you?"

Becker inhales sharply. "*No*, I—"

"Oh, this is absurd," she says, her mouth twisting in contempt. "It's completely *absurd*." She leans forward, snatching away his half-full mug of tea, whirling around and hurling it into the sink. "I want you to leave," she shouts.

"Please, Dr. Haswell, I don't think it's him, that's not what this is about—"

"Right now!" She points toward the door. "Out you go!"

Becker has no choice; she's giving him no choice. He grabs his coat and shuffles back into the hallway with Grace following on his heels, barking at him all the while. "You people! Trying to cook up some ludicrous, sensationalist nonsense to publicize your museum! You're really not all that sharp, are you? Julian Chapman went missing in 2002! *Division II* was made in 2004!" The date on the piece is 2005, Becker thinks, but he's not about to argue with her. "He'd hardly be dry bones in a couple of years, would he?"

"Well . . . I don't . . . I've really no idea—" Becker says miserably, turning to face her.

"I'm telling you he wouldn't!" Grace snaps. "Christ, if you'd only bothered to ask someone who knew what they were talking about! You *people*!" she says again. "You don't deserve to sit in her kitchen, to walk on her island. You don't deserve to hang one single piece of her work on your walls. Is this what you think of her? That she . . . *what*? Killed her husband and made a sculpture out of him?"

Vanessa Chapman's diary

I'm in Naples, where the air tastes of salt and sulphur and the sky at night is purple and you can walk by the sea and watch all the kids, all these ravishing Italian teenagers, laughing and shouting and kissing each other in the half-light.

By day, the heat and the men are relentless. Walking down the street is exhausting. The last time I was here I was a child, I remember the wolfish way men looked at my mother, how she smiled and laughed. I scowl and swear. Despite my vanity (maybe because of it?), I've never liked to be painted or photographed, I've never liked to be looked at.

I came to <u>look</u>.

I came to look at Gentileschi's Judith and Holofernes at the Museo di Capodimonte.

I remember that from when I was here last, too: then I think I was just fascinated by the horror of it, by the <u>gore</u>, now what I love is the way the two women are working together, seriously, really applying themselves to their task. Caravaggio's Judith is tentative and afraid, but this Judith— red-lipped, in her dress the blue of a Neapolitan sky—is determined, unflinching. Her sleeves are rolled up. And her servant is not just standing passively or helplessly to one side; she is fully involved, she holds him, presses him to the bed, her eyes on his face. You can almost imagine she relishes it.

I was standing there, in awe of these magnificent women, when a shadow fell over me. A man was standing too close, taking up all the light. Tall and broad-shouldered, square-jawed—he looked like he'd taken a wrong turn on the way to the bookies. I was about to move away when he said, are you Vanessa Chapman? I swear, my jaw dropped.

He said he'd seen my pictures at Cube. His name is Douglas Lennox, he has a gallery in Glasgow, and he says he's interested in representing me.

I let him take me for a drink and then, after a few, to bed. Probably not the best idea if we're going to work together, but he was very good—and he is married, so he shouldn't really cause me any problems.

––––––––

Julian has been home for five days, sulking. Apparently it is all over with Celia. He is broke and his father is refusing to lend him any more money. I don't have any to give him either.

––––––––

Douglas Lennox turned up yesterday. He rang me from the station in Oxford, said he was just passing.

From Glasgow??

He didn't like the paintings I did of Blenheim Palace, the ones everyone else admires. Sentimental, chocolate boxy. He loved the hedgerows. Bold, he said, ambitious—taking landscape in a new direction. That's what you want to do, isn't it? Julian came into the studio while we were talking, we were standing very close together, my hand was on Douglas's arm, or maybe he had his hand on the small of my back, we were touching at any rate—anyway, Julian—who knows how touchy-feely I am, with <u>everyone</u>—stormed out.

Douglas and I talked for a long time; I talked about wanting to move almost toward something three-dimensional, making marks with the palette knife that tend toward carving. He pointed out that the best work I have done has not been here—the pictures from Cornwall and Italy are more successful. This landscape—which once thrilled me—now palls.

When Julian came back to the house in the evening he confronted me about Douglas and I laughed at him. I thought for a moment he might hit me—I think I wanted him to. If he hit me then I could walk out, couldn't I?

––––––––

We have had thunderstorms three days running and I feel as though my body has absorbed the electricity in the air. I paint and paint; I feel revitalized, made new.

London tomorrow, going to the Art Fair.

––––––––

I thought I had been forgiven for the Douglas incident, but I was wrong. When I got back from London I got the old one-two.

The jab: he is seeing Celia Gray again—and it's <u>not</u> a fling, he says he loves her.

The cross: while I was away, he took one of my Italy pictures (<u>Naples Seafront</u>) to "a dealer friend of Celia's" and sold it.

I can't describe how I felt; it wasn't just despair, it was darkness like I have not known before, it was hatred. Sometimes his cruelty takes my breath away—as though his infidelity is not enough, he helps himself to my pictures, too, and the money I have worked for.

I have to be single-minded, I have to put work at the heart of my life.

And I have to leave because, if I don't, I think I might kill him. Or he me.

NINE

Driving back across the causeway, Becker thinks he sees something in the rearview mirror. A flash of blue, not the blue of the sky or the sea but something brighter, unnatural, out of place. A blue like a strobe of light. He stops the car and climbs out. The air is damp; there's a fog drifting onshore—already parts of the island are obscured from view. There's nothing at all on the hillside that looks like it doesn't belong there. He stands for a moment, looking around him, his body vibrating with the faint thrill of fear. Down on the seabed with the haar closing in, he can imagine the horror of getting caught by the tide. He is not a strong swimmer. He climbs back into the car and drives, too fast, bouncing over stones and thumping into potholes, all the way to the mainland.

So, he thinks grimly to himself, *that went well.*

At the far end of Eris village is a pub. Becker pulls into the car park and sits for a minute, hands on the wheel. He longs to be at home, but he cannot face the drive. The anxiety he felt earlier in the day has returned, a heavy sensation pressing against his temples, against the back of his neck; he is gripped by the certainty that if he starts off now, with dusk falling, he'll never get home.

He takes out his phone with the intention of calling Helena—she'll talk some sense into him, she never fails—but three missed calls from Sebastian make his mind up for him. He climbs out of the car and walks into the pub.

It is not quaint. A rectangular room with a dark wooden bar and a few tables, it's plain, shabby, and empty save for a trio of young men at a table in the far corner and a middle-aged woman reading her phone behind the bar.

The woman looks up and beams at him. "What'll you have, pet?"

"I was actually wondering if you had a room, just for tonight?"

"Oh we do!" she says, turning around to grab a couple of keys from the board behind her. "You've a choice, in fact, the big room or the wee one. Wee one's cheaper, but no en suite."

He opts for the larger room, which, like the bar itself, is functional but not welcoming. It seems clean, though, and above the smell of stale beer that permeates the place, he catches a whiff of something tempting. Pastry, he thinks. A pie?

Back downstairs in the bar, Becker consumes a very good steak and ale pie washed down with a pint of bitter while he reads through the rest of the notes and articles in his file. He is searching—hopelessly, he fears—for a way back in, for some piece of information, some point of connection that might allow him to get back through Grace Haswell's front door.

Chapman didn't give many interviews—perhaps because she was difficult, as the critics said, or perhaps because the critics insisted on devoting quite so many column inches to how difficult she was. Even at the height of her success, in the late 1990s and early 2000s, she rarely spoke about her work in public. After her husband's disappearance in 2002 and her subsequent withdrawal from the solo show planned at Douglas Lennox's Glasgow Modern Gallery, she never spoke to the press again.

He closes his laptop and slips it into his bag, picks up his glass, and returns it to the bar. The landlady has been joined by her husband, Becker assumes—a skinny man with a pink face who perches at one end of the bar, reading the local paper.

"That pie really was excellent," Becker says to the landlady, who inclines her head graciously. She eyes him for a moment.

"You looking for a holiday cottage out here?" she asks.

"Oh no," Becker replies, shaking his head, "I came out to see Grace Haswell. On the island."

"Oh, Dr. Haswell!" She raises an eyebrow. "You're a pal, are you?"

He shakes his head again. "No, no. I'm ... uh, a curator, at a museum. Down in the Borders. We—the museum, that is—inherited some of Vanessa Chapman's art after she died."

"Oh, aye. That's you, is it? We were ever so sad about Mrs. Chapman. She was a lovely lady. Kind. Bohemian, wasn't she? Glamorous. Popular with the gentlemen." She gives him a wink.

Her husband looks up from his paper and shoots her a dark look. "No trouble to anyone," he mutters, scowling at Becker. "Neither she nor the doctor. Kept themselves to themselves. No trouble to anyone."

"Well," his wife says pensively, "there was that thing with the mechanic—"

"Are you not needed in the kitchen, Shirley?" the landlord growls. Shirley shrugs, smiling sweetly at Becker, and disappears somewhere out back. Becker is about to take his leave when the landlord begins to mutter again.

"Retired, you know," he says.

"I'm sorry?"

"Dr. Haswell. Retired she was, and then came out of retirement to work at the hospital during the pandemic. Fifteen-hour shifts, they had them on. Worked to the bone." He glowers at Becker, as though he is somehow responsible. "I'd hate to see her bothered, after everything she's been through. She and Mrs. Chapman," he says again, "no trouble to anyone."

UPSTAIRS IN HIS room, Becker calls Helena.

"It's weird, you know, the locals seem to have been fond of her," he says.

"Why is that weird?" Helena asks.

"I was just surprised, you know. This incomer—a southerner, an Englishwoman, quite posh—turns up, buys an island, lives out there all by herself; and she's got this reputation for being cold and difficult and unfriendly, and yet the locals here—well, the landlord and his wife, anyway—have only good things to say about her."

"Mmmm." Helena seems distracted, as though she's only half listening to him.

"Mmmm? Mmmm what?"

She laughs. "Maybe she was a good customer? I don't know, Beck, I imagine she could probably be perfectly charming if she wanted to. And all those things the critics wrote about her—that she was . . . what was it?—disagreeable and prickly and *strident*—that's just what people say about a woman who knows her own mind, isn't it?"

"Is it?"

Helena laughs again. "Yes, it is! And really, when you think about it, *single-minded* and *selfish* are just synonyms for *childless*, in some circles."

"Are they?"

Helena tuts; he can almost feel her rolling her eyes at him. "Look, you need to go back and talk to her—to the friend, *companion*, whoever she is. Isn't that what you're there for? If you really want to get to know Vanessa, you need to find a way to make this Haswell woman speak to you. She's the one who knows where all the bodies are buried."

Becker hears a voice, from the corridor outside his room or over the line, he's not sure. "What was that?" he asks her.

"It's the pizza boy," Helena drawls huskily. "He's just getting out of the shower." Becker exhales loudly. "It's the *television*, Beck. Jesus. I'm bingeing *Kardashians* in your absence."

"I love you," Becker says.

"And we love you."

"You and the pizza boy?"

"Or pizza girl."

He ends the call and scrolls back through his Vanessa archive, reading with a rather more critical eye. Of course she wasn't that disagreeable, of course it was just misogyny! The critics were all men, the interviewers were men, as were most of the interviewees. They were men with agendas or men who bore grudges.

It is only on this latest pass through the articles that Becker realizes quite how *absent* Grace Haswell is. She's almost never mentioned—

except once or twice as Vanessa's carer in the obituaries—and even then, she's never quoted. It's possible that she didn't want to speak to the newspapers; it's possible that Vanessa asked her not to. But it's also possible that while the journalists were out chasing quotes from Turner Prize winners or prominent critics, no one thought to ask Grace Haswell, a provincial GP, what she thought, how she felt.

Becker closes the laptop. He is dog-tired, his back and shoulders stiff from the drive and from sitting hunched over his computer. He clambers off the bed and then pads over creaking floorboards into the tiny bathroom, drawing himself up, rolling his shoulders backward and his neck from side to side. He stands at the toilet, his head grazing the ceiling as he pisses, looking out through the Velux window at a solitary light in the distance.

How easy it would be, he thinks, not to see her. How easy to miss her altogether.

Back in the bedroom, he opens the laptop once more and begins to write.

Dear Dr. Haswell,

There are so many things I would like to talk to you about, so many questions I'd like to ask you. That bone—which I never for a single second imagined came from Julian Chapman's body—is the least of them. That's just something I have to do, a problem to clear up, a part of my job as curator of Fairburn's collection.

I'd like to ask you about your life with Vanessa, about the woman behind the work, the woman who only you knew. This is partly about professional curiosity, of course. I wrote my thesis on the development of nontraditional landscape art, and Vanessa's work was central to that. But my connection to her work goes back further; it has deeper roots. Like anyone who is interested in art, I have two sets of memories: personal memories and art memories. Sometimes, the two cross over.

My mother was a talented watercolorist. She went to art college but dropped out when she fell pregnant. She intended to return to her studies, but my father—a man I have never met—did not support her. My grandmother, who was already widowed by that point, didn't have the means to support all three of us, so Mum had to work.

She had a job at the supermarket in the center of Bicester, just down the road from a little art gallery called Harry West Art. It was, I'm sure you know, the first place ever to show Vanessa's work. Mum used to go there often, in her lunch hour or after work, to look at the pictures. At one show, she bought a tiny oil painting, eight inches by five. It cost her a week's wages and an almighty row with my grandmother.

The painting was of a hedgerow, its riotous greens studded with purple and yellow wildflowers, the scent of summer rising off it. The artist had pressed things—grass seeds and petals—into the paint. I remember being startled and delighted to find in it an iridescent insect wing. Small as it was, it was the kind of picture you never tired of looking at, the sort of picture that rewarded you with something different each time you studied it.

My mother hung it on the wall next to her bed.

A couple of years later, when she went into a hospice to die, she took only two possessions with her: a framed photograph of the two of us together, and that little painting. A year or two after that, when finally I found myself strong enough to look through the bag of belongings—her pajamas, her washbag—that had been returned to me after her death, I found that the photograph was there, but the painting was not.

I began to search for it. I was thirteen by this time, lonely and angry and completely clueless about art, but fortunately my grandmother remembered that the artist's last name was Chapman. This was in the pre-Google 1990s, but I was lucky enough to find in our local library a microfiched copy of an interview Vanessa had given to ARTNOW after exhibiting at the London Art Fair in 1995. Being a teenage boy, I was struck by how beautiful she was, but more than that, I was struck by what she said when she was asked what painting meant to her. I can quote her for you here, because I read these lines so many times I know them by heart:

"Art is legacy, it is solace. It soothes, consoles, arouses. It's work. It's what you do all day. It's how you work things out, how you understand the world.

It's the opportunity to start over, to shed your skin, to take revenge, to fall in love. To be good. To live long."

I found the little painting (*Hedgerow*, 1993) at an auction years later; I bought it with my first paycheck from Christie's auction house. My mother would have been astounded by what it was worth. Or perhaps she wouldn't! Perhaps she always suspected the world would one day value Vanessa's work the way she did. Either way, I think she'd be very happy to see that piece hanging on the wall beside my bed now.

I hope this goes some way to explaining why it would mean so much to me if we could talk again.

Yours,
James Becker

IN THE SMALL hours of the morning, just before the tide turns, Becker's phone buzzes. He jerks awake, heart thumping, thinking, *Helena.* But when he looks at the screen, he sees an email notification.

Dear Mr. Becker,
Thank you for your email. If you are still in Eris, you may come to the island today. Low tide is at eight.

Please understand that I will speak to you only on the condition that you ask your employers to stop pestering me.

If you are prepared to do so, then we can talk further.

Yours,
Grace Haswell

TEN

Becker wonders, as he climbs the steps to Vanessa's house, whether Grace will show him the studio. God, what he'd give to see it! What he'd give to go up to the top of the rock, to look at the view.

"You could go up," Grace says, when he asks her about it. She is pouring coffee into his mug: she's not been *welcoming*, exactly, but civil enough. There's been no sign of yesterday's anger. "But I wouldn't recommend it." She juts her chin toward the window, indicating the fog. "The last chap to go up there in a haar didn't come back down. Well, he did, but via the express route." She looks at him with raised eyebrows, a low whistle on her lips. "He washed up on the beach a week later."

Becker almost chokes on his coffee.

"It was in the papers," she says coolly. She sits down opposite him, blowing gently on the surface of her own drink. "A couple of years ago . . . maybe three? I lose track. Pre-pandemic, in any case."

"Good God. Who was he?"

Grace shrugs. "A walker. A tourist. Canadian, I think. Some poor soul far from home. I never actually saw him. His hire car was parked down on the track for a couple of days; that's how I knew something was up."

They sip their coffee. Becker shakes his head. "I had no idea it was so treacherous . . . the rock was one of Vanessa's favorite painting spots, wasn't it?"

Grace nods vigorously. "Oh yes, she was up there all the time. And in all weathers, too. The more you see a place, the more you can extract from it. That's what she said. She used to haul all her kit up, paints and canvases, the whole caboodle, on the quad bike as far as it went. And then on foot." Her brows rise toward her hairline again, a quiet smile on her face. "She lost more than one canvas to the wind. It used to put the fear of God into me, but nothing would stop Vanessa." She purses her lips. "Almost nothing."

There's no question: Grace is different today. There's more eye contact; she's less defensive, more effusive. The letter did the trick.

"She *knew* this place, you see," Grace says. "She knew every inch of this island, every rock and every root, every crevice, she knew where the ground was unstable, where the wind might catch you . . ." She shakes her head. "Not today; you'd be a fool to go up today. And I'm afraid I can't show you the studio yet either. It's not ready." Their eyes meet, and Grace sits up very straight in her chair. "*I'm* not ready. In any case, I need some assurances from you. I want to know how you plan to proceed from here on in."

Becker inclines his head, taking another sip of his coffee. Sensing that charm is unlikely to work, he opts instead for deference. "What I was hoping," he says carefully, "if you have time, of course, if you're willing, is that we—you and I, I mean—might be able to read through some of Vanessa's papers together . . ." He doesn't look up, just keeps his eyes on the table and his voice even. "In that way we might come up with a solution acceptable to both sides." Now he does look up, his gaze meeting hers. "I need your help," he says.

Grace presses her lips together, a faint flush spreading over her cheekbones . . . She is pleased. She is flattered. "That would be . . . I think that would be fine," she says, and Becker curls his hands into victorious fists under the table.

They come to an agreement. Grace will give him a sample of papers—a few notebooks, a couple of letters, perhaps—to take back to Fairburn. He will speak to Sebastian and ask—no, tell!—him to call off the dogs. From now on, Grace will deal directly with Becker, and only with Becker. There will be no more threats of legal action. Becker makes a solemn promise, crossing his ankles beneath his chair like a child.

"I'll fetch you some notebooks to look at, then," Grace says, getting up from the table. Becker waits until he hears the front door open and close again and then he seizes his chance. He slips out of the kitchen and into the darkness of the cluttered living room. Windowless and airless, it has the feel of a space rarely used. A faded screen in hospital-green linen rests against one wall; a small blue sofa vies for space with two ratty armchairs and an ancient television resting on a metal catering trolley.

On the floor are piled books, yellowing newspapers, ancient copies of *The Doctor* magazine. On every other horizontal surface—on every shelf and coffee table, on the mantelpiece above the gaping maw of the fireplace—are found objects: driftwood the color of milky coffee, orbs of pure white quartz, bright green glass worn smooth and shapely by the sea. Becker selects a stone, white with a line of rose running through it like a vein, and rolls it around in his hand, returns it to its place on the mantelpiece.

Beyond the living room is another corridor, off which is a bathroom and two bedrooms, a small one to the right, furnished with a neatly made single bed, a desk, and a wardrobe, a larger room to the left. Becker stops in the doorway of the larger room. The walls are painted white, the double bed is stripped, a chair is placed next to it at an angle. It is Vanessa's room, he knows, because through the window opposite he can see the sea and a lighthouse on an island in the distance. He is looking at the view depicted in *Hope Is Violent*, Vanessa's final painting, completed only months before she died.

Tears spring to his eyes. He retreats quickly, noticing as he makes his way back through the house that *all* the walls are bare, that the whole place feels stripped, robbed of everything that might once have adorned it. And he is among the thieves. As he walks back through the living room, he picks up the white stone again. Every pebble, Sebastian said, *every fucking pebble she picked up on the beach and arranged* just so. Becker slips the stone into his pocket; he makes it back to the kitchen table seconds before he hears the front door open.

"She didn't date anything," Grace is saying as she reenters the room, leafing through the pages of an A5 Life Vermilion notebook, "so finding what you're looking for might not be straightforward." She places the notebook, along with two others and a folder stuffed with loose papers, on the table. Becker knits his fingers together to stop himself from grabbing at them. "I don't think these books were ever really for reference," Grace says. "They were just . . . part of the process, I suppose, of figuring things out."

She catches his eyes and quickly looks away. Unwittingly, she has just made the case for Fairburn's claim on these notebooks: they were *part of the process*—part of Vanessa's artistic process. Becker lets the moment pass, unacknowledged.

"What was I saying? Not dated, that's it. So at least one of these is much too early, it's from when she first moved here, but I think you'll find it very interesting. She writes about sculpture in the second one, so that might be more relevant. I meant to go through all this," she sighs, "I honestly did."

"I know," Becker says quietly. "I understand, I really do." She smiles at him, grateful, and he feels wretched.

"There are sketches in the folder, and of course you can keep all of those—I've no idea whether any of them have any real value or interest; most of them just look like scribbles to me . . ."

Philistine, Becker thinks, unkindly. "What's fascinating for me," he says, "is the progression of her style, the development of it, both in terms of individual pieces and her whole body of work, so I imagine that almost all of those sketches will have value, provided I can get a sense of their order. I imagine the notebooks will help with that."

Grace looks doubtful. "I suppose . . ."

"One of the extraordinary things about Vanessa's work is that there's this real sense of coherence, even though her style changed so much over the course of her life. When you look at the paintings she did when she first got here, it's remarkable, isn't it, the difference between something like *South*, which I think was one of the very first completed on the island, and *The Tide Always Comes*, which was just a year later, and yet the change is quite radical, it's so much more *fluid*, and yet there's no question there's the same hand holding the brush, the same eye."

Grace sighs impatiently. "I wouldn't know about that," she says. "I'm no art critic. Everyone gets so bogged down in the theory, but sometimes it's just about necessity. You mentioned *The Tide Always Comes*—well, she had to paint that differently because she couldn't use a brush properly. She was just . . . squirting paint onto her fingers and applying it to canvas directly, and then using the brush, and she liked that effect, so it influenced how she did things later on, her brushwork became—"

"Looser!" Becker exclaims. "More expansive."

"Yes, I suppose—"

"And the paint becomes more sculptural . . . but hang on, you said she *couldn't* use a brush?"

"Well, no, because she'd broken her wrist." Grace looks at him, quizzical, half smiling, half frowning. "Did you not know about that? That was how we met."

ELEVEN

It was a slow day. Grace had a fifteen-minute break before her next appointment, so she'd grabbed the opportunity to make herself a cup of coffee she might actually have time to drink. That was when she saw her—saw *it*, rather—a small, battered green car lurching into the car park before coming to a shuddering halt, angled across three parking spaces. The driver's door swung violently open and a woman climbed out. She was tall and very thin with hair the color of pale amber—in dire need of a brush—hanging over her face. She carried herself awkwardly, chin tucked into her chest and her arms wrapped around herself, stumbling a little as she made her way across the car park toward the surgery entrance.

A drunk, Grace thought, gulping her coffee, scalding the roof of her mouth. From the waiting room she could hear the receptionist's voice, quiet at first and then rising slightly. A moment or two passed and then there came a rapping at the door.

"Sorry, Dr. Haswell, could you see a walk-in?"

The woman entered her office with her spine straight and her shoulders back, her left hand pinning her right forearm to her chest. "I think I might have broken it," she said quietly when Grace asked how she might help. As Grace moved closer to her, she caught a whiff of something sharp, like nail polish remover, but the woman's eyes were clear and focused. Not drunk, then, but clearly in pain, and wearing a wary expression, the sort Grace sometimes saw in victims of abuse.

"What happened?" Grace asked as, very gently, she examined the woman's arm. An ominous bruise was forming just above the heel of her hand. The veins of her forearm stood out against her muscles like ropes. Her fingernails were filthy.

"I tripped over this bloody . . . *thing*, this sort of manhole thing that covers the septic tank up behind my house." Her voice was soft and pleasantly gravelly, her English vowels rounded. "I was running to answer the phone—I'd been working in my studio, which is separate from the house—I just went flying." She winced, breathing in sharply as Grace turned the wrist. "It hurts like buggery."

Grace smiled. "I imagine it does. Mrs. . . ."

"Chapman. Vanessa."

"Vanessa," Grace said, inviting her patient to stand, "I'm afraid that you're right, unfortunately. I think it is a break. We'll need to do an X-ray to make sure."

"Oh, fucking *hell*." Grace flinched at the profanity. "How long will that take to heal?" Vanessa inhaled sharply, wincing again as she held her forearm to her chest, squeezing her eyes shut, giving Grace the opportunity to look at her, *really* look at her: at her dark brows and the firm line of her mouth, her straight nose, just a little too large for her face.

"That very much depends," Grace said, "on what we see in the X-ray. Did you drive here yourself?" She knew the answer but wanted to ascertain her patient's truthfulness.

"Had to," Vanessa replied. "I live alone."

"You should have called an ambulance," Grace said. Vanessa smiled briefly—*dismissively*, Grace thought. "You might have caused an accident," she said tartly, "driving with an injury like that."

"I couldn't wait for an ambulance," Vanessa said. "There wasn't time. I live out on Eris Island."

"You live on Eris?" Grace's heart tripped, as though she'd heard some sad old song, half forgotten, transporting her in time.

Vanessa nodded. "Do you know it?"

"I do," Grace said. She trundled the portable X-ray machine across the room. "I used to go walking there often. Such a beautiful spot, so peaceful—and the views from the rock . . ." Grace moved Vanessa into position, retreating behind a screen while she took the images. "I haven't been for a long while. Someone put up a gate at the end of the causeway."

"That wasn't me," Vanessa said. She sounded almost affronted. "It was the agent, the selling agent, for the man who owned the place before. I took the gate down, it's not been there for months and months, since the sale went through last year, in fact. There's right to roam in Scotland, isn't there? As there should be." She closed her eyes again. "I think of myself as the owner of the house, but I'm only the *custodian* of the island."

Behind the screen, Grace smirked. The pretensions of the rich! If Eris were hers, she'd put up barbed wire or get a fierce dog.

The X-rays done, she fetched Vanessa a couple of painkillers and a glass of water. "Surely if you could drive over an ambulance could have made it the other way?" she asked.

"The tide was coming in," Vanessa said. She popped the pills into her mouth and tilted her head back to swallow them, exposing her pale throat. She had a tiny scar right in the middle of it, as though someone had pressed a knife to her windpipe and then thought better of it. "I only had about twenty, maybe twenty-five minutes until the causeway flooded, and I didn't reckon they'd make it in time. I couldn't face waiting six hours."

Grace nodded. "No, quite. Although you probably ought to have called an ambulance from the phone box in the harbor rather than driving all the way up here."

"I suppose so," Vanessa said, chastened. "I really wasn't thinking straight."

"Pain will do that to you," Grace said, relenting. "The nurse will put a splint on your wrist for now. You may need a plaster cast, but we won't do that for a day or two; we have to wait for the swelling to come down. It will all be dependent on what we see in the X-ray film, in any case."

When she sat back at her desk to type her notes into the computer, she was suddenly all fingers and thumbs, conscious of Vanessa's gaze upon her. "How will you get home?" Grace asked, eager to focus on the practical. "It's really not a good idea for you to drive."

Vanessa pulled a face. "Well . . . I can't get back right away anyway, the tide's in now. I won't be able to cross until around four. I suppose I could get a taxi . . . I don't know what I'll do about the car, though."

Grace looked up at her. "How very odd it must be," she said, "living at the mercy of the tide." Vanessa shrugged and smiled and Grace felt irritated, as if she were being somehow mocked for the banality of her observation. And yet despite her annoyance, she found herself offering help. "You don't need to get a taxi," she said. "If you have to wait until this afternoon anyway, I can drive you. I'm only here until three on Mondays."

"Oh, I couldn't ask you to do that." Vanessa got to her feet, shaking her head firmly. "I wouldn't want to put you out."

"It's no trouble," Grace replied. "It's ages since I've been out to the island."

"But if you drive me, how will you get back?"

"I can walk across. It's only a mile or so, and there's a bus from the village back up here." Even as she was saying it, Grace wondered why she was making this effort, going out of her way for this woman. There was something about her—an air of entitlement, the sort that came with beauty, perhaps, or money—that both needled and attracted at the same time, and even though she was conscious of it, Grace found herself unable to resist.

THAT AFTERNOON, THERE was no wind to speak of. The water in the bay was like glass, and in the generous sunshine of midsummer, Eris Island shimmered green and purple and yellow, its steep hillside, thick with bracken, dappled with gorse and heather. Grace and Vanessa wound their windows down, the salty tang of seaweed filling the car as they approached.

"When was the last time you were out here?" Vanessa asked.

"Oh." Grace exhaled slowly, and it was only in doing so that she realized she'd been holding her breath. "Not for a long time. When I first got the job at the surgery in Carrachan, back in 1991, I used to come out here often. I used to cycle across and then walk up to the top of the rock. But then, I think it was '93, maybe '94, there were these terrible winter storms—I suppose that was before your time?"

"Oh yes, I only moved last year. I lived in England before that, in Oxfordshire."

"Well, the storms were really quite severe. In one of them part of the causeway was washed away, so it was no longer possible to cross. Not safely, anyway. No one was living on the island at that time, and it was months before anyone got round to repairing the road. And then not long after that, someone put up a fence, as I said . . . It's quite a treat to be coming out here again." Grace glanced over at Vanessa with a shy smile. "I've missed it."

Vanessa told her to drive up the track to the back of the house. No longer the shabby wreck Grace remembered, its pebble dash had been whitewashed and timber window frames painted a sunny yellow. The house formed an L shape around a courtyard—there had once been a third side at the rear of the yard, a barn probably—but that had long since collapsed. Grace parked the car in the courtyard and followed Vanessa as she walked up the hill behind the house toward an out-building.

"Watch out," Vanessa called over her shoulder as she strode on ahead. "There, you see, that's where I tripped." She pointed over to the left, where Grace could make out a concrete slab half hidden by the grass. At the brow of the hill was a barn with an enormous door—a vast, oxidized metal sheet—at its end. It was rolled back to reveal a cavernous interior, a window on the west side of the building letting in a generous slice of the afternoon sunshine. There were sheets of paper pinned to the walls, rough outlines sketched upon them, and in front of the window, toward the rear of the space, a potter's wheel.

"I thought you were a painter," Grace said, and Vanessa gave her a questioning look. "I mean, I remember reading, when the island was sold, that an artist had bought it. I assumed—"

"I *am* a painter," Vanessa said, smiling, raising her good arm to shield her eyes from the sun. "I do paint, although I've not been doing so much of it lately." She took a few steps back, inviting Grace into the room. They stood side by side looking at the sketches on the wall— little more, as far as Grace could see, than collections of shapes, all jumbled together. "Lately I find myself more interested in ceramics. I'm . . . going through a transitional phase, I suppose. Trying to find my feet. Or my hands." She looked at Grace with a smile. "Though what I really need to do is to develop my eye." Gently and deliberately, she slipped her left arm into Grace's right. Grace flinched with surprise, a fierce blush radiating from her neck to her face. "Shall we have some tea?" Vanessa asked. "Or do you fancy a walk through the wood, up to the rock?"

Grace withdrew her arm, stepping backward and knocking into a bench, sending a stone hammer rolling to the floor with an almighty clang. "Oh . . ." She fell to her knees, scrabbling to pick it up, muttering apologies.

"Don't worry about that," Vanessa said. "Do you not want to go up?" She laughed her throaty laugh. "Perhaps you think I lured you here under false pretenses. Like Ted Bundy, feigning injury so that I can have my wicked way with you?" She broke off. "Good God, Dr. Haswell, I'm *joking*. You actually look frightened!"

"Don't be ridiculous," Grace said, her face hot, a trickle of sweat prickling the small of her back. "Of course I'm not frightened."

Vanessa Chapman's diary

Healing. Can write a little, can't paint. No clay, of course. Weather beautiful, would swim every day if not for cursed wrist. Instead I comb the beach and the wood, bring things back, arrange and rearrange and rearrange again.

G thinks me very odd! She comes often with fresh food and village gossip. She knows everyone but, like me, prefers solitude to crowds. She knows stories about the island, about when the trees fell, about people being swept away trying to cross. She told me this, too: years ago, hundreds of years ago, the villagers used to bury the dead out here on Eris, to keep them safe from wolves.

TWELVE

Onions chopped, garlic crushed: a tip of the wrist, a scrape of the knife, a gentle sizzle as the vegetables hit heated oil.

On the Aga sits an ancient orange Le Creuset casserole dish in which Grace makes the tomato sauce for her pasta every night. Same pot, same ingredients, the same dinner on repeat. She used to cook properly—she's a good cook—but over time, in the face of solitude, her repertoire dwindled from a range of dishes to just a handful, and finally all the way down to one single supper.

She used to listen to the radio when she cooked, but at some point she stopped. She can't remember exactly when, but she knows she stopped at the point at which the consolation gained from listening to other voices was outweighed by the discomfort of silence ringing out when she turned the dial before going to bed. It's like a bell tolling, now, the silence she hears in the wake of Becker's visit.

She shook his hand when he left, holding on for just a beat too long.

Vanessa used to touch people all the time; it came as a bit of a shock to Grace at first, all that hand-holding and arm-linking, but other people seemed to like it. Grace watched them relax into her, allowing Vanessa to draw them closer into her orbit. Grace could never quite get that right.

So, Becker will think her odd. He will think her sad and strange. A lonely, frightened old woman, that's what he'll think.

And he'll not be wrong, will he?

After supper, she climbs the hill to the studio. She keeps the torch-light trained on the ground in front of her feet and does not raise her eyes, does not glance up at the tree line, behind which there is only darkness after all. What is there to be frightened of? There are ghosts in the wood, it's true, but then again there are ghosts everywhere. In the studio and up on the rock, in Vanessa's bedroom, right here on this path. And there, if she were to stray just a few feet over to the right, she'd find the concrete lid of the septic tank where Vanessa tripped, and she'd be haunted there, too.

She opens the studio door and turns on the light, pulls a space heater out from under one of the shelves and plugs it in. Rolls the door shut and slides the bolt across. Safe as houses.

Mr. Becker made her feel safe. Isn't that ridiculous? First he frightened her, then he made her feel safe.

He's the sort of man, she thinks, lifting the lid from the nearest box of papers, who'd carry your groceries to your car. Lend you a hand if you needed to move a sofa. Fetch you a saucepan from the top shelf. Step in if he saw you in trouble.

Would Vanessa have liked him? Grace thinks so. She didn't like a critic, but she loved an enthusiast. She would have smiled at him, charmed him, taken his arm or his hand. She was so tactile, so quick to touch, to embrace. All those things they wrote about her, that she was chilly, remote . . . those people didn't know her. Not really. She was warm when she wanted to be; she just knew who she liked. And who she didn't.

James Becker reminds her of someone. That's it, that's why she feels closer to him than she should. He reminds her of Nick Riley, a boy she knew at university. Mr. Becker has a similar manner, gives the same impression of gentility. Of decency. A slight physical resemblance, too: milky skin, long, pale lashes.

Is that why she feels like this? Is that why she feels this sudden, sharp pain in her side, why she has to hold on to the workbench, to catch her breath? Is that why she's blindsided by a sudden wave of grief? Because he's like Nick, who abandoned her?

Is that why she lied to Mr. Becker? Because she wanted him to think well of her? Because she wanted to please him?

She *did* see that Canadian boy. The one who fell. She was in the kitchen when he passed; he saw her at the window, smiled and waved. So young. She could have run out and warned him, told him to watch his step.

You can't save everyone.

She walks to the back of the studio, crouches down, and opens the store cupboard. There was a box of bones here, wasn't there? Maybe more than one. She reaches into the darkness and comes out with a rosewood box. There. It's full of tiny things, fragments, yellowing and dirty; she sifts through it, picking up the pieces, they are light in her hand, they are animal bones, without question. These haven't come from a human body. They are wrong, she's sure of it, the people at the museum in London. The bone is not human. It can't be.

She closes the box and stands up.

But of course it *could* be! That poor Canadian boy wasn't the first to fall from the rock. It's not likely, but anything is possible. A prickle inches up her spine, and she hears Vanessa's voice: *I dream about raking through ashes.*

She turns and rounds the kiln, undoes the latch and opens the door. She peers into the dark hollow, inhaling a faint scent of oil and soap. It's empty, long since swept bare.

Division II *is unquestionably Vanessa's work.* That was what Grace told Mr. Becker and that's the truth, only it doesn't *feel* like the truth, not the whole truth, because Vanessa was mad around that time. She was secretive, hostile, not herself; her back began to hunch and her eyes to yellow, a sour smell rose off her; it was as though she were transforming before Grace's very eyes, into someone else, some*thing* else. Something animal. She sat in the kitchen and smoked all day, only moving around at night after Grace had gone to bed. Grace used to hear her, bare feet slapping the floor as she moved from room to room; she used to hear the front door slam when Vanessa went out into the night. Where did you go? Grace would ask in the morning, when Vanessa was back at the kitchen table, smoking her cigarettes. Where do you go? She wouldn't answer.

I dream about raking through ashes, raking through ashes and finding bones.

But that was later, wasn't it? And she was talking about something else entirely. Still, Grace wonders whether somewhere in all these thousands of pages of notes and scribbles Vanessa wrote about those dreams. If so, Grace ought to find those words; she ought to weed them out.

Grace might have given Becker the impression that the papers she'd given him were snatched haphazardly from a pile, but that wasn't true either. She's not had time to read through everything, but she made sure to include a notebook from around the time that she and Vanessa met, and she made sure to hold back some of the later ones. She threw in a couple of those awful letters from Douglas Lennox, too, for good measure. Perhaps when Lennox's son gets a look at *those* he'll have second thoughts about making Vanessa's private correspondence public.

The time will come for honesty, Grace is well aware. The Fairburn people are not just going to forget the missing paintings. She'll have to come up with an explanation at some point. How much simpler things would have been if Douglas had been shot before probate was granted, rather than afterward!

She makes a start on the first box of papers: there is no order, everything is jumbled—notebooks and photographs and sketches and letters and postcards, notes on scraps of paper, shopping lists. Grace begins by arranging everything into preliminary piles: notebooks to one side, letters to another, and so on, and with that done, she moves on to a second box, and then a third. She tries not to let her eyes linger, tries not to read. If she starts reading, she will never finish: she will be derailed. But every now and again she cannot help herself, her eye slides over faded blue ink and snags on a capital G, generously looped and rich with promise.

The winds lately are soft, warm—G and I swim when the tide is in, it is heaven.

Her heart feels suddenly tender; her eyes fill with tears. She brushes them away with the back of her hand and lets her eyes travel to the top of the page:

G has time off—she chooses to spend it here. I asked would she not like to go away—on holiday, to visit family? She looked at me as though I were mad. I am grateful, in any case. We drink wine in the evenings, picnic on the rock. The winds lately are soft, warm—G and I swim when the tide is in, it is heaven.

THIRTEEN

It has been a hellish summer, uncomfortably hot, pollen and carbon monoxide and recrimination hanging in the air. But finally, <u>finally</u>, J and I have struck a deal. We go our separate ways, he moves in with Celia, and we sell the house. He gets three-quarters of the proceeds, I get the rest, but I get my money <u>up front</u> so that I can put in a bid for the island.

Celia has signed off on all of this—it'll be her money, after all.

My heart breaks, but I hardly feel it, because the rest of me vibrates with joy.

I will be <u>free</u>.

Becker is reading when Helena walks into the study. It is early, barely light, wet flakes of snow falling but not sticking. He doesn't turn around to look at her but allows himself the anticipation of the feel of her hands resting soft on his shoulders and then the warmth of her lips on his neck.

"Hello." Her morning breath is sugary sweet. She perches on the edge of his desk, burgundy robe loosely belted across her bump, her hands wrapped around a mug of steaming tea. "How is she, your Vanessa?"

He pulls a face. "Strange," he says, and he reads her the paragraph he has just finished. "She loves him and she longs to be free of him, she *vibrates with joy* at the thought of leaving him. She's a riddle."

Helena shrugs. "Not at all," she says. Becker raises his eyebrows at her, and she laughs, lifting a foot and placing it in his lap. He obliges her by massaging her sole. "You can love someone with your whole

heart and be desperate to be rid of them. Some people are just—"
She breaks off, exhaling softly over the surface of her tea. "Hard to be
around, no matter how much you adore them. And Julian was awful
to her, wasn't he? Notoriously so. Selling her work to pay off his debts,
sleeping around. That affair with Celia Gray was so public, so humiliating. She must have hated him for that."

"But that's just it—she didn't hate him," Becker replies. "She loved
him. Her heart breaks; she says so here."

"But that's just her heart, isn't it?" She smiles at him. "What about
the rest of her?" She bites her lip, sliding her foot gently up his thigh.
"Hearts can be overridden, other parts maybe not so much."

He laughs breathlessly as he reaches for her.

Sex between them lately is intense, verging on brutal. He means to
show reverence and respect for her condition, but in the moment he
always forgets, and his satisfaction gives way—almost as soon as he's
come—to guilt. This dissolving of boundaries between their bodies,
between his self and hers, is a source of joy, but it's complicated now by
something else. *Someone* else.

AFTERWARD HE STRUGGLES to look her in the eyes and she shoves
him so hard that he smacks his head on the foot of the desk. He gets
to his knees, rubbing the back of his head. "What was that for?" As if
he doesn't know.

"Don't Madonna-whore me, James," she says sternly, pulling her
robe back around her. She allows him to help her to her feet, but the
second she's upright, she snatches her hand from his. "I invited Sebastian for supper," she says, flinging the words out casually, like someone
skimming stones across a lake. "Can you make sure we've got some
good wine? *Not* Tesco Finest."

A DELIVERY VAN is parked at the back entrance of the big house, which
means they're receiving a new piece. Since no one has informed Becker
about this, he imagines it's something either very old or very new. Four
men—two in the van itself and two on the ground—are offloading

what appears to be an enormous carpet. Becker steps in to support the central section, and they carry it in together.

Sebastian and his mother are waiting in the central hall, their faces lit with anticipation. Lady Emmeline's mouth twists in distaste when she spies Becker. She shoots him a look to freeze the blood and then turns to her son. "Let me know when it's in place," she says. She walks off in the direction of the drawing room, heels clicking briskly on the parquet.

"Morning, Emmeline!" Becker calls out loudly to her retreating back.

Sebastian shakes his head. "At least give her her due, for Christ's sake."

Becker eyeballs Sebastian. "It really doesn't matter how I address her, does it? I'll always be the filthy, working-class interloper."

"You'll always be the man who broke up her son's engagement," Sebastian says, not quite under his breath. He turns to the delivery-men. "We're putting it in the blue room," he says brightly, extending his right arm like a tour guide. "It's this way, I'll show you."

In his office, Becker scrolls news sites, headlines rolling past unread as quietly he chastises himself. Why did he say that? There was no call for him to be spiteful.

There was an argument not long after he'd first arrived at Fairburn, over the placement of a sculpture—an unforgivably ugly sculpture— that Sebastian had bought, and for some reason he can't quite remember now, Becker allowed it to get heated: he raised his voice, used bad language. Later, when he was sitting on the steps to the east lawn, smoking a cigarette, feeling foolish, Helena came to find him. *Oh, here we go,* he thought, *the posh girl with a trust fund and a 2.2 in art history has come to tell me off, to teach me how to behave.*

But she didn't. She asked him to roll her a cigarette and, while he did so, offered a word of advice. *Don't let them ruffle your feathers,* she said. *Don't let them get under your skin. You're too passionate.* He remembers how he blushed when she said that, how he stiffened. *These people have ice in their veins,* she told him. *Don't show your hand. Don't let them see so easily who you are.*

He's annoyed that he didn't follow her advice this morning, but annoyed as he is at himself, he is angry with Sebastian, too—

irrationally so. He doesn't want to be reminded of all the wrongs he, Becker, has done to his employer.

He's still smarting when, an hour or so later, Sebastian puts his head round the door. "Beck. Do you want to come and see the Aubusson in situ?"

Dutifully and in silence, Becker follows Sebastian along the hall to the blue room, so-named for its curtains, in which they have laid in the center an antique Aubusson rug in shades of blue and cream.

It is not at all to Becker's taste. "It's very fine," he says.

"Isn't it?"

Becker nods, pressing his lips together firmly. "*Very* fine. Where did you get it? You didn't tell me you were looking for one."

Sebastian crouches down, brushing the back of his hand against the wool. "Mother got it, at auction. Without telling *me*," he says, rising back to his full height. He gives Becker a knowing look, and they both smile. "I'm sorry about earlier," he says.

"Not at all, I was . . . a dick."

"You were." Sebastian laughs, slapping him on the shoulder. "But even so. It's not just about Hels." He turns away, and Becker follows, heading back down the hallway toward Becker's office. "Mother not liking you, I mean. There's more to it than that."

"I know," Becker says.

"It's not *just* because you're a filthy, working-class interloper," Sebastian says, chuckling. "You know it's complicated. It's about my father, and Vanessa, and you being . . . well, a constant reminder of Vanessa, and all that went on—"

"But you know Vanessa's work would be here with or without me."

"It would, of course. But you're sort of . . . the *embodiment* of some pretty negative associations for her." He shrugs. "Ah, look—she's been in a foul mood since she saw the doctor last week anyway."

They've reached his office door. "There's nothing wrong, is there?" Becker asks. He's ashamed to realize how much the idea of Lady Emmeline being unwell pleases him.

THE BLUE HOUR   87

Sebastian scoffs, shakes his head. "Lady Em will outlive us all," he
says. "The doc's told her that the reason she's not sleeping and feeling
so . . . *antsy* all the time is that she might have post-traumatic stress
disorder, of all things. As you can imagine, she's not best pleased about
that." He walks before Becker into the office, strolling across to the
window behind the desk. The snow is still falling; it's heavier now,
stickier. "To be fair, they do say it about pretty much *everyone* these
days, don't they? PTSD, I mean. Used to be you had to have been
blown up by terrorists or pinned down under enemy fire. Nowadays
all you need to do is hit the family cat with your car." He turns, smiling ruefully at Becker, who nods and looks away. "I know what you're
thinking: Ah, but she didn't run over a cat, she accidentally shot her
husband in the neck and he bled out in front of her. I *know*." Becker
never ceases to be astounded by the stiffness of Sebastian's upper lip
in the face of this—and other—misfortunes. "I know, you know, but
the doctor doesn't. He got the official line, like the police and the press
and everyone else, which was probably a mistake. I think we could
probably have counted on the doc to be discreet . . ." Sebastian smiles,
shaking his head. "That's just the way it went."

The way it went was that Mr. Bryant, the gamekeeper, who is not
much younger than Sebastian's mother and has worked for her family
since he was a teenager, claimed that the stray shot came from his gun,
sparing Lady Emmeline the ordeal of a police investigation and all
the press intrusion that would go with it. There *was* an investigation,
which cleared Bryant of any wrongdoing—the fault, if there were any,
lay with Douglas himself, who had walked ahead of the guns and put
himself in harm's way—and he retired a few months later. Quite possibly, Becker thinks, with a rather more generous pension than he might
have been expecting.

"I'm sorry, Seb," Becker says. "I forget sometimes just how much it
is you're dealing with."

Sebastian scoffs. "A bunch of octogenarians running around with
high-powered rifles, what could possibly go wrong?" His smile has

become strained. "They had no business going out there, any of them, but what can you do? Imagine me trying to get in Emmeline's way."

Becker steers the conversation toward the mundane—an auction Sebastian is planning to attend in Edinburgh, the house tours they are considering launching next spring, for which Seb has managed to rustle up a little publicity.

"I persuaded the *Sunday Times* journo to ping over her copy just to make sure there are no literals. I'm going to email it to you—you'll give it the once-over, won't you?"

"Sure," Becker says. "Any good?"

Sebastian rocks his head side to side. "She'll not win a Pulitzer."

DARK DELIGHTS AT FAIRBURN HOUSE

*Maria Atwater gets a sneak preview of
the expanded Lennox collection.*

The past few years have been a roller coaster for Sebastian Lennox. In 2016 he was appointed director of the Fairburn Foundation, the charitable trust founded by his father, Sir Douglas, and his stewardship received a surprise boost when Fairburn inherited the Vanessa Chapman estate the following year.

Heartbreak and tragedy, however, were waiting in the wings. In the summer of 2019, Sir Douglas Lennox was killed in a shooting accident on the family estate. A few months later, Lennox's fiancée called off their wedding. And then Covid happened, laying to waste plans for the foundation's first major exhibition at the Lennoxes' ancestral home in the Borders, Fairburn House.

"It has been tough," Sebastian tells me, "though no tougher than many people have experienced over the past couple of years. And we now look to the future with great excitement."

Perhaps the most intriguing part of the Lennox collection are the Chapmans, many of which have never been seen before. Highlights include a number of small but powerfully intense seascapes and paintings of Eris Island in all tides and weathers. *Hope Is Violent*, believed to be the last picture Chapman completed before her death, is particularly poignant, giving us a dramatically rendered view of Sheepshead Island, as seen from Chapman's bedroom window.

Most thrilling of all, though, is the group of five works the late artist referred to in her diaries as her "black paintings"— large canvases straining under the weight of thickly applied paint in lustrous shades of green and blue, black and grey. Three are pure abstractions, but two of them feature figures smiling wolfishly, engaging in transgressive acts; they are bleak fairy tales, the most narrative of all of Chapman's works.

Spaciously displayed and sensitively lit in Fairburn's Great Hall, the black paintings are astonishing and strange. "They have this very sinister, nightmarish quality to them, but we don't really know what they're about," Lennox says. "At the moment, we can only speculate—is the figure in the paintings [Vanessa's late husband] Julian Chapman? Or is it an embodiment of the cancer that killed her? We hope that with full access to Chapman's papers, we might be able to discover more about where these extraordinary paintings came from and what they represent."

Other surprises in the bequest included a small number of sculptures, including *Beached*, *Division I*, and *Division II*, which were displayed in Paris at the Musée d'Art Moderne's much-praised *Twenty-One* show.

"The sculptures are fascinating not least because they seem to reference an earlier period in Chapman's work," says James Becker, creative director of the Fairburn Foundation. Becker, an old university pal of Sebastian Lennox's, is a Chapman expert. "Before [Chapman] became known as an expressionist painter, she was a practitioner of assemblage, arrangements of objects she found near her home in Oxfordshire. Those early works were belittled by critics—dismissed as 'folk art'—and as a result, Chapman seemed to have lost faith in the practice and abandoned it. But the discovery of these sculptures proves that she never lost her interest in the use of found, natural objects. Here we see them used in conjunction with created forms to powerful effect."

A selection of Chapman's sculptures is included in Tate Modern's *Sculpture and Nature* exhibition, which runs until November. Tours of Fairburn House open to the public early in 2022.

FOURTEEN

"What did you think of the *Sunday Times* piece?" Sebastian stands at the kitchen counter, running a knife through a bunch of parsley with chefly grace. He has a dishcloth flung over his shoulder, and a burning cigarette balances in the ashtray at his side. He looks like he owns the place. He *does* own the place.

"It was all right," Becker says ungraciously. He wants to say, *It was fine, I suppose, except for the bit where you started blethering on about the black paintings, ascribing narrative and meaning to the work of an artist you know almost nothing about.* But he bites his tongue. He is just back from driving a thirty-mile round trip to the nearest wine shop stocking not Tesco Finest; he has come home to a warm house, a fug of cooking, his pregnant wife laughing and drinking wine with her ex-fiancé, his lord and master; he feels ungracious.

"I thought it was good," Helena says. She's at the hob, tipping a pan at an angle with one hand, spooning melted butter over fillets of Dover sole with the other.

"I thought we were having beef rib," Becker says flatly. She turns and looks at him, the trace of a smile on her lips. He holds up two bottles of Barbaresco.

"Oh." She tilts her head, wrinkling her nose. "Sorry, darling. Changed my mind. It's all right, though, Seb brought Chablis."

Becker yanks the fridge door open with unnecessary gusto. Neither Sebastian nor Helena seems to notice. He pours himself a large glass of white and takes a sip. It's very good. He slams the fridge door and this time gets Helena's attention. She shoots him a look, gives him a tiny warning shake of her head.

There's an agreement between the three of them, unspoken but binding. They will behave like grown-ups; they will be civilized. It's the only way they can continue to live and work together, to remain friends. The hurt and the damage have to stay beneath the surface so that eventually, at some point, it will rot away. That's the theory, anyway. The odd thing is that, of the three of them, it is Becker who finds their little triangle uncomfortable and unrealistic. Helena is unfazed, inured perhaps by a lifetime of men competing for her affections, and Sebastian—the loser—has taken it on the chin. Becker won, so why can't he get over it?

"I thought it was a good piece," Helena says again, "considering the readership. The stuff about the black paintings was great—what did she say? Astonishing, sinister . . . it was all very selling. And you did well to get the Julian angle in there, Seb. That's the sort of stuff people are intrigued by, isn't it?"

As opposed to his witterings about assemblage, Becker thinks bitterly, but of course she's right. Selling isn't his strong suit. Selling isn't what he's here for.

Over dinner, they talk about upcoming exhibitions in London, a band Helena wants to see who are playing next month in Glasgow, old friends, people Helena and Sebastian knew when they were younger. Their families have known each other forever—Helena's mother went to school with Emmeline. Sebastian is charming, Becker is quietly civil; he tries not to grind his teeth. Helena sits between them, now peacemaker, now hand grenade; she can defuse a tense situation with a wave of her hand and then somehow stir up another with a word, a look.

When talk turns to Emmeline, Helena places a hand on top of Sebastian's. "Of course it's impossible for her to talk about, Seb. What happened was . . . unimaginable. In any case, her generation, her class, they don't talk, do they? They don't do weakness. You, though, it's different for you." Sebastian smiles at her affectionately, rolls his hand out from under hers as she adds, "You definitely ought to talk to someone."

"I'm not sure she'd like that," he says, and then he drains the last of his wine, shaking his head as though dismissing something. He turns to Becker. "Tell us about Eris," he says. "You haven't told me anything about the wicked witch."

Becker raises his eyes heavenward. Helena gives him a kick under the table. "Come on, Beck. What was she like?"

"She was nice," he says. "A bit frightened. And very lonely, I imagine. The house is rather run-down. It looked . . . stripped. I felt sorry for her." He slips his hand into the pocket of his jeans, rolling between his fingertips the white pebble he took from the house. "We've already taken a great deal from her."

"Did you press her about the missing works?" Sebastian asks, clearly unmoved. Ice in his veins, indeed.

Becker sighs, topping up his glass. "We don't actually have evidence that there is anything missing. Douglas said he remembered Vanessa promising him certain paintings for an exhibition, but that exhibition never even happened, so—"

"He saw them!" Sebastian interrupts. "My father went to Eris a few months before the exhibition was due to happen, he saw the pictures in her studio. He told me this. He saw the pictures, as well as dozens of ceramic pieces destined for her solo show. They were there"—Sebastian jabs the tabletop with his forefinger—"in the studio, ready to go—it was part of the reason he was so shattered when she suddenly canceled." Helena tries to intercede, but Sebastian holds up his hand. "Look, even if she had sold the paintings privately, it simply isn't credible that we wouldn't have found a single trace of any of them."

Becker shakes his head. "No, you're right, you're absolutely right about that, it's not credible. But that's still not evidence. We have no proof of anything; all we have is—"

"My father's word."

In the chilly silence that follows, Helena pushes her chair back. Sebastian half rises from his seat, but Helena shakes her head at him. Leaning back in his chair, Becker catches the tips of her fingers with his hand, squeezing them in a gesture of apology. "I'll do the dishes," he says.

"I know you will," she replies, jutting her chin out at him. "I was going to make tea. Do you want one? Or a coffee, or . . ."

"Whisky," Sebastian says. Now he leans back. Stretching his arms up over his head, he yawns expansively. "I'll have a whisky."

Becker gets up to fetch a bottle of Springbank from the cabinet. "What about *Division II*?" he asks. "When are we getting it back?" He finds the bottle, turns around.

Sebastian is only half listening; he's watching Helena as she clears the table.

"Sebastian?"

"It's . . . uh . . . it's with this private lab in London, they have better facilities—"

"Jesus Christ!" Becker slams the bottle down on the table. Helena flinches and cuts her eyes at him; she places the teacup she is holding on the counter and leaves the room. Neither Becker nor Sebastian says a word as they listen to her footfall on the stairs, the slam of the bedroom door.

Sebastian throws up his hands. "I asked the people at the Tate to get another forensics guy to look at it, just like you suggested, and they did. They agreed with the chap who wrote the letter—they think the bone is human. A human rib. So now we are duty bound to investigate, at least until we get an idea of how old it is. We don't have a choice."

They come to an agreement: the testing will go ahead, but Becker will be there when the case is opened. That, Sebastian reckons, is unlikely to be for a few weeks at least. It's not a priority case.

"We'll need to let the insurers know," Sebastian says to him.

"And Grace Haswell," Becker replies.

Sebastian shakes his head, bemused. "It's none of her business, Beck." They finish their whisky, and Sebastian says goodnight. Once he's gone, Becker does the washing-up, tidies the kitchen, and puts everything away save the bottle and a glass. He pours himself another drink, turns off the lights, and sits in the darkness in front of the dying fire.

He didn't argue about Grace Haswell, but now, sitting staring into the embers, he makes his case in his head. It *is* her business. If you'd talked to her, if you'd listened to Grace talk about Vanessa's fingerprints, her DNA, her breath—you'd think so, too.

He didn't argue because he doesn't want to argue with Sebastian, just as he doesn't want to alienate Grace. He wants to please everyone. He does not have ice in his veins.

Here's the crux of it: he already feels guilty, and he doesn't want to exacerbate his guilt. He has behaved badly in the past; he wants somehow to balance the scale, though he knows full well he cannot. He cannot turn back time. He cannot go back to his early college days, when he befriended Sebastian not because he liked him—back then, he regarded Seb as just one among the herd of entitled, public-school mediocrities that populate Oxford colleges—but because he knew that Sebastian was Douglas Lennox's son and that Douglas was Vanessa's gallerist. No more can he go back to the afternoon when, just three days after Douglas's death, Becker brought Helena back to this house and spent the afternoon in bed with her.

Nor would he want to.

But he can do this right. He can do the job that Sebastian has given him as well as he possibly can; he can make a success of the museum, show the collection in its best light, he can honor Vanessa's work and his mother's memory.

He will do all this, for Sebastian and for Grace, and for Vanessa, too.

Vanessa Chapman's diary

I have mice.

Mice, a leaking roof, rotting floorboards, and damp. The electrics are lethal, and there is a foul smell from the septic tank.

I've not felt this happy in years.

The Aga works, so I live in the kitchen and work outside when I can. I paint all day—yesterday the light was good until almost ten o'clock. I climbed up to Eris Rock—the highest point of the island. An extraordinary soft sunset, sky fondant—pale greys and soft whites at first, then came dusky pink and amber turning darker, an orange fit to eat, a molten yellow almost the shade of a Van Gogh sunflower. I could barely get the paint onto canvas quickly enough. The sky is one thing; the sea a different beast. The sky challenges, but the sea confounds: restless, ever-changing, the deep round swell of it, the violence!

Impossible to capture.

———

I have been going to the beach to make studies of the sea, not terribly successfully. I can make out the wave, the drag of a current, the build of swell, but it is the critical moment that eludes me, the moment of breaking, when all that stored power is unleashed, that moment of terrible chaos.

Impossible.

———

There was a violent storm yesterday, water pouring in through the roof in the kitchen and living room. Everything shorted. Candles only now. I'm unable to get to the mainland, and I think the weather is set to last two to three days. It's frightening and exhilarating—I've been sketching constantly. There is something in the sketches, but I cannot quite get at what. Whenever I try to grasp it, it moves away.

I have biscuits and a bottle of whisky and enough tobacco to last two days. Three if I'm careful.

Work has begun on the house: roof first, a new window in the kitchen to let in more light. Replace floorboards in bedroom, deal with damp. New kitchen to go in. Whole place to be rewired.

Then the barn. Large picture window looking south, widening doorway on the east side—that end will be almost entirely open when the door is rolled back, so the space becomes three-sided, light from the south & east & plenty of ventilation.

It will use up the rest of the money from J. But since the house went for more than we thought, he still owes me 15k. I also have two completed paintings to give to Douglas—<u>South</u> and <u>Low Tide</u>—and another of the barn with the wood behind that is not quite finished. I will tell him to get what he can for them.

————

Squalls blow in and out, threatening to rip the roof off and making it impossible to paint outside. I keep busy: the wood is thick with finds: cones and seeds, teeth and old bones. The beach is fruitful, too. Sumptuously rounded pebbles in dusky pinks and terra-cotta and purest white. Jellyfish! Shells, of course, kelp in rust and the most lurid green, bright blue glass. At low tide you can walk the seabed, more than half a mile out to sea. I come back with pockets bulging.

I feel overwhelmed with ideas.

The sheer expanse of landscape—sea and sky—is invigorating. The air so unleaded! It lends itself to a completely different aesthetic. I no longer feel hemmed in by dusty plane trees and houses and hedges. I no longer feel weighted down by England's dreary white skies. Here the sky is miraculous azure or threatening gunmetal, glorious orange and peach and primrose.

————

Getting things done. Drove into Carrachan to see the dentist. Crown fitted. This afternoon I'm seeing a man about a quad bike so I can transport canvases up the hill more easily. The man in the village shop (Sandy?) is trying to sell me a boat. I think I prefer to remain at the mercy of the tide—and in any case, I'm not sure I'd feel brave enough to use a boat—the currents here are terrifying. One of the reasons I rarely paint on the beach: I'm afraid of getting caught.

Douglas came on Thursday, stayed the weekend. I enjoy him, but he demands a lot—body and mind. He wants me to start thinking about a solo show—he worries I will be forgotten out here . . . I'm not ready. I want to allow myself to settle here, to enjoy this feeling of vibrancy and creativity without having to think conceptually, without having to <u>plan</u>.

A journalist from the <u>Sunday Telegraph</u> came yesterday. Douglas's idea. For a feature on "how artists live." Not at all the right time for me—the studio is not finished, and I have no work I want to show—not to a journalist in any case.

D complains that I hold too tightly to my pieces—he thinks it is about confidence. It isn't. It's about <u>choice</u>. I will surrender my work to the world only when I feel ready, I will not be hurried or harangued or bullied. Those days are over.

———————

Mark says he will drive up in the van next week, he is bringing Frances's old kick wheel.

———————

Fetched 20kg porcelain paper clay from Carrachan. Roof still leaking, man came out yesterday, he is quoting £2k to repair!

J not responding to my letters. I shall have to go south to wring the money out of the bastard. No idea why he is being so tight, Celia is filthy rich—it's the thing he likes most about her.

———————

Studio finished at last. I fired the kiln for the first time yesterday!

———————

I work at least from dawn to dusk, often well into the night. I barely notice time, I hardly eat, hardly write. I am consumed, feel I need nothing else. Working with ceramics is a joy. None of the anxiety I feel when painting—there is such freedom with clay: nothing is set, nothing decided, nothing finished until it is fired. I'm working almost solely at the wheel—

tall, elegant pieces, long-necked and fine. I'm experimenting with colour. Moving here has opened up a new palette for me. I breathe in air that is cold and crisp and crystalline: it feels white, and sometimes blue or violet. I imagine it as needles in my lungs (that sounds violent, but it is not). My mood feels lighter, and I start to find a fluidity that I lacked before.

———————

D sent over the <u>Sunday Tel.</u> piece. Beautiful picture taken from the top of Eris Rock, another of me, in the studio, looking daggers. I am described as attractive, prickly, sullen, uncommunicative. Not much about the work. (D says this is my fault because I was so ungenerous.) Quotes from "friends" (which friends???) about how work consumes me, how I never have time for anything else (i.e., my marriage), I am single-minded, obsessive. All the usual shit they say about women who fail to devote themselves body and soul to family aka dreary domesticity. At the end there is a line saying I was "instrumental in the breakup of Mark Brice's marriage." Unfair and untrue. Bet that came from Isobel, the vindictive bitch.

Have not felt so pissed off since I got here. Rang D and told him it's the last fucking time I talk to a fucking journalist. Afterward, I walked up the hill, right to the top of the rock, looked out to the sea, to the islands, I turned round and saw that the tide was in. I was cut off from the world, nowhere to go and no one to bother me. I ran back down to the studio, put it all out of my mind, and was serene again.

Now, in the kitchen, darkness fallen, I long to create something that conveys that feeling of breaking from the rest. How to capture? The feeling of cleaving—clean and painful and freeing.

———————

J writes, furious that I should be airing our dirty laundry in the newspapers???? Threatening to come here. I threw his letter in the bin and went back to the studio, worked all day, didn't think of him once.

———————

Darkness here is sudden, complete, inhuman. With the haar in there is no light at all save the flash, every twenty-three seconds, from the lighthouse on Sheepshead.

———————

Some days, the sun barely rises.

———————

No light, no shadow, and yet I find I am desperate to paint.

———————

A while ago (two days or three?), I went to my southern spot to finish my Sheepshead painting. Strange weather: it was bright when I left the house, but by the time I set up, the sky was a peculiar yellow—like gas in the atmosphere—and the sea was still, black and terrifying. Like the end of the world! I started a fresh canvas and painted with a sense of urgency I cannot explain, only that the darkness and the fear seemed to draw me in and consume me.

Now that canvas—completed in a matter of hours—is in the spare room and I hardly want to look at it. It is a haunting presence, disquieting. A black painting.

FIFTEEN

Holding his cigarette lightly between his lips, Becker rubs his hands together to warm them. He is leaning over the guardrail on the foot-bridge, the water beneath it covered with a thin layer of ice. His head swims. A black painting! And it wasn't about cancer or Julian Chapman or any of those things Sebastian came up with; it is a painting of the sea. The impossible sea! She found a way to paint it.

He spent much of the night going through the first notebook, lux-uriating in it, taking his time, making his own notes. Vanessa mentions bones just once—*the wood is thick with finds . . . teeth and old bones . . .* Why *old* bones? Did she know they were old? Or is that just a figure of speech? Bones are always old, aren't they? The fact is she might have found the rib on one of those early forays into the wood, right back when she first came to the island, more than twenty years ago. It might have been hanging around in her studio for years before she found a use for it.

(He wonders, briefly, about the teeth. What sort of teeth? Surely *those* couldn't have been human? After all, you don't have to be a forensic anthropologist to recognize a human tooth.)

In any case, the bone question is moot now, isn't it? The experts have deemed it human, and they're to test it. It's out of his hands.

His cigarette finished, he walks up to the main house, entering at the back as usual. He can see, as soon as he turns into the hallway, that the door to his office is ajar. He strides quickly along the corridor, hands clenched into fists, indignation bubbling up: yes, the house is Sebastian's, but surely he is entitled to some privacy in his workspace? He pushes the door open hard, keen to provoke a reaction.

From the opposite side of the desk, Lady Emmeline looks up coolly at him. Spread over the desk are pieces of paper covered in fine pencil and blue ink—the contents of the folder he brought with him from Eris.

"Are you planning to put these on display?" she asks.

"Uh . . . some of them, yes," Becker replies. "I've not had time to read everything yet. There's a lot to go through and I—"

She holds up a hand to silence him, expression pained; she squeezes her eyes shut for a second. "What is it that you find so interesting," she asks, turning away from him slightly so that her face is hidden, "about Mrs. Chapman? She reminds you of your mother, Sebastian said, is that right?" Very slowly she turns toward him again, lips drawing back from her teeth. "She died of cancer, too, didn't she?"

"Sh . . . she did, yes." Becker stumbles slightly over his words. "When I was a child—"

"And was she also a whore?"

Becker is stunned into silence. Emmeline moves around the desk toward the door, but her eyes do not leave his. "If in the course of your work as curator here you choose to humiliate me, Mr. Becker, I will make certain that you pay for it. Do you understand? And if you think that an elderly woman such as myself is incapable of causing you harm, I assure you you're mistaken."

She moves past him, a waft of L'Air du Temps and the sound of heels clacking along the marble tiles. For a few moments, he cannot move.

He feels as though he's been slapped; he is ashamed to find himself close to tears. Closing the office door, he crosses quickly over to his desk, pressing his hands down on the desktop, breath coming painfully sharp. He reaches out and takes hold of the letter Emmeline was looking at when he entered the room; he turns the page around so that he can read it.

November 1999

Vanessa,

Since your last visit I struggle to think of anything but you. Right now I would leave my wife and son to perish in a burning building if only I could have you again, spend a night with you, an hour. I think of nothing but your luscious mouth, your delectable cunt.

I have to see you.
Douglas

Becker feels his face grow hot. He tugs at his collar, embarrassed, as though he and Emmeline now share some filthy secret. Rounding the desk, he sits down and starts to gather the papers she has spread out, shuffling them into some sort of order. Sliding them back into the folder, he spies letters from Vanessa to her great friend Frances Levy, another from a potential buyer, a rough sketch of the studio, and a note, written on headed paper from Douglas Lennox's Glasgow Modern Gallery, in Douglas's spiky hand.

I should cut your fucking throat for what you've done to me

SIXTEEN

In bed, he lies behind Helena, his right hand on her hip, his lips pressed against the back of her neck. She smells ripe, *almost overripe*, he thinks, and in the darkness he smiles. She raises a hand and drapes it over his leg, lightly grazing his thigh with her fingernails.

"I found Emmeline in my office this morning," he says.

"Oh?"

"She called my mother a whore."

"*What?*" Helena wriggles away from him, rolling over and propping herself up on one elbow.

He pulls a face. "Actually, that's not *quite* fair. She was calling Vanessa a whore and then asked if my mother was one, too."

Helena shakes her head, incredulous. "Beck, that's horrible. She's . . . I honestly think she's becoming deranged."

Becker rolls onto his back. "I don't know," he says. "When I arrived, she was looking through some of those papers I got from Grace Haswell. She'd found a letter from Douglas to Vanessa. It was . . . *explicit*."

"Really?" Helena slides one leg over his. "How explicit?" she breathes into his ear. When Becker laughs, she lies back down, sweeping her hair out of the way so that she can rest her head on his shoulder without it catching. "Obviously that can't have made pleasant reading, but it's not like she didn't know. From what I've been told, Douglas was not discreet. And it wasn't like Vanessa was the only one—he was monstrously unfaithful."

"I suppose we really ought to feel sorry for her," Becker says. "The whole thing must be humiliating."

"Well, maybe," Helena murmurs. "But it's not your fault, is it? Or your mother's."

"No, quite." Becker is looking up at the crack in the ceiling, which starts in the far corner and has been tracing its spidery way toward the center of the room ever since he moved into the lodge three years ago. He ought to do something about that, he thinks, get someone to look at it. Leave it too long and the whole lot'll come down on them. "Has Emmeline always been like this?" he asks, but Helena doesn't answer; she shifts in his arms, her breath slowing, deepening, as she falls asleep. He lies awake for a long while listening to Helena's soft breath, looking up at the crack in the ceiling, praying the roof's not about to cave in.

SEVENTEEN

Grace sits at the kitchen table, a pile of correspondence in front of her. It is almost two o'clock in the morning; the tea she made an hour ago sits in the pot, cold and stewed. Within the hour, the tide will be in and she will go to bed, but for now she continues her work, reading, considering, sorting everything into neat little piles.

The windows rattle, and she looks up. The darkness is thick as pitch, but she can tell that weather is coming. She makes a note to close the shutters on the south side of the house—it bears the brunt of the wind—and to make sure the studio doors are secured.

Pulling a blanket up over her shoulders, she returns to the letter in front of her. It's one that Vanessa wrote to Frances Levy, an artist friend, part of a stack of correspondence that Frances's daughter, Leah, returned to Grace after Frances died of Covid last year. Grace is putting the letters into sequence, making sense of their call-and-response, a twenty-five-year conversation that is concerned almost entirely with the art they were making, Frances down in Cornwall and Vanessa in Oxfordshire and up here in Eris.

Vanessa: The paint is the thing! Since I broke my wrist I feel I'm so much more aware of the <u>materiality</u> of the paint. I love this feeling of moving into a more sculptural space on the canvas. Sometimes I wonder though if all this change, this constant metamorphosing, makes the work seem incoherent?

Frances: Developing an aesthetic language, in the way a writer cultivates a voice—isn't that what we aim for? Your shift from figuration to abstraction and back, that is part of your language, and it is right that it should morph sometimes, it should develop—after all, we must change if we are to stay relevant.

Vanessa: I'm not bothered about relevance. I'm not interested in unmade beds or sharks cut in half! But still I shift, as sands do. I think what you make should be influenced by where you make it, how you make it, and with what. Every day I wake and am thrilled to be here—divided from the land by sea—speaking the language of nature and tide, not of politics or human society.

Grace grits her teeth. The letters are written in what she thinks of as Vanessa's "art voice," the pretentious one she used to impress people she thought were her social superiors, one she never used with Grace. She finds most of the correspondence with Frances either baffling or banal. How could they take themselves so seriously? They were painting pictures, for Christ's sake, not curing cancer. Still, she imagines Becker will find this all thrilling, and so she places the letters about art in the pile of papers destined for Fairburn. Others, those where life—love affairs, friendship, enmities—intrude, she places in a separate, "private," pile.

Frances: Dora came to see me. She and Mark have split again. She was very distressed, begged me to intervene on her behalf—to ask you to finish things with Mark. I told her I had no control over you! But I will say this: if Mark is not important to you (as a lover, I mean to say, I know he is important as a friend), end it. Do not pursue it or let him come back to you. She is so broken. It was ugly and sad to see. The baby is only eight months—I worry Dora isn't coping.

Vanessa: Frances, you know that this thing with Mark isn't really my doing. I break it off and break it off (I have broken it off again) and still he comes back. I am sorry for Dora. I am sorry that she is hurt. But I think her problem is with Mark, not me. Awful to think of her struggling with the child—I cannot imagine how that feels, I have always been so grateful that I couldn't get pregnant when

Julian wanted me to. It has always seemed to me that family is the antithesis of freedom.

When Leah first handed the letters over, Grace was surprised—did she not want to keep her own mother's letters? Grace kept them to one side, thinking Leah might have acted rashly, as people do in grief, that she might change her mind and ask for them back, but she hasn't done so. Reading through them now, Grace thinks she understands why. Leah is rarely mentioned, and when she is, she's a postscript. Or worse.

Frances: You are wrong about family! You <u>absolutely can</u> be a mother and be free. And work, too! Look at Hepworth. (Though, if I am honest, I do sometimes wonder why we kept going. One baby is enough! Why stretch love so thin?)

Leah is the youngest of three.
Grace places the letter in the "private" pile, noticing as she does her own name mentioned toward the end; she picks it up again.

Frances: Is G still there all the time? You need to be careful, V, you know how you have a tendency to attract hangers-on. I imagine she finds you very glamorous. Her life must be so dreary—endlessly doling out antibiotics and scolding people for smoking and drinking too much. So joyless! I suppose we ought to feel sorry for her.

Grace's hand clenches to a fist, scrunching the paper with it. With a huff of impatience she smooths it out again, pressing it into the wood with the heel of her hand. Idiotic to let it rankle so and yet . . . *doling out antibiotics*! It's laughable. Yes, there were coughs and colds, but there's also a fisherman who kept the use of his right hand thanks to Grace's skill and quick thinking; there was a three-year-old who came into the surgery for her MMR vaccine and left with a referral to a kidney specialist. If it hadn't been for Grace, her rare cancer would likely have gone undiagnosed for months; it might not have been caught in time. That little girl got married last year and is expecting a child of her own now. *She* is Grace's legacy—what has Frances left behind? Earthenware pots?

Grace moves on to the next letter in the sequence, and as she reads she feels her heart swell in her chest, tears springing bright to her eyes.

Vanessa: I don't think you need to feel sorry for G. She has a real life, a real job! She is rooted, connected to this community in a way I will never be. I envy her that. People rely on Grace. I rely on her! She is not a hanger-on. She is a good friend. I relish her lack of interest in the art world—she thinks it's all pretentious crap and she's (mostly) right. We rub along together very happily, and if (when) I need to be alone, I tell her so. It is never a problem.

Glowing with pride, Grace places this letter on top of the pile she intends Becker to read. He will see how Vanessa loved her; he'll see that she's a fundamental part of Vanessa's story. After a moment's hesitation, she plucks the letter in which Frances mentioned her children from the private pile and adds that to the one for Becker, too.

There is another cache of letters ready for sorting, the Carlisle letters, as she thinks of them, but she can't quite face these yet, so instead she turns to the photographs. Most of these she is happy to relinquish: the majority are pictures Vanessa took of the island. Although she didn't like to paint from them, she found them useful as reference points, or to remind her of the way the light might have looked at a certain time on a certain day.

A few photos date back to her life in Oxfordshire—at parties, mostly, with groups of people dressed up and holding drinks in gardens—and a few snaps of people taken here in Eris, too: Frances and Mark and a few other "art" friends, an unflattering one of Grace sitting stiffly on the bench overlooking the sands, one of Douglas and Emmeline Lennox, date-stamped 1999.

THE BLUE HOUR   111

In the picture, the Lennoxes are tanned and glamorous, both of them in sunglasses, smoking, leaning against the hood of Douglas's Aston Martin. A rifle rests between them. They were going on somewhere, Grace seems to recall, to hunt. Emmeline liked to shoot; she went off one afternoon on the island and came back with two rabbits, for cacciatore. She skinned them herself.

While Vanessa was showing Douglas what she'd been working on, Grace helped Emmeline with the stew, chopping onions and celery and carrots, listening to her complain about her staff and the ramblers wandering all over their estate. The weekend before, she told Grace, she'd shot a dog that was worrying the cows.

"How awful," Grace said.

Emmeline's mouth turned down at the corners. "Walkers," she said, shrugging. "They let it off the leash." *Orf*, Grace remembers. *They let it orf the leash.* "They had a child with them. It cried and cried. Dreadful carry-on. As if I'd shot its mother."

Grace disliked her intensely. She remembers scrubbing the potatoes, the skin across her knuckles red and raw, and she remembers the pleasure she took, in that moment, thinking that Vanessa was likely not showing Douglas her work at all.

She picks up the photograph and squints at it again, examining Emmeline's expression, the firm line of her mouth, the upward tilt of her chin. She remembers the dismay on Emmeline's face when Douglas and Vanessa came down from the studio, late for dinner, their clothes disheveled, stinking of sex. Grace remembers how her feeling of pleasure dissipated like smoke.

SHE WAKES JUST before nine, pulling back the curtain to let in the light. The window is spattered with raindrops, a soft sky dappled with clouds. She opens the window and leans out and tastes salt on her tongue. The hillside is burnished with damp copper bracken; the deep, soft green of the wood is an invitation.

She dresses quickly and leaves the house before she can talk herself out of it. She has become fatter, less fit over the past year; she needs to stop the rot. Living out here on the island all alone requires a certain level of fitness.

The tide is falling, the water in the bay stippled like pebble dash. On the far end of the causeway she spots a figure on foot. She cannot tell at this distance who it is, but they seem to be carrying something—a bucket, perhaps? A mussel picker.

She turns her back to the sea and heads up the hill, alarmed at how quickly breathlessness sets in. She's never been svelte, but she's always been strong: hands like a butcher, a man once told her, legs to kick-start a jumbo jet. The slope up toward the wood is steep, but she used to walk alongside Vanessa—taller and slimmer with much longer legs—and keep pace. Now she stops every twenty paces or so, breathing hard, sweat prickling between her breasts and in the small of her back.

At the brow of the hill lies the studio, and then a small stand of trees, and beyond another, more gradual slope to the wood. The wood has been left untended and is sunless as a cave, cold, too, and pungent with leaf mold. Once you enter its embrace, the sound of the sea is deadened; you hear only the ominous creak of old pines, the cry of gulls.

Keeping her pace steady, Grace makes her way along the path as it meanders north to the heart of the wood and then hairpins back to the southwest, ascending once more. She has just turned that sharp bend when, out of the corner of her eye, she catches a glimpse of color, bright red. Her breath catches, her heart rate rocketing. It's nothing, it's no one. It's a Coke can. For God's sake! She grits her teeth and walks over to pick it up. Hikers usually clean up after themselves, but not always. Sometimes you get kids out here, huffing glue or gas or whatever else they can get their hands on. Not so often in winter.

She carries the can with her toward the western end of the wood, where two enormous trunks, trees brought down in a storm almost thirty years ago, once forced the path into a sharp detour. The trunks eventually rotted away, but this part of the wood still feels different: a gap in the canopy allows the light in, so smaller plants grow here, witch elm and holly and inhospitable hawthorn, its berries gleaming like gouts of blood. The ground beneath her feet is firm and undisturbed. Grace scuffs through the leaves; she crouches down and presses her hand against the cold earth, tracing her fingers along the ground. The dank smells of the thicket stir something in her, a memory of a camping trip, of sleeping under the stars. Another life.

With some difficulty she straightens up and turns, walking briskly down the hill toward home. It isn't until she has passed the studio that she notices someone sitting on the bench overlooking the sands—the mussel picker. A child, wearing a high-vis jacket, a blue bucket at their feet.

"Hello?" she calls out hesitantly. She has no desire to cope with a lost child. But they turn, and Grace sees with relief that it is not a child at all, it's Marguerite, her wrinkled face breaking into a smile. She slips off the bench and picks up her bucket.

"'Allo!" She is wearing a pinafore and Wellington boots, the high-vis jacket swamping her tiny frame. She holds out her bucket, showing Grace a small collection of mussels and some kelp. "You want some?" she asks, eyes wide, expectant.

"Oh no," Grace says, shaking her head, "not for me, thank you."

"You don't like?"

Grace shakes her head. She does like mussels, but she'd think twice about eating anything picked on the coastlines; you can't go a day without reading a story about water companies pumping sewage into the sea.

"That's a snazzy jacket you've got there," Grace says. Marguerite giggles. "It doesn't look terribly warm, though." Marguerite shakes her head, looking up from beneath lowered lashes, as though she's been caught doing something she shouldn't. "Will you come in for coffee?" Grace asks, and the old woman nods and smiles again, trotting along at Grace's side toward the house.

Marguerite is in her seventies now, but unlike Grace she remains wiry and agile, her tanned forearms lean and muscled. She places the bucket outside the door and takes off her Wellies, padding into the house in damp-socked feet. Her eyes light up when she sees the table piled high with papers; after a few attempts to stop her picking things up and putting them down in the wrong place, Grace gives up. She makes coffee while Marguerite marvels at sketches and old photographs, smiling toothily at Grace whenever she recognizes something or someone.

Suddenly, she stops. She looks at Grace, her expression grave. "There is a man at the harbor," she says solemnly. "He is watching you."

Out at the harbor? Grace walks over to the window and picks up the binoculars on the sill. "Now?" There are no cars parked at the harbor wall; she sees no one at all.

"*Non, non, il y a deux jours.*"

"In English, Marguerite," Grace says, replacing the binoculars. "I don't understand you otherwise."

"Not today." Marguerite shakes her head. "There are two days, maybe three days, four, five. A man. Watching, waiting."

Grace nods. "It's all right, he was just someone who needed to talk to me." Marguerite probably means Becker, though she might not. She's been drifting into dementia for years now, a slow decline at first, but it's picking up—almost two years of lockdown-induced isolation have surely not helped; she is frightened of strangers and her memories are jumbled, characters from one life popping up in another. "You don't have to worry about him," Grace says. "He came over to see me, but he's gone now."

"He comes back?"

"Yes, maybe . . ."

"Oh." Tears well in Marguerite's eyes, her fingers working at the ends of her hair.

Grace sits at her side. "It's OK, Marguerite. He's not a bad man. You don't need to be frightened of him. You don't need to be frightened at all."

"Yes," she says, shaking her head as she says it, "yes, yes."

"He's not . . . he's not Stuart. Stuart is not coming back."

"No," Marguerite says. Tears run down her cheeks; she wipes them away with the tips of her fingers. "But maybe yes? *On ne sait jamais.* We can never know."

Grace takes hold of Marguerite's hand and squeezes her fingers. "We do know, don't we? I've told you. He's not coming back." Stuart was Marguerite's husband; he's been gone more than twenty years and she's still terrified of him. "Come on now, look at these pictures, there you go." Grace pushes a shoebox full of unsorted photographs toward her. "You take a look at those while I get the coffee." Marguerite does as she's told, chattering away to herself quietly—possibly in French, Grace can't make out any words. Grace makes a strong batch of coffee—she knows just how Marguerite likes it—and places a mug and the sugar bowl on the table, watching in amusement as Marguerite spoons sugar into her drink, *one, two, three . . .*

"That's enough," Grace says, laughing as she stays the older woman's hand. Marguerite giggles.

Blowing on her coffee before tasting, she sips, smiles. "Good," she says. "Very good." She takes another sip, swinging her legs under her chair, and looks around, cocks her head to one side like a fox listening for prey. "Where is he, your friend?"

"My friend? You mean Vanessa?"

"Yes." Marguerite nods. "Where is he?"

"*She's* gone, Marguerite, a while ago now, you remember? You came to her funeral." The smile drops from Marguerite's face. "She was very sick, for a long time, and then she died."

"*Ah, non.*" Vanessa always had time for Marguerite; she was kind to her without ever intruding on her privacy. One of Vanessa's gifts, knowing how to give people what they needed.

Now Marguerite is tearful again, and this time Grace's attempts at distraction with more photographs and sketches are unsuccessful. "But where is he, your friend?" Marguerite asks again, her brow knitted.

This is how it goes. There is always another question, another friend, another man, another something or someone to be afraid of. And a moment later, it's forgotten.

When Grace offers to drive her back across the causeway, Marguerite demurs. "Good for me," she says, grinning, mimicking marching. "Keep me young!" Her front tooth, a porcelain replacement for one lost years ago, has become discolored by nicotine and coffee; it gives her a neglected air. "Thank you, thank you," she sings, kissing Grace on both cheeks. "Thank you, thank you, thank you." And off she goes, bucket swinging, down the track toward the sea, chattering her thank-yous into the wind.

Back in the kitchen, Grace restores order to her stacks of letters and photographs; she flicks quickly through the pictures in the shoebox, most of which are unlikely to be of great interest to anyone. Becker is welcome to them.

Finally, she turns to the Carlisle letters: the ones she and Vanessa wrote to each other over an eighteen-month period when Grace left the island and took a temporary job in the north of England, the year following Julian Chapman's disappearance.

These are hard to read.

January 2003

Dear Vanessa,

I'm not claiming to understand how you feel, of course I'm not. How could I? I don't pretend to understand how you could spend hours describing to me his faults, his infidelities, his manipulations, his deceits, and then welcome him as you did into our home, taking him to bed, making plans to travel with him to Morocco or Venice or wherever else you were planning to run off to. But it doesn't matter now, does it?

None of that matters now, the only thing I care about is <u>you</u> and your happiness. You know that I love you dearly, that I would do anything for you, and that includes letting you be, if that is still what you want. But I worry terribly about you all alone, I know how frightened you get. If you need me, send word, and I'll come back, to Eris and to you.

Love, always,
Grace

Reading this, Grace is amazed that she had managed to sound so rational, so resigned. When she reads Vanessa's response, it feels as though a wound has opened in her chest, a gaping hole for the wind to whistle painfully in.

I don't know how to respond to your letter, only to say that I <u>don't</u> want you to come back to Eris. You know things you shouldn't, and I'm not sure how to be around you again. I hope you understand what I mean.

There is more, but Grace cannot bear to read it. She turns the page and picks up another letter, one that bears just a few words.

I need you. Please, come.

There are notes from later on, too, little shopping lists Vanessa left out, requests for more paracetamol, more whisky, oranges, cigarettes; sometimes little sketches, of the view from the kitchen window, the clouds, an idea for a vase, funny doodles of seals sunning themselves on the beach, curved like croissants, flippers raised in jaunty salute.

Looking at these little bits of paper now, Grace is grateful to her younger self, the one who knew to throw nothing away, to save every scrap, treasure every word she wrote down. Vanessa stopped drawing altogether toward the end, and her notes became sporadic, often incomprehensible. She stuck them to the fridge or simply threw them on the floor for Grace to pick up, scraps of paper covered in a tight, barely legible scrawl:

please help please you help me grace please help me

Vanessa Chapman's diary

I have been thinking about what Frances said, all those years ago, about blurring the boundaries between abstraction and representation—I thought she was being so obvious, trite even, but she's right in a sense—that is what I'm looking for. To be unbound. Maybe not to blur but to dissolve the lines—between abstraction and figuration, organic and inorganic, ordinary and uncanny.

So. Have been working on creating a new object—a vessel—made from some of the broken fragments of ceramic. The pieces do not all come from the same broken thing, I am creating something new, uneven, uncanny— bowl but not bowl, vase but not vase. Thinking of suspending found objects above it, so that they have a direct relationship to the vessel but are not contained by it. Moving toward a sort of sculpture, I suppose. Hard to explain, but I am starting to see it. Sketching a great deal.

————

The suspended forms will be static, they can be seen & appreciated & interpreted from different angles, so the form of the whole changes.

The space between the objects is as important as the objects themselves, shadow as important as light.

I had an idea to enclose the whole thing in glass??? But I am of two minds: I like the distance this creates but worry will there also be a loss of immediacy? A loss of connection?

But to whom am I connecting, after all? I have no plans to show anything. Who would show it for me?

All my bridges burned, the tide is in.

————

Division is complete.

I picked up the glass from the glazier on Friday and assembled everything yesterday. It took a long while to get all the pieces arranged just right; it was fidgety and difficult. But this time I very much enjoyed the process; it felt like creation rather than just repair.

I so enjoyed weighing each object in my hand, feeling it drag on the filament, gauging the mass of one object in relation to another.

It was very late by the time I finished, and once it was all done and the glass set in place, I stepped back and found myself turning to one side, as though to say, Well? What do you think? And there was no one there. No Julian, no Douglas, no Frances, no Grace. Not even a moon! Just a whole island in darkness. I felt so sad.

I went down to the house and drank a whole bottle of wine by myself in consolation/celebration.

At least I do like the piece—everything else I have made recently has felt like a failure. So, progress! Next time, though, maybe I should try something on a larger scale? More complex? Something to consider. A new direction to explore! Creative work is such a ballast against despair. For the moment, I must be content with my own appraisal, with these green shoots. I know this will not be forever.

The tide cannot stay in forever.

Can it?

It is good that it is summer, because I think winter darkness now might kill me.

I dream of Julian all the time, of his beautiful face and his cruelty.

I had another letter from Isobel. She's so angry with me. I don't know how to meet her anger; she didn't respond to anything I said in my letter, I wonder whether she read it at all?

I dream of Julian so often I thought I would try to paint him, see if that might exorcise the ghost? When I try, I can no longer conjure him.

Perhaps I don't deserve to.

———————

Rain, and a haar stole in during the night and wrapped itself around us and was so thick I could not see the water from the bedroom window. I waited and waited for it to lift, but it didn't and so, stir-crazy, I went for a walk in the wood. It was eerie, frightening, the mist hanging like phantoms between the trees. I couldn't walk more than a few paces before looking behind me, so sure there must be someone there.

Sometimes I imagine the most terrible things.

———

I found a perfect bird skeleton. Tiny, a tit maybe, or a sparrow. I came all the way back to get a box to put it in and carried it back to the studio. I have no idea what to do with it, but it thrills me. Lately I find myself so excited by thoughts of death.

———

For some reason I keep thinking of the time I broke my wrist. The crack! The impression of whiteness, of my mind clearing. The clarity that comes from pain.

Pain is clear, grief a fog.

Solitude, too, is clarifying, revelatory.

Love, like grief, obscures.

Creation from destruction takes courage; it is an act of will, it is violent, like hope.

———

I found a small, hard lump in my right breast, rigid, almost like a little lump of cartilage beneath the skin. I must see someone about it, but I don't like the doctor they've brought in to replace Grace, he is young & sly and when I went in to see him last he looked at my body not the way a physician looks at a patient, but the way a man looks at a woman.

EIGHTEEN

Becker recoils as though struck. Is this it? The start of Vanessa's illness? For the first time since he started reading her notebooks, he feels as though he is intruding. It is not just the feeling of someone sneaking a look at a private diary, glimpsing something deeply personal; it's worse than that: he knows what the author does not, he has seen the terrible ending before she has even conceived of it.

He puts the journal down. It is late, past midnight; his head buzzes with exhaustion, and yet he knows he won't sleep. He's alone and ill at ease. Helena has gone to London, suddenly but not entirely unexpectedly. Her sister is having one of her periodic relationship crises, during which Helena is generally summoned to advise, console. Conspire. Thick as thieves, the two of them.

She'd already left by the time he got home this evening. He'd had to drive all the way down to Penrith to look at a couple of sculptures Sebastian is interested in—very nice, but the seller is asking too much for them—then on the way back, a digger somehow slipped its moorings and fell off the back of a lorry on the M6. Miraculously, no one was hurt, but it added two hours to his journey.

He found a note when he arrived home:

Crisis in Chelsea! Seb's giving me a lift to the station. See you Saturday. xxx

Now he feels anxious and frustrated. Does her sister really need her? There will be another boyfriend next month, and another breakup a month or two after that.

He reaches for his wineglass and brings it to his lips. It's warm and tastes sour. Getting to his feet, he pours it down the sink, rinsing out the glass and filling it with water from the tap. He takes a long draft, watching his reflection in the window. He looks pale, his eyes sunken into their sockets. Turning away, he returns to the table and sees that the pages of the notebook have turned by themselves. He is looking at a fresh page.

Cold, a fine mist hanging over the island, the sea restless.
Walking in the wood this morning I found a bone, picked clean.

If he believed in signs, if he believed in ghosts, he would think that she was here in the room with him, that she had turned the page on her illness herself, guiding him toward the thing he was looking for:

Walking in the wood this morning I found a bone, picked clean.
Perfectly white, almost luminous, dry and smooth. When I picked it up, I found that it was broken, cracked almost all the way through. I knew at once what I wanted to do; I could see the whole of the new piece.
I took the bone to the studio—it is elegant, slender, and tactile, light and yet somehow substantial. Sheep, perhaps? Or deer? G would know.
The feeling I had, when I held it, I think it is a feeling of control.

He reads those last few lines over and over: this is it. This must be it. She found the bone, and she thought it was sheep or deer. There is nothing strange or sinister about it. He leans back in his chair, exhaling slowly. He is relieved, he realizes, genuinely relieved—which means that he must on some level have suspected something of her. How stupid of him! Grace said it was stupid, and she was right.

He reads on.

Marguerite came to see me this morning. She asked after Grace and seemed confused not to find her here. When I told her that Grace is in Carlisle, that she's been gone more than a year now, she got terribly worked up, she kept shaking her head, saying no, no, no.

I gave her a brandy, which cheered her up a little. She started speaking to me in French; I could only understand one word in three, but there was a lot of talk of bad men. She seems to be losing track of the here and now—just a few moments after I told her Grace was in Carlisle she said that she had seen her. I asked when did you see her? Today? Last week? She kept saying "before the sun rises."

I felt frightened. I started to imagine Grace had come back, that she was here somewhere, on the island, in the wood, watching me. It seems utterly stupid now, but after M left I actually phoned the surgery in Carlisle and asked to speak to her. They said she was with a patient, that she couldn't come to the phone. I felt so ashamed. How could I be afraid of her? What has become of me? Of us?

Becker closes the notebook. He feels bewildered—he has no idea who Marguerite is or why Grace is not on the island—but his overwhelming sensation is simple relief. Vanessa found the bone in the wood; she found the bone and picked it up, just like she'd pick up a pebble from the beach, there's nothing more to it than that. There will be no fundamental reassessment of who Vanessa Chapman was, there will be no disgrace—not for her and not for James Becker, her cheerleader in chief.

Vanessa Chapman's diary

I borrowed a shotgun from Mr. McAndrew, the farmer I get eggs from.

I don't think you're supposed to borrow guns?

Well, anyway, the quad broke down, and the man who came to fix it was surly and strange. When he came to the studio to get his money, he stood blocking the doorway, and when I tried to get past him, he moved into my way and smiled the most terrible smile. I gave him his money and he left. I could hear him laughing as he walked down to his van. He wanted to frighten me.

I felt vulnerable as I never have here before.

I told Mr. McAndrew about it, and he gave me the gun.

NINETEEN

It is eight o'clock in the morning, and Becker is standing in the Great Hall in Fairburn House. It is barely light. He has turned on a spotlight to illuminate a single painting: a large canvas, four feet by three, painted in blacks and grays. Somewhere in this wash of darkness is an archway, a doorway, perhaps, and within it, a figure, a person with a face like a mask, disturbed only by the suggestion of movement around its mouth, the red and white of a smile.

In Becker's right hand, resting against his hip, is one of Vanessa's notebooks. He holds it up and turns to a page he bookmarked very early that morning.

I painted him. The man in the doorway, I painted his smile.

There is no mention of *Black II*, and yet Becker is sure this is the painting Vanessa is referring to: a man in a doorway, smiling. An innocuous-enough description and yet the painting is anything but. Through deft application of paint and sparing use of color, treading that fine line she walked between abstraction and representation, Vanessa has articulated her terror in a painting so vivid you can almost smell the fear.

It's not Julian, it's not Douglas. It's just a man who came to fix something, a man who frightened her. Some people might find this revelation disappointing or anticlimactic, but Becker is *hooked*. With every line he reads, he gets to know her better, to understand what compelled her. Now he knows this: Vanessa painted what she loved, she painted her freedom, she painted the sea. She painted what she feared.

If he is right. He can't really see how he couldn't be right—she *must* be referring to *Black II*, surely? The only person who would be able to confirm that is Grace.

AN HOUR OR so later, he finds Sebastian sitting at the breakfast table in the back kitchen, a pot of coffee at his elbow, dripping raspberry jam onto whatever it is he is reading. He hears Becker approaching; he looks up and grins. Becker returns the smile, though it falls from his face as he realizes, watching Sebastian wipe a page with a napkin, that what he is reading is one of Vanessa's notebooks.

Sebastian catches his expression. "It's a tiny bit of *confiture*, Beck. Chill."

The *gall*, Becker fumes, the casual disregard for what is precious. *Chill?* He could punch the entitled arsehole. "Where did you get that?"

Sebastian smiles at him—charming, infuriating. "I swiped it yesterday, when I went to fetch Hels. Don't look at me like that. It's my property."

"What is?" Becker snarls. "The book or Helena?"

Sebastian pushes his chair back, dusting crumbs from his lap. "That's beneath you," he says mildly as he gets to his feet, and he is right, it is, and Becker hates himself for showing himself up, showing himself to be the lesser man again.

"The book is not *your property*," Becker says, sticking his chin out, arms folded over his chest. "It belongs to the foundation."

"God, you're so possessive over her, aren't you, Beck?" Sebastian says, taking a step closer to him, so close they would be nose to nose, were Becker an inch taller. "Over Vanessa, I mean, not your wife." Becker takes a step back, and Sebastian thrusts the notebook toward him. "Have you read this one yet?" Becker glances at it, shakes his head. "Well, take a look at the back page. Go on, take a look—there's a list of the works that were due to be shown in the exhibition at my father's gallery."

Becker takes the book, turning it over in his hands, inspecting it for further damage. Sebastian exhales loudly. Becker turns to the back page as instructed.

Glasgow Modern Sep 2002

CERAMICS:

Sea series 1–9, Eris series 1–12, Flourish
     1–3, Breathe 4, 7, 8, 9 & 12
Possibly a few other smaller works?? Flare-lip vases?

PAINTINGS:

To Me She Is a Wolf
Darkness Causes Us Not Discomfort (Black I), Black II, Follow Me
Totem
North
The Tide Always Comes: Summer & Winter
Eris Rock: Arrival, spring, winter & winter II
Hollow
Sea series: Sundown, Storm I & II, Wreck, Revival

Now it is Sebastian who is standing with arms folded, expression defiant. "By my count, that's at least twenty-nine ceramic pieces and *eighteen* paintings," he says, an edge of triumph in his tone.

Becker scans the list, does the math in his head—Sebastian is correct. And yet when the works were delivered to Fairburn, there were fifteen ceramic pieces in total, and he can see right away that a number of the paintings listed here are missing.

"My father was right!" Sebastian says. "You wanted evidence? Well, this is it, isn't it? She can't start going on about private sales—we've talked to all the auction houses, we've canvassed collectors, there's *no trace* of them."

Becker sits down heavily at the kitchen table, frowning at the list in front of him. "It doesn't make sense," he mutters. "We have . . . four of the black series, but there's no *Totem*, no *North*, we have *Wreck* but no *Revival* . . . There's at least . . . Christ, *six* of these not accounted for."

"Right? Haswell is lying to us, Becker. She's been lying all along, and honestly I no longer see any reason why—"

"It's possible," Becker interrupts, "that Vanessa changed the names of some pieces. Some artists do that, although I doubt—"

"Oh, come *on*!" Sebastian throws up his hands, exasperated. "You're clutching at straws."

He is, and he knows it. He nods, rubbing his forehead hard with his fingers, squeezing his eyes tightly shut. "So . . . what are we saying? We're suggesting she's hidden the paintings somewhere?" He looks up at Sebastian, who nods vigorously. "But to what end? She can't sell them, not legally. Who would give her money for them, without provenance?"

Sebastian sits back down and shrugs extravagantly. "God knows! Maybe it's not about the money—maybe it's about spite? Or anger? Maybe she expected Vanessa to leave everything to her, and then it turned out—"

"She was left with nothing."

"*Nothing?* She got a house! She got a fucking island!" Sebastian points to what he presumably believes to be the direction of Eris. "Look, God knows why she's hung on to them, I don't know, all I know is that she has our property, and it's time you dealt with it. It's time you dealt with *her*. And if you don't think you're capable of that—"

The kitchen door leading out to the courtyard slams shut, and they both start. Emmeline, dark and crooked as a witch, accompanied by her canine familiars, back from their walk.

"Hello there." Sebastian's tone is transformed; he is cheerful, respectful. He gets up from the table and goes over to say hello, but Emmeline turns her back on him, steadying herself on the kitchen counter as the dogs circle her legs, whining excitedly. Emmeline takes off one of her Wellington boots and then pauses, her stockinged foot dangling, knee bent like a horse favoring a hoof. "Mother?" Sebastian says. "Are you all right?"

"I'm . . . fine," she says crossly, but she's clearly not. Sebastian is at her side at once, holding her elbow. She pulls away. "Don't *fuss*, Sebastian, I'm fine."

"You're bleeding—"

"Blasted bitch keeps getting under my feet," Emmeline spits. "She's a liability." She allows Sebastian to support her as she takes off the other boot. She has blood on her hands, and even from ten feet away Becker can see that she's trembling. He stands, slipping the notebook Sebastian was reading into his pocket, and slinks silently out of the room without a word.

Vanessa Chapman's diary

A terrible start to the new year. Celia Gray is dead—a car accident in the South of France. No one else involved—she went off the road and into a tree. Julian wasn't with her, thank god.

Poor, poor Julian. My heart aches for him—he wanted this so much. Her, obviously, but the life she offered him, too. All that money! So tantalizingly close, and now it is gone.

God knows what he will do.

TWENTY

Becker writes to Grace that afternoon and is surprised to receive a reply almost immediately, saying that he is welcome to come to Eris on the weekend. Saturday would be good. You mean tomorrow? he replies. Yes, tomorrow.

He calls Helena to let her know that he'll be gone by the time she gets back from London, but her phone goes straight to voicemail. He is tempted to look at her Instagram, knowing there will be evidence of lunches in fashionable restaurants and drinks in bars, trips to the theater perhaps, a glimpse into another life, one he feels excluded from. The fact that his exclusion is self-imposed doesn't make it feel any better. He doesn't look. Too dangerous.

This feeling—this longing for her—makes him oddly nostalgic for the days when she wasn't his, when he could only fantasize about being with her. It is strangely thrilling, the idea of her as forbidden object of desire rather than *wife*.

In the early days, when he first came to work at Fairburn, Helena was always dropping by unexpectedly, popping her head around the door, always in a hurry, breathlessly asking him some question that might just as easily have been answered by someone else—her husband-to-be, for example? If anyone else happened to turn up, she became flustered, color rising to her cheeks.

Becker thought he must have been imagining things. He had to have been! But then, on one impossibly glorious spring evening, swifts swooping low across the lawn and a golden light illuminating the creamy magnolia flowers outside his office window, she turned up just as he was shutting down his computer. She was dressed for company, a silk slip in sunset colors, high heels, red lipstick. She entered the office quickly, closing the door behind her. She walked around his desk and, before he could say a word, leaned down and kissed him on the mouth. Then she stood up straight and stepped away from him. She waited a moment for him to say something and, when he didn't, smiled sadly. "The invitations are due to go out next week," she said, and was gone before he had the wit to respond.

He thinks of it now and cringes; he was such a coward. He did nothing, said nothing. Worse: he hid from her, turned and fled whenever she appeared in the corridors of the house. The wedding invitations were sent.

That was that.

Only fate—in the unlikely form of Lady Emmeline Lennox— intervened. A stumble in the heather, a misfired shot, and Douglas was gone. The wedding had to be postponed. And while Sebastian was comforting his stricken mother and mourning his father, Becker stepped in.

Late summer, when the meadows were purple with heather and rosebay, Becker went to fetch Helena from the train station. He was there on Sebastian's request, Sebastian having to take his mother into town to see about funeral arrangements. Becker met Helena from the train and drove her back to Fairburn, only instead of driving her up to the main house, he took her to the Gamekeeper's Lodge.

It floors him still to think about it, the heat of the day, windows flung open, shadows lengthening as the long afternoon wore on, the knowledge that Sebastian wouldn't be back until that evening, that Becker had her for hours.

In the blue of dusk he got up to fetch glasses of water from the kitchen. When he returned, he plucked up the courage to ask her directly: "What is this, Helena? Cold feet?"

She was sitting on the bed, flushed and damp-haired, her legs drawn up to her chest. "You think I would do this lightly?" she asked, hurt. "You think I would betray him on a whim?"

Becker shook his head, handing her one of the glasses as he clambered back onto the bed. "I don't," he said, "but I don't understand, really, why you would do this, what it is you want." He was shaking, he remembers that, hands trembling as he brought the glass to his lips.

It seemed an eternity before she spoke. "The first time I met you," she said carefully, "that night we all had drinks—do you remember? Me and Seb, Emmeline and Douglas and you, up at the house. You were so quiet, so soft-spoken . . . What a *mouse*, I thought. Handsome, but not like Seb is handsome . . ." Becker winced. "It's true," she said, shrugging. "You know that." She crossed her legs, pulling a pillow onto her lap. "But then Douglas started asking you questions about work, about Chapman, and you weren't so quiet any longer . . . You disagreed with him about something, something curatorial, about how best to display the collection. Douglas was bellowing and boorish, adamant that everything should be strictly chronological, but you were talking about how the sculptures you'd just discovered were so directly linked to those early Oxfordshire landscapes, the ones where she took bits of grass and seeds and things and pressed them into the paint, that this was another way of using found objects and nature . . ."

"And he said I needed to get my head out of my arse," Becker replied, pulling a face. "He said I needed to stop thinking like a PhD student and start thinking like the curator of a *commercial space*."

Helena laughed. "Yes, and then Seb tried to join in—he was siding with his father, of course—and I don't remember what he said, probably because he had nothing to say, everything that came out of his mouth was so glib and so facile, and you were so . . . *controlled*." She smiled, blushing. "It was very attractive. I kept thinking about it afterward, how steely you were." Her blush deepened. "It struck me then, right then, that first night, that you had *substance*, and that, as sweet as Seb is, there's nothing to him."

Becker relives it now, the pleasure he took in Sebastian's belittling, delicious and hot and shaming.

"It's not his fault," Helena added. "He's had everything handed to him, he's never really had to work, he's never had to struggle . . . and do you know, neither have I? I'm the same. I'd blow away in a stiff breeze. I need someone to tether me. I want it to be you."

Later, when she was in the shower and Becker was downstairs in the kitchen, pouring a glass of wine and trying to think of what he should say to her before she left, he was blindsided by the realization that he'd have to resign his post. He'd have to give up Vanessa if he was going to have Helena. And he froze, the glass an inch from his lips. He wanted this so much, this opportunity to study Vanessa, to read her words, to write about her, to immerse himself in her. His whole life had been leading toward this point, and now he was going to have to walk away from it.

It's not worth it, he thought. She's not worth it. He only thought it for a second—a fraction of a second, perhaps—but he *did* think it.

When Helena came downstairs, her long hair combed back and twisted into a bun, her face scrubbed clean of makeup, her eyes were a little red, from shampoo or tears. She was breathtaking. *Of course* she was worth it. "I'll resign," he said. "We'll leave; we'll go somewhere else."

She made a face. "Why?"

"*Why?*" he spluttered. "You're . . . *engaged* to him, Helena, and we—"

"Becker!" She kissed him, open-mouthed. "Don't be so bourgeois! Yes, it'll be messy. He'll be angry, it'll be painful at first, but he'll get over it. There'll be another girl in a month or two, and another one a month or two after that. Don't worry about Sebastian."

So he stayed. They stayed. And Sebastian—sweet, stiff-upper-lip Sebastian—did get over it. He disappeared for a few months, he went diving in the Maldives and hiking in Spain, he picked up girls and discarded them and, when the pandemic hit, he returned alone. No hard feelings, he swore. All's fair and all that. The best man won.

BECKER SPENDS THE rest of the afternoon clearing his desk, sending emails, speaking to a couple of auction houses about forthcoming sales, contacting a private collector about the possibility of a loan for the exhibition they're planning to hold next summer.

Just before he is due to leave, Sebastian sticks his head around the door. He is wearing an evening suit, his tie not yet done, his jaw artfully stubbled, like a man in an aftershave advertisement. "Did you by any chance swipe that notebook I was looking at?" he asks. "The one with the list?"

Becker sighs in exasperation. "I'm going to Eris tomorrow; I need to show her that—it's the only thing resembling evidence of missing works that we have."

Sebastian nods. "Fair enough." He half turns to go and then appears to think better of it. "You'll keep me informed, won't you? I want to know how she reacts when confronted with the smoking gun." Becker nods but doesn't reply. "I mean it, Becker, I want results this time— you need to start playing hardball with her."

"All right," Becker replies, "but I still think it's worth at least trying to keep her onside." Sebastian rolls his eyes, but Becker presses on regardless. "I have a feeling this may turn out to be more complicated than you think—after all, Grace gave us the notebook with that list in it. Why would she do that if she were trying to conceal something?"

Sebastian shrugs, shakes his head, glancing at his watch. He has the attention span of a gnat, Becker thinks, he's already on to the next thing, he's out the door, on his way to dinner. "Just keep me in the loop," he says. He has his phone in his hand now, reading something as he walks away; he's almost out of sight and then he stops. Turns back. "Have you ever asked yourself, Beck, why it is that we got everything?"

"I'm sorry?"

"Do you not think it's odd?" Sebastian asks. "That this Haswell woman was Vanessa's friend, her carer, her companion for *twenty* years, and yet Vanessa left her—as *you* put it—with nothing. Why was that, do you think?"

Vanessa Chapman's diary

I don't really know how to write about this. I will recount everything I remember, though I doubt this is wholly accurate.

I was working in the studio around four, it was dark, night not quite fallen but the sun had not shown itself all day.

Cold and blustery.

I thought I heard the noise of a car and I went outside but saw nothing, no lights on the causeway or the track, so I went back inside and carried on working. I had just put some pieces into the kiln for glaze firing when I thought I saw something moving past the window.

A second or two later, a man appeared in the doorway. I knew immediately that he was going to hurt me. I recognized him as the man who fixed the quad last winter.

The shotgun was leaning against the wall and I grabbed it. He started to come toward me—he didn't say anything, didn't make a sound, just came toward me. I raised the gun. He kept coming and I tried to fire but it jammed. I tried to hit him with it, but I was too slow.

He grabbed hold of me and pushed me to the ground.

I was screaming and screaming, he had one hand on my throat, the other trying to undo my jeans.

I must have closed my eyes, because the next thing I knew there was a horrible gurgling sound and he was no longer on top of me. I realized that someone else was in the room.

Grace had wrapped one of my clay cutter's wires around his neck and was pulling him backward. He was kicking out, trying to free himself. He was trying to get his fingers under the wire, to stop it from slicing into his throat.

He struggled for a while, kicking and making an awful choking sound.

I don't think I did anything at this point. I was on my knees, I think. He stopped struggling after a bit. Grace pushed him forward, so that he was on his front. She kept the wire around his neck and shouted at me to call the police.

I still didn't do anything. I was shaking so violently I felt I could not control my movements.

She shouted again, for god's sake, go call the police, take the gun, call the police.

I got up then, ran to the house. I called the police. I was crying on the phone, I told them, a man attacked us, my friend killed him. I couldn't really answer their questions, I was just crying and crying.

He wasn't dead.

When I went back up, I could hear him shouting and screaming—Grace had secured his ankles with twine and strapped his wrists together with her belt. The wire was still around his neck.

We stood there until the police came. Grace knelt in the small of his back holding the wire and I stood over him with the gun.

All the time we were waiting, he did not stop talking, all that time he kept telling me all the ways he'd hurt me, the things he'd do to me, the tools he'd use.

The police took an hour and a half to come.

Grace stayed the night.

I owe her my life.

I owe her everything.

TWENTY-ONE

Grace remembers an evening, a rare evening when they were together at the studio, talking. Drinking wine, maybe? The sun was still high in the sky; it was summer. Vanessa was at her wheel, she was talking—in a way that she rarely talked to Grace—about work.

"The thing about clay," she was saying, "is that you can make it look like anything." Her head was bent, her hair tied at the nape of her neck; one hank had fallen forward over her eye, and every now and again she shrugged it away, sweeping her cheekbone against her shoulder. "That makes it tricky."

She dipped her fingertips into the water and returned them to the form spinning on the wheel. "I don't mean tricky to work with. Stoneware is quite simple; porcelain is harder, of course, but I don't really mean tricky like that. I mean that if you *can* make anything—*anything!*—then what should you make? There are too many possibilities."

Another dip, another trickle, another shrug of the shoulder. "There's this sculptor Isamu Noguchi—a brilliant, brilliant man, he died in the eighties—anyway, he once said that clay is *too* fluid, *too* facile, it gives you too much freedom . . . Oh!" She sat back laughing. The form had lost its center, crumpled in on itself, bent double like a drunk on the pavement at closing time. "I don't think I could ever have too much freedom . . ."

She smiled at Grace, drying her hands on a cloth, taking a sip of her wine. It's rosé, Grace thinks, or maybe something with bubbles in it. "Don't you want to have a go?" Vanessa asked, holding out her hand, beckoning for Grace to come closer, and Grace laughed, shaking her head.

"Then again," Vanessa said, wiping her hands, working the clay back into a solid mass, centering it once more, "maybe he's right, because when you're as plagued by doubt as I am, having so many options is a bind . . ." She started over, dipping her fingers into the bowl of water, kicking the wheel into motion once more.

"The thing *I* love about working with clay," she said, "is that when things go wrong, it doesn't matter. You throw it back, you start again, you make a new shape, every time you start over, something new . . . It's not at all like painting, where all your false marks and mistakes remain. Even after you scrape away the paint and start over, the lost images remain like ghosts. With clay, once you've made the new form, the old one is gone, obliterated! Even if you wanted it back, you couldn't have it. No point searching for it. So you have to learn"—she leaned forward, her teeth biting into her lower lip, her brow furrowed in concentration—"to let go of what went before. To let go of the past."

Grace is in her bedroom, which has also been known as the back bedroom and the spare bedroom—in fact, she still thinks of it as the spare bedroom even though it is the one she sleeps in, just as she still thinks of the house as Vanessa's house rather than her own. It will always be Vanessa's house, and the room on the southern side of the house, the one that overlooks the sea, will always be Vanessa's room. But while Becker is here, if he chooses to stay the night, Grace will take Vanessa's room, and he will take the spare room.

There are moments that for the sake of her own sanity Grace does not allow herself to contemplate, and the last meaningful hours she spent in Vanessa's room count among them. Since then, the room has been left empty. Not *untouched*—Grace cleans from time to time; in the summer she opens the windows to allow the sea air in, so that the room smells of salt and seaweed and not dust and damp—but essentially the room looks much the way it did the day the ambulance came across the causeway to take Vanessa's body away. The furniture remains in place, the bed and the desk and the dresser by the wall, even the chair next to the bed where Grace used to sit.

Grace does not have to sleep in this room—she could take the sofa or offer Becker the sofa, but it would raise questions, wouldn't it? It would seem awkward and strange. And after all, it's just a room. It's not a shrine, it's not sacred. It is not haunted.

First things first. She needs to ready the spare room: strip the bed, wash the sheets, clear her personal things away: the shirts that lie draped over the back of the armchair, the hairbrush and moisturizer on the dressing table. There should be no call for him to look inside her wardrobe, but even so, she removes the two canvases stacked behind her coats and takes them through to the living room. She shifts the old linen screen and opens the door behind it, which leads to a small, windowless room. They have never known what it was for. *A priest hole!* Vanessa liked to claim, but they didn't have those up here. Vanessa used it as a darkroom. Now, Grace uses it for storage.

As she pulls aside the screen, she feels a corresponding tug of conscience. The paintings are not rightfully hers. Until now she has allowed herself to think of them as an oversight, a pair of canvases stashed in a wardrobe, forgotten. Now she is deliberately going against Vanessa's wishes, and that feels uncomfortable. Although, if she is honest with herself, it wouldn't be the first time.

Besides, she has plenty to give Mr. Becker: boxes in the living room full of sketches, two unfinished and unframed canvases, yet more notebooks, and a stack of letters. She has taken care to put the letters from Douglas Lennox at the top of the pile, the ones that show him needy and aggressive, smarting from her rejection, bitter to the point of derangement: *How can you claim it meant nothing? Are you really going to use my wife as an excuse? You've never seemed to care much about the wives of your other lovers.* This, Grace knows, is petty of her, but there is a point: it is not easy to lay yourself bare to public scrutiny; it is not easy to have those you loved laid bare either.

She wraps the smaller of the canvases in an old towel and takes it to the little storeroom. The space is mostly bare, save for a couple of ancient, empty suitcases and a few boxes of her own personal papers, which she brought over after she let the cottage in the village go. She rests the small canvas against one of the old suitcases and goes back to fetch the larger piece. As she turns it around, so that the canvas will be facing the wall, the sheet she has wrapped around it falls away slightly, revealing, at the top of the wooden frame, Vanessa's mark: *Totem*.

Letting go of the past is necessarily a selective enterprise. Some things you hold on to, and some things you release. When it comes to the portraits and the letters she has chosen to keep, Grace is holding tight to what she and Vanessa were to each other. This is not a matter for explanation or interpretation or speculation; it belonged only to them. Now it belongs only to her.

All those years, she slept in the spare room and was called, when Vanessa was written about, a companion or a carer, a friend, sometimes a partner—each word wrong in some fundamental way, though neither of them ever explained how. Vanessa because it was in her nature to resist explanation and Grace because she was never asked.

What could she have said if someone had asked? How could she have explained, when all other loves are seen as subordinate to romantic love? What she and Vanessa had was not romantic, but it was not subordinate either. *Just a friend*, that's what people say. *Oh, she's just a friend.* As though a friend were something commonplace, as though a friend couldn't mean the world.

My beloved, Grace could have said, were she asked. She was my beloved.

In the kitchen, she sits at the table and makes a list of things she needs to get before Becker arrives: milk, bread, eggs and bacon for breakfast, a chicken to roast for dinner, vegetables. Wine. It's a long time since she's had to cook a proper meal for anyone, a long time since there have been guests at the house. In the very old days, before Grace moved into the spare room, Vanessa's art friends would visit often, and sometimes people from the village came for lunch or drinks, though they didn't usually stay, unless they missed the tide. Probably the last person to stay the night was Julian. And he wasn't really a guest; he just turned up one day, uninvited.

TWENTY-TWO

There was a man in Vanessa's kitchen. His blond hair was receding a little; his torso was deeply tanned. He was wearing shorts, the baggy sort favored by younger people, and nothing else. When he turned to face her, Grace saw that the shorts sat so low they revealed a deep iliac crest and a tuft of pubic hair.

"You must be Grace," the man said, holding out a hand for her to shake. "I'm Julian. What are you cooking for us tonight?"

Grace ignored his hand, hoisting the shopping bags on to the kitchen table. "I'm not cooking. I picked up a few things for Vanessa," she said. "If she were left to her own devices, she'd starve."

"Good of you," Julian said. Peering into one of the bags, he drew out a packet of butcher's minced beef, raised an eyebrow, and replaced it. "Did you get fags?" he asked, looking up at her with a smile.

Grace turned her back on him. "She'll starve, but she won't forget those," she said, and left the room. She walked into the hallway and out the front door; she marched across the courtyard and straight up the hill.

Vanessa was throwing, her foot on the flywheel, her attention wholly focused on the task at hand, and yet before Grace could speak, she said, "I'm working." A warning tone.

"I brought some shopping," Grace said.

"Thanks." Vanessa did not look up; instead, she turned her shoulders very slightly, angling herself away from the door. Away from Grace.

Grace didn't move. She stood in the doorway for a minute, two, in complete silence, waiting for Vanessa to look at her, to explain—to explain herself, to explain why he was here—to say *something*.

But Vanessa did not yield. Frustrated, Grace turned away and saw that he had followed her from the house. He was standing on the path, halfway up the hill, cigarette in hand, watching. Smiling his dumb smile.

She was going to have to walk past him. She was going to have to endure his gaze all the way down to the car, feel his eyes on her pale, fleshy limbs, on the sweat patches blooming under her arms, on her face, puffy with summer allergy. As she walked down the path, he didn't move, only stood and smoked and, as she went past, said quietly, *"À bientôt."*

IN THOSE DAYS, Grace still had her cottage in the village, so she could have avoided seeing Julian again. Only she couldn't bear to stay away. It needled her so, his presence on their island, she had to know *why*, she had to know *for how long*.

The day after that first encounter, she drove back over, hoping against hope that he'd be gone. But the little red sports car was still parked in the courtyard.

Grace parked next to it and went once more up the hill. The studio door stood open.

"Vee?" Grace called out. The studio was empty.

Empty! Vanessa had barely left it for weeks, she had been working obsessively, preparing for the Glasgow show. Grace had not been exaggerating when she told Julian that if she didn't bring food, Vanessa simply wouldn't eat. Sometimes she begged Vanessa to take a break, to walk a little, to swim like she used to; *it's not good for you*, she said, *cooped up like that all the time, breathing in all the dust and the paint, you need to take breaks.* Vanessa bridled, refused, worked even harder.

And now, as soon as *he* turned up, the wheel stopped spinning and the studio stood *empty*?

All the things Vanessa had said about him—that he was unfaithful, profligate, shallow, self-centered, prone to outbursts of temper—had she simply forgotten? Did it all fly out of her mind when he showed up in his flashy car with his tan and his smile? Anger began to build in Grace like a storm front, clouds of rage gathering behind her eyes.

She stomped back down the hill to the house. The front door was closed. She hesitated, listening; she even considered knocking. But this was her house, too, wasn't it? Hadn't it become hers, over the weeks and months they had lived together? She pushed the door open, calling Vanessa's name.

The house was warm and silent. She walked through the living room to Vanessa's bedroom, its bed unmade, the air thick with the smell of cigarette smoke and sex. The kitchen was a mess: dishes in the sink, coffee grounds spilled on the counter and on the floor. A bottle of cognac stood open on the kitchen table next to an overflowing ashtray. The food Grace had brought the day before, the items she had carefully selected from the supermarket shelves, bearing in mind Vanessa's needs and wants, sat sweating in shopping bags next to the Aga.

Grace was on the point of leaving when she heard a scream. She rushed to the open window and looked out. Vanessa was on the beach with him; he was chasing her, grabbing at her, she was shrieking. They were playing, like children.

Grace knew she should leave, but she could not, just *could not* walk away without looking Vanessa in the eyes. She put the kettle on and made a cup of tea; she tried to drink it, but her throat felt painfully constricted. She gave up, stood at the window, and waited, watching the top of the stairs. Eventually, they appeared, stopping breathless on the top step to kiss, Julian sliding his hand roughly between Vanessa's legs. Her face burning with shame and anger roiling like acid in her gut, Grace forced herself back to the table. To be caught watching would be unbearable.

"Gracious!" Julian laughed when he saw her there. "You're here. And what have you brought us today? Champagne? Oysters? *Mince?*" He laughed again. "We were thinking of building a fire on the beach, what do you think? Have you brought us anything to barbecue?"

"It'll be damp," Grace replied sourly. "The tide is coming in."

"Oh, Grace, *ma petite boule*, such a killjoy. Isn't she a killjoy, Nessa?"

Vanessa sat down at the table and reached for Grace's hand, squeezing the tips of her fingers. Her face was deeply flushed, with excitement or exertion or, who knew, embarrassment?

"You should go," Vanessa said, smiling at Grace without meeting her eyes. She squeezed Grace's hand again. "Go on, I'll come and see you soon."

Grace left. As she passed beneath the open kitchen window on her way back to the car, she could hear, above the music of Vanessa's laugh, Julian's voice. "Why *is* she here all the time? What does she want, *la petite boule de suif*? Is it a piece of you, Ness? Is that what she wants?"

EARLIER THAT YEAR, Grace had been promoted, moving from Carrachan to run the new village surgery in Eris. At lunchtime, in good weather, she could usually be found on one of the benches along the harbor wall eating her sandwiches, and it was there that Vanessa found her the next day.

"You're upset," Vanessa said as she sat down at Grace's side.

She was; she'd had a wretched morning, half an hour before lunch spent with the mother of a child who'd fallen into the quarry pool a few miles north of here. The child drowned. The mother was half mad with grief, sleepless, desperate. *Please, Doctor, give me something.* But Grace had already prescribed all the pills it was safe to give, so she had to send her away. She wasn't going to tell Vanessa about that; Vanessa wouldn't be interested. Vanessa was too selfish to understand.

Doggedly chewing her tuna sweetcorn, Grace didn't look at her. "He spoke to me as though I were the help."

Vanessa laughed. "Julian speaks to everyone like that. I wouldn't take it personally."

"Does he speak to you like that?"

"Well, no, not me," Vanessa said. "I'm his wife."

Grace looked at her then. "Are you? Is that how you see yourself? As his *wife*?" She spat the word at Vanessa, who recoiled.

"Well . . . I'm not saying it's a *vocation*," Vanessa said, her cheeks reddening. "It's just a fact. We're not divorced." She got to her feet. "We're not divorced yet." She looked away from Grace, out across the water. "Look, just . . . don't come to the house for a day or two. He'll only annoy you. OK? I'm going to Glasgow on Thursday to see Douglas about the show; I'll be back Saturday, or Sunday at the latest. He'll be gone by then."

Grace raised her hand, shielding her eyes from the glare off the sea. "He'll be out of our lives?"

Vanessa turned to face her, her expression quizzical. "He's not *in* your life, Grace," she said. "He's in mine."

As she walked away, Grace called after her, "I heard you talking about me, you and him. I heard what he called me, I looked it up. Ball of fat, it means. He called me a ball of fat, and you laughed."

Vanessa slowed her pace momentarily but did not turn around.

THE FOLLOWING AFTERNOON, when Grace came home from work, Vanessa was sitting on her front step in the sun, an almost-empty bottle of wine at her side. She swayed as she stood up.

"Did you drive here?" Grace demanded, storming up to her. "You're drunk, Vanessa. You drove through the village. Past the school! I ought to . . ." She grabbed the collar of Vanessa's shirt, scrunching it up in her fist. "I ought to call the police!"

"Grace!" Vanessa clutched at Grace's forearm with both hands. "Please . . ."

Grace relinquished her grasp. She snatched the car key from Vanessa's hand and marched past her into the house, slamming the front door behind her.

Vanessa found her in the kitchen, drinking water directly from the tap.

"Butterball," Vanessa said. "That's what it means. It's . . . it wasn't meant cruelly."

Grace stood up and turned off the tap. "Yes, it was." She looked at Vanessa, at her glassy eyes and her petulant expression; Grace wanted to slap her. "Men like him . . . they have a special kind of contempt for women like me—*ugly* women. I've felt it all my life. An ugly woman is barely human to a man like your husband. It's sickening but not all that shocking. What's worse, what is utterly *abject*, is the way that women like you—the pretty, the *chosen*—the way you collude in that contempt. Simpering like a schoolgirl, because a man has paid you some attention. Laughing cravenly at his cruelties. It's pathetic."

"It's not like that," Vanessa said. She bit her lip and began to cry; Grace turned away in disgust. Vanessa grabbed hold of her wrist. "*I'm not like that.*"

Grace placed her hand over Vanessa's, trying to pry her fingers open, but Vanessa wouldn't let her go; she put her arms around her, encircling her waist, crying into the fabric of her shirt. Grace stood stiffly, hands at her side, taking long, deep breaths.

"I don't know why I let him do it," Vanessa said. "I don't know why I let him back in."

"He flatters you," Grace said. "He exploits your vanity."

"Yes." She spoke into the nape of Grace's neck. "Yes, he does. When he touches me I feel as though my bones will melt, I feel—for a few moments, a few hours—so *wanted*. There's such power in it, the feeling of being desired." Grace tried again to disentangle herself, but Vanessa held on. "He flatters me, charms me, seduces me, and it's so good." She lifted her head, looked into Grace's eyes. "The sex is so good. It's so self-affirming, isn't it, to be made to feel that way in bed?"

Grace wrenched herself free of Vanessa's stifling embrace. She wanted to put her hands over her ears, to sing like a child to block out the sound of Vanessa's voice, but Vanessa, following her across the room, kept talking. "Then of course he's barely come and he starts talking about money, the things he needs, how much he owes, the places he wants to go . . . He calls *me* selfish!" She shook her head. "He wants to know why, when I have all I need—the house and the studio and the island—why can't I just *share*?"

Grace scoffed, incredulous. "He surely can't think *you* have anything to give him? For Christ's sake, you can barely keep the lights on."

Vanessa sniffed, wiping her eyes. She went over to the sink and turned on the tap, taking a glass from the cupboard. "He's desperate," she said in between gulps. "He hasn't said so, but reading between the lines I think he's borrowed money from people he oughtn't to have borrowed money from."

"And he expects you to bail him out? If he's been stupid, he needs to take responsibility for that . . ."

Vanessa turned back to face her, her eyes filled with sorrow. "It was the thing with Celia Gray, you see, he thought he'd bought the winning ticket. He thought he didn't have to worry any longer. But then she died, and they hadn't married yet because *we* were still married, so he got nothing—"

"He blames you!" Grace was astonished. "He blames you, and worse, you feel sorry for him!"

Vanessa drained the last of the water and placed the glass on the counter. "I do," she said. "Isn't that stupid? I feel sorry for him, and I let him turn my head, I let him talk me into things, I lose the thread . . . of where I am. *Who* I am. I neglect the things that really matter to me, my work . . ." She scraped her teeth over her bottom lip. "And you." Grace lowered her head. "God, I never should have let him cross the threshold, the fucking *vampire*." Vanessa approached Grace once more and reached out, placing the crook of her forefinger gently beneath Grace's chin. Grace closed her eyes. "He *was* being cruel to you, Gracie. He was, and I don't know why I laughed, because it wasn't funny. I didn't find it funny then, and I don't now. It's unforgivable."

Grace sighed. "But I forgive you," she said softly. She did not open her eyes.

VANESSA STAYED THE night. Before the sun was up, she rose to beat the tide and drove back across to Eris Island. The next day, on the Thursday, she left early again, this time driving to Glasgow to finalize plans for the show with Douglas.

That lunchtime, while Grace sat eating a sandwich on her bench overlooking the harbor, she saw Julian's little red sports car come racing across the causeway, haring up the hill and into the village at twice the speed limit.

On Sunday, the shops in the village were closed, so Grace drove to the market in Carrachan to buy food and flowers to welcome Vanessa home, but when she got over to the island that afternoon, Vanessa's car was already parked in the courtyard. The front door was open, but when Grace called for her, no answer came. Grace found her in the studio. She was kneeling on the floor.

She had blood in her hair and on her clothes and hands.

TWENTY-THREE

The first thing Becker sees is the gun. Right there in the hallway, leaning against the bench. Grace clocks him looking at it. "Don't worry," she says with a wry smile. "It's just for show. I'll not be requiring you to shoot your dinner."

Becker laughs nervously. "Is it the same one?" he asks.

Grace's brow furrows. "The same as . . . ?"

"The . . . one Vanessa borrowed, you know, from the farmer . . ."

"*Oh.*" Grace nods, recognition registering in her eyes, face flushing. "You read that part."

"It's . . . *horrifying.*"

Grace nods again. "Yes, it was. A fat lot of use the gun was, too." She looks thoughtful. "Although I suppose we could have beaten him to death with it." She turns, leading Becker into the living room, where three boxes of papers sit atop the coffee table. "Those are for you," she says, waving a hand at them. "That should keep your boss happy."

It won't, of course, far from it, but Becker has already decided he won't broach the subject right away. For the moment, he expresses enthusiasm and gratitude, following her into the kitchen, where she fills the kettle while he stands at the Aga, looking out of the window, toward the mainland.

"Who was he?" he asks.

"Who was . . . oh, we're back on the gun? Just a man. Stuart Cummins. A lorry driver and sometime mechanic. His wife, Marguerite, used to come into my surgery fairly regularly—broken fingers, split lip, minor head wounds. Some other things, women's things." She hands him a cup of tea. Her face is shuttered, eyes cast down. "She never pressed charges.

They lived in one of those cottages over at the harbor, you can see it from here." She points. "Theirs is the last one, on the left."

"The one on the end?" He remembers the anguished face at the window, the one that wasn't there. "But they don't live there any longer?"

"Marguerite does. Stuart's long gone, thank God."

So it *was* her. "Marguerite . . ." he says out loud. "She was married to the man who attacked Vanessa? She's mentioned in one of the notebooks, she visited Vanessa, she was confused about something . . ."

Grace smiles ruefully. "Marguerite's been unwell for years. She has Alzheimer's now, but even before that, her mental state was pretty fragile. Her husband did many cruel things to her, but do you know I think the cruelest of all was never to tell her when to expect him?" They are standing side by side, looking over the water at the cottages. "He'd go off on a job, and she never knew when he'd be back, whether it would be a couple of hours or a couple of days. So she had no peace. For years, she was always waiting, standing at the window, watching out for him."

There is a break in the clouds, and suddenly the room is filled with warm light. Grace beams at him. "Look at that!" The sands have turned golden, the clouds primrose and pink. They are silent for a while, watching the wind work its magic, whipping green water to white horses. Then a cloud moves in front of the sun and the light is lost. Grace turns away. She sits down at the table with her tea and motions to him to join her.

"What became of him?" Becker asks. "The husband, I mean, the mechanic?"

Grace shrugs. "I've no idea. He got a shorter sentence than he deserved. If they'd known about all the things he did to Marguerite . . ." She interlaces her fingers to make a bridge on which she rests her chin. "After he attacked Vanessa, I moved out here. I kept my cottage in the village because I was still on the on-call rota and, in any case, between the tides and my work schedule, I couldn't be here all the time. But I stayed as often as I could. Vanessa was very shaken up, very afraid. For a time, she stopped walking in the wood on her own; she started stashing weapons all over the place." Grace gives an odd little laugh. "Knives in the studio, a hammer by the front door . . ."

She shakes her head, pressing her lips into a line. "It made me very angry." Her dark eyes look black in the flat light. "Makes me angry still. To have a place tainted like that . . . it's *another* violation on top of the original one. It happens all the time—you go walking somewhere, or swimming or running—whatever it is, your *thing*, the thing you enjoy—you go to a place, and it's beautiful and unspoiled, and you are doing that thing you love, and then someone—not *always* a man, I suppose, but usually a man—comes along and transforms it into an ugly place. And you never feel safe there again. And you are never the same again. The place is changed and you are changed, and neither for the better."

She is talking, Becker feels, half to him and half to herself; she sounds angry and bitter and he feels stupid, awkward—he wants to apologize to her, but for what? For casually invoking a traumatic event? For the behavior of men? All men? Some of them? While he's searching for something to say, her mood changes, her weather. The clouds are blown away and her face brightens. "Would you like to see the studio?" she asks.

IT LIES IN the lee of the hill, its slope a somber green now that the sun has dipped behind Eris Rock. A footworn path takes them up a steep incline that levels out after a couple of hundred yards into a plateau on which the studio sits.

Becker gnaws at his thumbnail, twitching with anticipation as Grace fiddles with the padlock; he holds his breath as she pushes back the enormous metal door, rolling it away like the proverbial stone. And there it is: a cavernous space with shelving running along the wall on the right-hand side and an ancient kick wheel on the left, the kiln at the far end.

Becker steps inside. The air is colder and drier within; it smells of dust and sulfur. Through the long picture window Vanessa had cut into the wall there is a view to the south, over the grassy slope toward the sea and Sheepshead Island.

In the middle of the room stands a trestle table on which yet more boxes are piled. "This is the stuff I've still got to sort through," Grace says. "As you can see, there's quite a bit." She motions toward the nearest box. "I found a whole load of photographs, I'm not sure if you'll want those?"

Of course he'll want them! They make a fascinating record of Vanessa's years on Eris; there are dozens and dozens of shots of the house, of works on the roof, the renovation of the barn. And dozens more of the island itself, of its changing landscape, rusty bracken and purple heather, electric yellow gorse. "Did she paint from these?" Becker asks, as he sifts through shots of the sea at every hour in every weather, trees fallen in the wood, piles of seaweed strewn across the sands like bodies.

"Not often. Well, not in the early years anyway," Grace replies. She is opening and closing the cupboards at the very back of the studio, looking for something. "Though she did later on, when she fell ill, when it became harder for her to work outside. She liked to have them, though, just in case. To remember the light, she said, although then she'd complain that the light never looked the same on film."

"She's right," he says, selecting another photograph, "the light never does." In the picture he's holding, two people stand side by side, elbows propped on a railing, against the background of a wild sea. One of the people is Grace—many years younger but essentially the same, with her bowl haircut, her soft, round face, her chin receding beneath a shy smile. The other person is tall, coltish, and leggy in a vest and shorts, dirty blond hair falling over bony shoulders—Vanessa, he assumes, though he cannot say for certain because her face is obscured. No, not obscured, *erased*. It has been scratched out.

"Oh, God." Grace appears at his side. "That's a very old picture, that's mine." Becker turns it over: *Grace and Nick, St. Malo '81*.

"I thought it was Vanessa," he says, and Grace shakes her head, taking the picture from him. She studies it a moment. "No, it's not. It's Nick. I don't know why she did that . . ."

"Vanessa did that?" he says. He finds he's not altogether surprised—she shows her temper in her diaries, with an occasional flash of spite.

"She could be quite funny about things sometimes. Quite possessive," Grace says quietly, "which I always thought was a bit unfair when you consider that she demanded complete freedom for herself. Nick Riley was a friend of mine, at university. We were flatmates for a while. We went on a camping holiday once, with another girl, Audrey. She must have taken the photo." She seems uncomfortable, a little embarrassed. "Nick and I were very close for a while. It wasn't a romantic involvement, but . . . he was special to me. He was quite beautiful. And Vanessa always saw beauty as her purview."

Grace slides the picture into the pocket of her cardigan. She moves away from him, over to a small wooden cabinet underneath the window, and opens a drawer. "That makes her sound awful, which she wasn't at all," she continues. "She had a bit of a temper, that's all. Ah, there it is."

She takes something from one of the drawers, a wooden box. "Look," she says, placing it on the table. "Come and take a look at this." The box is rosewood, inlaid with mother of pearl. Grace opens the lid: inside are bones. Bones and fragments of bone, broken, discolored things, none so pure as the one in *Division II*. They all look tiny to Becker, as though they come from some sort of small animal, like a rodent, but really, what does he know?

"Could I take these?" he asks. "I think they might be useful, and in any case, they are . . . they are things she collected to use in her art, aren't they?"

"Mmm." Grace nods. "All right." She turns back to the cabinet. "There's another box somewhere, filled with pebbles and shells and another with feathers, and oh, look here . . ." She pulls out a little box, a plainer one, and opens it to reveal a tiny bird's skull. Carefully, Becker takes it between his thumb and forefinger. He turns it over, examining its eye sockets, the neat little beak. "Sparrow, maybe?" Grace says.

Becker shrugs; he has no idea, but it reminds him of something he read in one of the notebooks. "She wrote about finding a bird's skull . . .

or perhaps a skeleton? It was around the same time, in fact, that she wrote about completing *Division* . . . I think you were away at the time. Have I got that right?"

Grace ignores the question, picking over bits of bone. "Pretty sure none of *these* are human," she says. "Feel how light they are." She hands him one of the larger pieces. "Human bone is much denser than animal. That's probably from a lamb. I had a feeling there were some larger ones somewhere." She holds up her fingers to her lips, head tilted backward a little, considering. "She made copies, you know, she'd make molds in plaster and then cast them—that's how *Division II* was made; she would find bones, or pieces of bone, and she knitted them together with ceramics, which is rather neat, since it's actually what you use to repair and replace bones in medicine these days—"

"Grace." Becker sees an opportunity and takes it, interrupting her. "About the ceramics—I wanted to ask you about the ones she made for the Glasgow Modern show." Grace turns her attention back to him, her eyebrows raised, expression expectant. "In the back of one of the notebooks you gave me to read, there's a list, a list of the works that she and Douglas agreed on for the show. Do you remember that? There are around thirty ceramic pieces on that list, but almost none of them came to Fairburn. Do you know where they went? Did she sell them? Are there any records of sales?"

Grace closes the rosewood box. "Did you know that I set her wrist?" she asks. "I told you, didn't I? That was the first time we met. She tripped over that bit of concrete out there, just to the right of the path, the lid to the septic tank." She returns the box to its place on the shelf. "We met over a broken bone," she says, turning to face him, smiling brightly, "and then later she started to use broken bones in her work. I like to think that's significant." She pauses for a second, and then her face takes on a serious cast. "Can I trust you, Mr. Becker?"

"Of course you can," Becker says, hoping that at last she is going to answer the question.

But she doesn't; she just smiles again and says, "Good. Then I'll leave you to poke around here by yourself and I'll get on with dinner. Half

THE BLUE HOUR   157

an hour, maybe? Lock up when you're done. There's a torch there on the right, you can bring that with you so you can see what you're doing. Watch out on the way down, the ground is pretty uneven."

He watches her making her way carefully down the hillside until she disappears into the darkness. He hears the front door close.

He is alone.

A fine sliver of moon hangs behind a veil of cloud; the beam from the lighthouse sweeps across the sea. Slack water, the tide turning. A cry, sharp and anguished, makes him jump. A herring gull swoops overhead, and he retreats into the studio.

At last, he has Vanessa to himself.

He sifts through the pages in the box nearest to him, sorting through rough sketches, many of them little more than a few lines on the page. Among the drawings of the islands and the wood, he finds figure sketches, too, a kneeling figure, another lying down, viewed from different angles. Studies, perhaps? Though not for any paintings he has seen.

Looking at these pages, at these boxes, he has the impression that no matter how many of them he sorts through, somehow there will always be more, and more, and more: Grace is like a magician, conjuring letters and sketches and bones out of nothing. Or a cat, perhaps, bringing her treasures to lay at his feet. Only they're not *her* treasures, are they? And treasures aren't what cats bring in any case; they bring kills.

Grace is hiding things from him. The way she ignored his question about the missing ceramics makes that clear. She may *literally* be hiding things: the house is not big, but there is bound to be storage: a cellar, perhaps, or an attic. Didn't she mention a storeroom at some point? He will, he supposes, have to give her a chance to deny it.

He walks to the back of the studio, opens up the kiln, inhales the scent of old dust and ash, his skin prickling as he imagines her here, his Vanessa, opening this very door, heart in mouth, to see whether her work had survived the firing. If he could, he would happily stay here all night among her things, despite the cold. But he can't be rude. And he still has work to do, questions to ask.

He rolls the metal door across and, holding the torch between his teeth, locks the padlock. He has barely turned away when the torch flickers once, twice, and then goes out altogether, leaving him completely blind. He pulls his phone from his pocket and after a few moments manages to turn on its torch. There. The beam illuminates a narrow strip of grass in front of him; outside of that strip the darkness presses in. Becker starts down the path, holding the phone in front of him, noticing as he goes that there is no phone service here at all.

THE HOUSE IS warm and light, the kitchen a fug of smells—roasting chicken, woodsmoke. Grace is opening a bottle of red wine, her pale face flushed, patches of damp under her armpits. "Do you drink wine?" she asks, and hands him a glass before he can answer. "Sit, sit." She fusses around him, muttering to herself, *where did I put, where was that* . . . She finds the matches she's searching for and lights a candle. With the wine and the low light, the candle burning on the set table, the scene appears oddly romantic, and Becker feels a sudden twinge of panic. He thinks of the landlady in the Roald Dahl story, luring young men to her establishment only to poison them and stuff them. He reaches into his pocket for his phone.

"There's no service here," he says plaintively.

"Only if you climb to the top of the rock," Grace says, "and I wouldn't recommend that in the dark. Do you need to call someone? There's Wi-Fi. You can use the whatsit."

He smiles. "WhatsApp."

"Although"—she frowns—"I've no idea what the password is."

"It's usually on the router . . ."

"Oh yes—that's in Vanessa's room. I'll just go take a look."

She disappears, returning moments later with a piece of paper on which she's written the code.

"Thanks," he says, getting up from the table. "I just want to check in on Hels. I'll make the call . . ." He indicates that he's going to go into the living room.

"Of course."

Helena doesn't answer, so he messages her instead, telling her there's no phone service, that she should WhatsApp if she needs him. He waits for a moment, to see if she'll reply, but the little ticks remain stubbornly gray and so he returns to the kitchen, sits back down at the table, and takes a long slug of wine. He tries not to imagine Sebastian dropping by to check on her.

"Everything all right?" Grace asks without turning around.

"Everything's fine," Becker says. He takes another sip. Now he's thought of Sebastian, he can hear his voice, telling him to *just bloody get on with it.* "Grace, I need to ask you about the paintings and ceramics that were on that list, the one I mentioned earlier?"

Grace bends to open the oven, lifting a roasting tin to the stovetop, clattering it down.

"I was always here for Vanessa," she says.

"Yes," Becker says, frustrated, "I know that, I—"

"No, you don't." She turns around to face him, removing the oven gloves and wiping her forehead with the back of her hand. Her expression is somber. "I was always here for her, from that very first time we met, when she broke her wrist. I was the person she relied on—she'd get lost in her work and forget to eat, so I brought food. I cooked for her. I fixed things when they broke, or if I couldn't fix them myself, I found someone who could. I fetched and carried for her. I made her life easier. I listened when she talked, even if half of what she talked about was alien to me. I was here when that man attacked her. I protected her. And I was here to pick up the pieces, after everything fell apart. After Julian." She opens a drawer and takes from it a carving knife and fork, which she thrusts toward him. "Will you do the honors?" she asks, nodding at the bird. "I've something I need to show you."

As Becker hacks inexpertly at the chicken, he steels himself for the dreaded confrontation. He knows what she's going to say: that for all that she's done, she deserves some recompense, and there's a part of him that would agree. It does seem fair that after all she did for Vanessa she should be rewarded, but he knows—just as Sebastian knows and she herself must know—that this isn't about what's fair; this is about what Vanessa Chapman stipulated in her will.

When Grace comes back, she frowns at the mess he's made of the chicken and hands him a bit of kitchen towel. She places a piece of paper on the table in front of him and picks up the carving knife and fork herself. "Read that," she says, as she sets about finishing the job he has started.

It's a note, Becker sees, written on paper stained with dark brown smudges, in Vanessa's now familiar hand.

J, we can't keep going round and round and round!

I'm going to be back on the weekend and you <u>must</u> be gone. There's no more money in the pot.

We have loved each other and we have hated each other and now we can be free of each other.

Isn't that wonderful?

You must find your own way.

Love,
Nessa

"They had been *together* that week," Grace says, as she hands him a plate. "Spending time together, sleeping together. They'd argued, too, because as usual he was after money. I left them to it; I went back to my cottage in the village. I didn't want to be around all that. And to be frank, I didn't like him." She serves herself and sits. "In any case, he arrived on the Saturday. They had a few days together, and then Vanessa left on Thursday to drive to Glasgow to see Douglas Lennox, to finalize arrangements for the show—it was just a month or so away at that point. Vanessa took a few of the paintings in the car—the ones you have now. The rest—all the ceramics and the largest canvases— were to follow later, in a van. Most of it was laid out in the studio, ready to be packed.

"So, as I say, Vanessa left that Thursday, early because of the tide. Julian was still asleep, so she left him that note." Grace takes a bite of her food. She chews, shaking her head as she does. "This *cannot* come out, do you understand, Mr. Becker? She never wanted any of this to be made public."

"Yes, all right," Becker replies impatiently. "But any of *what*? What are you saying?"

"Vanessa left the note for him next to the bed, and she found it when she returned on Sunday, among the debris in the studio. All the ceramics had been smashed, the canvases slashed. Everything destroyed."

TWENTY-FOUR

When she arrived that Sunday, Vanessa's car was parked in the court-yard but the house was empty, so Grace set off up the hill toward the studio. As she approached, she heard a strange sound, a scraping sound, like a turning tool against the wheel, only louder, much louder.

When she reached the doorway, she realized that it was Vanessa; she was crying, keening, the noise was coming from her throat. She was on the floor, and she had blood on her: in her hair and on her clothes and on her hands. There was blood on the floor, too.

"Vanessa!" Grace ran to her, falling to her knees. "What happened? Vanessa, are you hurt? What happened?" Vanessa didn't speak; she just kept making the awful noise, kept squeezing her hands into fists until blood dripped from between her fingers.

"Vanessa! Stop, *stop*." Grace was trying to open Vanessa's hands, trying to prize her fingers apart; she was starting to cry herself, starting to shout. "Where are you hurt? Answer me! Please tell me what happened."

"All of it," Vanessa whispered. She swept one hand to the side, open-ing her fist, shards of bloodied porcelain falling from her hand. "It's all gone."

Grace could hardly bear to look. There was debris all around them. Obscene gashes in the paintings against the walls gaped like wounds.

"Your hands," Grace said. Vanessa opened her right fist, and from it Grace took a scrunched piece of paper, a note. To Julian. "Vanessa, where is he?" Grace said. "Where is Julian now?"

Vanessa shook her head and closed her eyes.

When eventually she opened them again, Grace helped her up from the floor and, with one arm around her shoulders and the other holding tightly to her left wrist, guided her over to the basin. Vanessa did not resist as Grace placed her hands under the running water; she stood silent and unmoving as Grace did her best to remove the remaining splinters of porcelain from her fingers and palm.

Neither of them spoke.

A WHILE LATER, Grace took Vanessa back down to the house. She sat her on the edge of the bath while she cleaned the blood from her skin, disinfecting and dressing her hands. She gave her a sleeping pill and put her to bed. Then she went back up the hill to the studio. She collected up the larger pieces of ceramic, placing them carefully on the table in groups, trying to figure out which fragments belonged with which. She swept and washed the floor, sluicing the last of the blood and debris out onto the grass, where it soaked into the soil.

It was a beautiful, mild evening, a soft breeze coming off the sea and over the gorse bushes, carrying with it the scent of kelp and coconut, but every breath Grace took tasted of blood and disinfectant. When finally she was done, she sat in the kitchen and drank whisky to purge the taste of metal from her mouth.

She checked on Vanessa, who was still sleeping, and then she phoned the emergency contact for the surgery to tell them she wouldn't be able to come in the next day. It was the first time in a decade she'd miss a day of work.

She fell asleep at the kitchen table, the whisky bottle open in front of her.

Sometime after midnight she jerked awake. Sitting up, she wiped the spittle from her mouth, rolled her aching shoulders, tipped her head from one side to the other to stretch out the muscles in her neck. She was about to get to her feet when she realized that she was not alone, that in the darkness Vanessa was sitting on the other side of the table, her face white, like a death mask.

"Jesus!" Grace gasped. "You scared me." She moved to turn on the light.

"Don't!" Vanessa snarled. Then, more gently, "*Please.*"

Grace sat down. "How do you feel? How are your hands?" When Vanessa didn't reply, Grace added, "I've taken tomorrow off. I'll phone the police first thing."

"No."

"It's criminal damage, Vanessa."

"*No.*"

Grace exhaled slowly. "Well . . . We need to get in touch with the gallery at least, we—"

"No, Grace. *We* don't need to get in touch with anyone. Don't phone anyone. Don't tell anyone. Don't do anything."

"You have to tell them, you—"

"Don't tell me what I have to do!" Vanessa snarled. "Everything is gone. Do you understand? *Everything.*"

"I know, I . . ."

"Please, leave me alone. For pity's sake, go to bed and leave me alone."

WHEN GRACE ROSE in the morning, the phone was ringing. Vanessa was sitting in the kitchen, drinking coffee, unraveling the bandages from her hands. "Don't answer it," she said when she saw Grace move toward the phone. "Could you go to the village and get me some cigarettes?" Her eyes were ringed with circles the color of bruises and her face was puffy, but she was clear-eyed, her voice steady.

"Of course," Grace replied carefully. "Do you need anything else? Shall I make you something to eat?" Vanessa shook her head. When Grace came over to inspect Vanessa's hands, she turned her face away, but she didn't resist. "Keep them clean," Grace said, "and dry. Don't try to do too much."

"Too much of what?" Vanessa asked, and she started laughing, a high, strange sound.

———

THE PHONE RANG all the time. Vanessa didn't answer it. She did nothing; she barely moved from the kitchen, just sat there and smoked and drank coffee and stared at the sea, at the causeway, as though waiting for someone to come.

And then, after six days had passed, late on Saturday afternoon, someone came.

Grace was relieved, at first. She was walking on the beach when she saw the police car driving slowly along the causeway. *At last*, she thought, *she's come to her senses.* Quickening her pace, she hurried toward the steps: she wanted to be there for Vanessa when she spoke to them.

They were all in the kitchen—two young men in uniform, standing awkwardly near the door, and Vanessa, still sitting at the kitchen table, smoking. Grace bustled in, shoving one of the officers out of the way as she did.

"I'm Vanessa's friend," Grace announced. "I also live here."

"Well, not really," Vanessa said, squinting at the cherry of her cigarette.

The police officers exchanged a quick look.

"We were asking about Mr. Chapman," the older of the two said. "About the last time you saw him."

"He's missing," Vanessa said quickly, looking at Grace for the first time since she'd come into the room.

"Missing?" Grace repeated.

"That's what Isobel says. Apparently he didn't show up for her birthday."

Grace let out a short bark of laughter. "So . . . does that mean he's *missing*? Because he didn't show up to a birthday party?"

Vanessa shrugged. "It *is* odd. He didn't call her or anything. That's unusual. They're very close."

"I understand that he was here visiting?" the first policeman said.

It took Grace a moment to realize he was talking to her. "That's right," she replied. "He was here last week . . . no, the week before that.

He left on Thursday. I wasn't here, I was staying at my cottage in the village, but I saw him . . . I saw his car, that is. I saw it going through the village on Thursday, around lunchtime."

"You saw his car?"

"Yes, it's bright red, a sports car—you don't see many of those round here. And he drives like a lunatic, so he stands out."

The second policeman, the younger of the two, smirked. "Like a lunatic? He was driving fast, you mean?"

Grace nodded.

The older one turned to Vanessa. "And there was nothing . . . odd about your husband's visit, no quarrels, nothing like that?"

Vanessa frowned. "Well . . . you know that we're separated? We're getting a divorce. But it's fairly amicable. He came to see me to talk about some money things and—"

"He came all the way up here?" The younger one again. "From Oxford? He couldn't just have called?"

"We're still friends," Vanessa said, her soft, gravelly tones turned hard as glass, "as I said. You do understand what *amicable* means?" The policeman turned pink to the tops of his ears. Vanessa directed her attention to the other one. "It's strange, as I said, that he missed his sister's birthday, but it's not completely out of character for Julian to go AWOL. He has . . . lots of friends, usually a few girlfriends, no end of creditors, and he drinks quite a bit. He's not here, as you can see." She wafted a hand in the air. "Do feel free to take a look around if you wish. As far as I know, he left on Thursday, like Grace just told you, not long after I drove to Glasgow. When I came back here on Sunday around midday, his car was gone, so I assumed he'd driven back south."

THEY DIDN'T LOOK around. They just took her word for it, gave her a card and the usual spiel about *if you remember anything*, and off they went.

As soon as the police officers were in their car and heading back to the mainland, Vanessa got up and left the kitchen. She walked outside and up the hill, with Grace trailing after her. "Why didn't you tell them?" Grace called out.

Vanessa ignored her, and when Grace called out again, she whirled around, her expression furious. "Tell them *what*, Grace? That he destroyed all my work? What if something's happened to him? If I tell them what he did, they'll think *I* did something to him. The press will find out, they'll be camping on the beach, crawling all over my island. They'll never leave me alone."

"But . . . how could they think you had anything to do with it?" Grace protested. "You were in Glasgow, Vanessa, you were at the gallery, how could you have done anything to him?"

Vanessa said nothing; she just stood there, biting her lip, her gaze shifting off to one side. She blinked furiously and then, tossing her hair over her shoulder, she turned and marched off toward the studio.

THE PHONE RANG and rang; Grace was forbidden to answer it.

Another policeman came back a few days later, a different one, a man in plain clothes, from down south, who insisted on talking to Vanessa alone. Grace lingered in the hallway; she heard him pose the same questions the other police officers had put to her, plus a few more besides.

What is the *precise* nature of your relationship to Mrs. Haswell? he asked Vanessa. Where does she sleep? How did Mrs. Haswell and Mr. Chapman get on? Did *they* argue at all? At the end of the interview, the detective told Vanessa that while a number of people could confirm that the red sports car had been seen driving through the village that Thursday lunchtime, one witness claimed to have seen it heading back across the causeway later on that day, in the evening.

"I wasn't here!" Vanessa snapped at him. "How many fucking times?"

Grace reentered the room then, quickly stepping in to defuse the situation before Vanessa got herself into trouble. "Thursday evening, did you say?" she asked. "What time on Thursday evening?"

The detective peered at her, eyes narrowed. "Where were *you* on Thursday evening?"

"Well, I . . . I was at work on Thursday," Grace said. "I was in the surgery until six, I suppose, or maybe a little after. We've got a review coming up and there's a lot of paperwork, and after that I took Marguerite her Diovan because she forgot to pick it up again, and—"

"Marguerite?"

"She's a patient."

"Is it usual for you to make house calls?"

"Not really, no, but Marguerite lives just around the corner from the surgery, in one of the harbor cottages, and she's . . . well, she's rather lonely, so I try to drop in on her from time to time. As I say, she'd not picked up her blood pressure medication, so I took that round and then she offered me some supper, which was very welcome as I'd been rushed off my feet and hadn't got round to doing any shopping, so we ate and—"

"What did you eat?"

Grace shrugged. "Um . . . French onion soup. Salad. We each had a glass of red wine and then coffee."

"What time did you leave?"

"I stayed a little while, because, as I say, she's lonely. It was still light, though. Still light, but the water was over the causeway, so . . ." Grace looked at the tide chart on the kitchen wall. "Sometime between eight thirty and nine thirty it must have been."

"The tide was in?"

"It was coming in." Grace glanced at Vanessa, who was staring out the window, didn't appear to be listening at all. "It was just about too late to cross over."

"Just about?" the detective repeated.

"Well," Grace said, "if you were in a four-by-four and you knew what you were doing, you could have made it . . ."

"The island isn't private property, you know," Vanessa said, suddenly rejoining the conversation. "*Anyone* could have come across. People do, especially in summer, to walk up to the rock."

"At *night*?" the detective asked.

"In the *evening*," Vanessa replied pointedly. "Depending on the weather, the sunset can be breathtaking."

Grace frowned, chewing her lower lip. "Vanessa," she said quietly, "you don't think . . . he wouldn't have tried to get back over, would he? When the tide was coming in?"

Vanessa raised her hand to her mouth, eyes suddenly bright with tears. The detective, though, was shaking his head. "That can't be it, our witness would have seen that, wouldn't they? And in any case, his car would have been found by now."

Vanessa scraped her teeth over her lower lip. "There was an incident a while ago—six, maybe seven years?" She looked to Grace for confirmation; Grace nodded. "It was before I lived here. Someone got into trouble on the causeway, their car was washed away, and it was weeks before it was found."

"But there was a storm then," Grace said. "There was a terrible storm."

The detective looked at her for a long while. "And the day we're talking about?"

"Calm," Grace replied. "It's summer. Most of the time this bay is dead calm."

The detective nodded slowly, looking back at his notes. He turned once more to Vanessa. "Can you give me the name of the hotel you were staying in while you were in Glasgow?" he asked.

Vanessa tipped her head back, sighed. "I wasn't in a hotel," she said, looking him dead in the eyes. "I was staying in Douglas Lennox's pied-à-terre on Blythswood Square. If you ask him, he'll probably deny it. He's frightened of his wife. He thinks if she leaves him, she'll take him to the cleaners."

The detective looked from Vanessa to Grace and back to Vanessa again. "You have a sexual relationship with Mr. Lennox?"

Vanessa pressed her lips together, as though to stifle a smile. "He's a gallerist who shows my work. We sleep together occasionally."

The detective pushed back his chair and got to his feet. "All right if I take a look around, Mrs. Chapman?"

TWO DAYS LATER, more police came, a dozen of them, roaming all over the island just as Vanessa had feared they would. They searched the house, they went up to the rock and looked over the edge, they hunted through the wood. They found nothing save, in the studio, traces of blood. "*Mine*," Vanessa told the detective. "I dropped a vase and cut myself picking up the pieces." She held up her still-bandaged hand.

In the house, the phone kept ringing, and Vanessa couldn't afford to ignore it any longer, not with the police hanging around; she had to field angry calls from Douglas, hysterical ones from Isobel.

She glided through it all, glacially detached, her face a mask. She answered all their questions: was he depressed (a little, sometimes, he was grieving, his girlfriend died in an accident six months ago); did he have money problems (yes, yes, yes, I've told you, yes); do you think he might have taken his own life (—).

The blood turned out to be Vanessa's, just as she'd said it was.

A month or so after the police visited, a fisherman in a boat a couple of miles southwest of Sheepshead Island found a black wallet in his nets; it had Julian Chapman's credit cards inside it.

They found no other trace of him or of his car.

He was gone.

TWENTY-FIVE

"He just . . . he destroyed everything?" Becker has repeated this a few times; he can't seem to take it in. The details of Julian's disappearance—the missing car, the wallet—all of these were reported at the time, but *this*? This act of vandalism? He has never heard mention of it. "He destroyed everything she'd made, everything she'd been working on? And that's why she pulled out of the show?" Grace nods. She is sitting opposite him with her hands in her lap and her head bent almost to her chest. She brushes the back of her hand against a cheek. "But . . . why didn't she explain to Douglas, at least? She could have saved herself so much pain and *expense*—God, the court case, years of recriminations . . ."

Grace looks up, moves her head gently from side to side. "Douglas would have wanted to go to the police, she knew that. He would have wanted her to claim on insurance or to appeal for criminal compensation, and she . . . just *wouldn't*. Believe me, I tried to persuade her, but she was afraid . . ." She tails off, bends her head again.

"Afraid? Of the police, you mean, that they would suspect her?"

When she looks up again, there is a guardedness in Grace's expression. "Ye-es," she says warily. "She was afraid they would suspect her, she was afraid of what it would do to her sanctuary, to Eris, if people thought Julian was somewhere out here. But more than that . . . I think that she was also just heartbroken. And in shock. She didn't want to face up to what had happened, to the violence of it."

She pours herself a little more wine; as she refills his glass, he can see her hand is trembling.

"I'm sorry," he says, "this must be very upsetting to talk about."

Grace inclines her head and gives him a sad smile. "It changed her," she says softly. "What happened that summer, it changed the way she looked at the world . . ." She touches her face again and looks away, out the window. A car crests the hill across the water, headlights on full beam. "I'm not sure she was ever the same again."

For a minute or two, they drink their wine in silence. Becker's mind is racing, he has so many questions, not least whether he can keep this confidence—it's not as though he's sworn to, has he? He said he understood that Vanessa didn't want this made public, but he's made no promises. And, realistically speaking, he *cannot* keep this from Sebastian.

"Grace," he says eventually, "I do understand why Vanessa was afraid of what might happen if this became public, but I think I have a duty to let Sebastian Lennox know what happened to those works."

"No you don't!" She shakes her head vigorously. "We're talking about pieces that were destroyed twenty years ago, long before Fairburn inherited Vanessa's estate. They've nothing to do with Lennox. Please, Vanessa would hate to have all this picked over, to have everyone speculating again about what she did or didn't do. If you have any respect for her memory, you'll let this lie."

He is torn between the idea that Vanessa really would hate this being known and the idea that this is part of her story, a *fundamental* part of her story. It will surely have informed everything that came after. He thinks of *Division II*, its delicate components enclosed in a glass case, protected from the world.

Until now.

"Can you remember," Becker asks, "any details about the pieces that were destroyed? What they looked like, I mean, what sort of forms they were? Vases, bowls, something more sculptural . . . ?"

Grace shakes her head. "I'm sorry, I really don't remember the ceramics all that well . . . The paintings I can recall a bit better, but the porcelain pieces sort of . . . blend into one for me." She shrugs guiltily.

Becker feels a brief flash of anger. *You lived with a genius,* he thinks, *and you weren't even paying attention.*

"The names didn't help," she goes on. "They were always so vague. *Flourish* or *Breathe* . . . I never understand why she didn't just call things what they were. I expect it means I'm a philistine, but why *Hope Is Violent*? Why not *Lighthouse on Sheepshead*? Why *Totem*? Why not *Grace with Bird*?"

"*Totem*?" Becker repeats. "*Totem* was a portrait? Of you?"

"I was holding a wood carving," she says, her voice gruff, "of a little bird."

He's not sure if it's because he's had too much wine or because the light is so dim in the kitchen, but it takes him a while to notice that Grace is crying.

"Grace," he says, "I'm so sorry . . ." He reaches across the table, awkwardly patting the top of her wrist. She rolls her hand over and takes hold of his fingers, squeezing their tips momentarily. She inclines her head, brushing tears from her cheek against the fabric of her shirt. They sit like this for a moment, until, mercifully, Becker's phone pings, giving him an excuse to withdraw his hand.

"Sorry," Becker says, glancing at the message. It's from Helena— she's exhausted, she's going to have an early night. He glances at his watch, frowning—it's barely 9:30.

Grace sniffs. "Is everything all right?" she asks.

He nods. "Yeah, it's fine, it's . . . my wife."

"Is something wrong? You look concerned."

"Oh"—he smiles—"it's nothing. It's nothing."

Grace pats the tips of her fingers to her cheeks. "It's clearly not *nothing*."

Becker shakes his head. "It's just me. I worry about her. The pregnancy and the stress of the situation at Fairburn . . ."

Grace raises her eyebrows. "The situation? You mean *our* situation?"

"Oh, no," Becker says, shaking his head again, "I don't mean that."

He's drunk, he realizes, he must be, because he's started to talk too much, and before he knows it, he's running his mouth, pouring his heart out. "Helena was engaged when we met," he says, "to Sebastian Lennox." Grace's eyebrows creep closer to her hairline, and Becker blushes, fidgeting with the tassels of the tablecloth. "She . . . uh . . . she changed her mind." He looks up. "It wasn't really my doing," he says, and Grace smiles. "No, no, honestly. It wasn't like I *tried* to take her from him. I would never have imagined for a minute that she would leave him for me. He's a great deal more eligible."

Grace tips her head to one side, her eyes meeting his. "Your Helena sounds a good judge of character," she says. "Not everyone *wants* someone flashy or obvious or terribly rich. Some people see past that, don't they? And sometimes people like us have our own quiet attractions."

Becker nods, smiling idiotically, unsure of what she means. *People like us?* Does that mean her and him? What does she imagine they have in common?

"So this Sebastian," Grace says, leaning forward as she tips the last of the red wine into Becker's glass, "he wants rid of you?"

"Actually," Becker says, his blush deepening, "Sebastian has been a lot more forgiving than I would've been in the circumstances." He laughs nervously. "It's Seb's mother who's the problem. She didn't like me in the first place—she thinks I'm common—but she loathes me now, and she's become quite . . . *unpleasant.*"

"Oh, Emmeline was always unpleasant," Grace replies, getting to her feet.

"Of course." Becker pushes his chair back, rising to help her clear the table. "I'd forgotten you know her."

Grace waves off his offer of help, and he collapses back into his chair. "Barely," she says. "She came out here on a couple of occasions with Douglas, but she didn't have much time for the likes of me."

Becker can just imagine: to Emmeline, Grace would appear little more than a servant. "I suppose I ought to be more sympathetic to her, after all she's been through . . ."

Grace scoffs. "After suffering decades of his infidelities you'd think she'd be happy to see the back of the old goat."

"The circumstances were so shocking," Becker murmurs, "and there's guilt as well as grief . . ."

"Guilt?" Grace repeats, turning to look at him. "Why *guilt*?"

Becker's wine-addled brain takes a few moments to process the fact that he has said too much, but it's too late now; he can see from the expression on Grace's face that she has figured it out. "Emmeline was the one who shot him?" she says. "Good lord. How extraordinary."

"The family kept it out of the papers," Becker says, inwardly cursing himself. "Everyone wanted to protect her . . . she'd suffered enough."

"I see," Grace says. She is leaning against the kitchen counter, folding and unfolding the tea towel in her hands. "*Extraordinary*," she says again. "That woman could hit a rabbit through the eye with an air gun."

Becker sits up straight. "I'm sorry?"

Grace nods. "Oh yes, Emmeline's a crack shot. She used to boast she could've gone to the Olympics, if they'd allowed women to shoot back then."

Becker pushes his wineglass away, rising unsteadily to his feet. He's struggling to think straight—has she really just suggested that Emmeline could have shot Douglas *on purpose*?

"I . . . I probably ought to go to bed," he says.

"Oh." Grace is clearly disappointed. "I wanted to show you something else. Discuss something with you, before you take the notebooks back to Fairburn. But I have to be sure, Mr. Becker, that I can trust you." She looks at him, her eyes enormous, imploring. "I can trust you, can't I?"

Grace crosses the kitchen, turning on the main light. Becker sits. Narrowing his eyes against the glare, he watches as she reaches into the box she fetched earlier, the one from which she drew Vanessa's note to Julian, and plucks out a notebook. "These, as I'm sure you've guessed, are the things I would rather have kept to myself. You can take the notebooks, but I would ask you not to put them on display. *Please*. For her sake," she says, handing him the book, "and for mine."

The notebook, another Life Vermilion, is identical to the ones he has been reading back at Fairburn, only in this one, Becker sees that

Vanessa's handwriting is not elegantly loose and looping; it has become spidery and erratic. Her hand no longer follows the lines on the page but wanders all over the place, scribbling into corners, veering off at odd angles. Many of the pages are blank except for faint, seemingly unconnected traces of pencil, a few barely legible phrases.

"When the cancer came back," Grace explains, "it metastasized. It went to her brain." She chews her lower lip, watching Becker leaf through the book. "She had terrible headaches; the sight in her right eye started to go. She'd long since stopped working with ceramics— she just wasn't strong enough to handle the clay—but by this time she could no longer paint; she struggled even to draw. She became—on paper and in real life—a lot less coherent. You can see that sometimes she appears to be writing not for herself, as with the older books, but *to* someone. To Frances, sometimes, or to me."

Becker scans the pages, trying to make sense of her scrawl. Some of it sounds very much like Vanessa:

I seek substance: literal, physical substance. Wood, again, or stone?

Some of it less so:

where did he go where did you go where did I go?

Some of it is unbearable:

is the light failing, or am I?

And some of it desperate:

You have to help me. You owe me this

The last sentence underlined so forcefully that she has ripped the page.

"She begged me to help her," Grace says. "After a certain point, everything became about that. All our conversations. When she spoke to me, she spoke of nothing else, she begged and begged and, in the end, I did it. I did what she asked me to do."

For a long moment, Becker is speechless. "You *helped* her?" he repeats at last, his skin prickling despite the warmth of the room. He has a lump in his throat, hard as a peach pit.

"I don't think there's anything conclusive in the notebooks," Grace says quietly. "Vanessa writes about morphine at some point, but there's nothing to damn me. Nothing to *convict* me, I wouldn't have thought. I doubt much would happen at all, were this to come out—I'm sure it's too late to prove anything. We were careful. I gave her the dose the night of a storm; it was three days before the ambulance came to take her." She looks him dead in the eyes. "It's not the law I'm afraid of, and it's not a matter of my professional standing either, since I'm pretty sure I've retired for good this time." She sighs, breath shuddering out of her. "But if people were to read this, there would be speculation, *controversy*, the press prying once more. She *loathed* them, you know, she always did. She would hate to have them picking over her bones." As she leaves the table, she places a hand gently on his shoulder. "Everything is for her protection, you see. Everything I did, everything I do."

For a while, Becker sits alone in the kitchen, trying to make sense of everything he has heard: about Julian and about Emmeline and about what Grace did for Vanessa. To Vanessa. His head is thick, he can't seem to unpick the ragged knot of his thoughts; every thread he pulls at only seems to cinch the tangle ever tighter.

Eventually, he makes his way to bed, weaving through the gloom of the living room, trying not to crash into the furniture. He sits on the bed, head in hands, listening to the waves, willing the room to stop spinning. What happens now? What happens tomorrow? Is he going to tell her the truth, that *Division II* is to be broken open? That for all he knows, it might have already happened, that Vanessa's last breath may be gone?

———————

HE IS WOKEN by a loud beeping. He forgot to turn off his alarm. He sits up in the darkness, head thumping, stifles a groan, scrabbles around on the nightstand for his phone. He knocks something over.

Shit.

It's not his alarm, it's a WhatsApp call, it's Helena.

"Beck? Can you hear me?" Her voice is full of tears; there's an echo, as though she's in an empty room.

"Yes, I can, what's going on?"

"Oh!" She starts to cry and his heart stops.

"Helena, what is it? Where are you? Helena?"

"There's blood. I'm bleeding."

"Jesus, where are you? Are you in London?"

"No, I'm home, I'm in the bathroom, I—"

"OK, OK." He tries to keep the panic out of his voice. "Is it . . . how much blood? Is it spotting?"

"I don't think so." Her voice is tiny.

"Call an ambulance. No, *I'll* call an ambulance. No, *fuck*, I can't. I don't have service. *You* call the ambulance, I'm going to call Sebastian and tell him to go round to wait with you. Get out of the bathroom, Hels, go downstairs, unlock the front door. Do it now, I'll ring Seb."

"OK." She makes a strange noise, somewhere between a laugh and a cry. "I'm frightened, Beck."

His hands are shaking as he calls Sebastian. It rings and rings; he hangs up, tries again, and again. The third time, Sebastian picks up.

"Helena's bleeding, you have to help her." He is trying not to raise his voice, struggling to keep the lid on his terror. "You have to go to her, now! Don't ask questions, please, please, just go!"

"I'm going," Sebastian says. "I'm going now!" Becker has barely ended the call when he remembers the tide. He throws his clothes on, sprints through the living room to the front door, he runs outside. Water is just starting to lap the causeway. He runs back into the house, grabs the rest of his things. He needs to leave a note for Grace;

he can't find anything to write on. He grabs handfuls of paper from the box Grace left, letters and cards—he can't write on those. He finds a receipt in his inside coat pocket and scribbles on that. As he's writing his eye snags on a word on the letter at the top of the pile: *Division*. He grabs the letter and stuffs it into his jacket and runs out the door.

TWENTY-SIX

When Grace opens her eyes, she sees the chair at her bedside, its upholstery a dull, faded orange, and behind it a bare wall. She feels disoriented for a moment, and then she remembers that she is in Vanessa's bed. She stares at the wall, trying to remember what used to hang there, which of the paintings it was that Vanessa would look at over her head when Grace sat at her side.

What was it? *Dawn in Winter*. A painting of the channel, an ice-green sea drawing away from the land, the causeway leading the eye to the mainland, to the snow on the hills. One of Vanessa's earliest Eris landscapes, one of her enduring favorites. So many of those early ones were morning pictures; she loved to be out on the sands or on the hill with the day dawning, hope springing, reveling in her freedom. Fairburn has *Dawn in Winter* now. Grace wonders where it hangs; she can't quite picture it under spotlights in some grand, vaulted gallery. It was a humble, everyday sort of picture.

She can ask Becker! It occurs to her then that she is not alone, that she has someone to talk to.

Glancing at the clock next to the bed, she realizes that she has slept through low tide. She rolls over; through the gap between the curtains, she spies a blue sky. She feels a little surge of joy: she's heady from last night's wine, though Becker drank quite a bit more of it than she did. And she is rested, she has slept long and soundly, and it's thanks to him. Thanks to the comfort of having him here with her.

It was *wonderful*, last night. Cooking for someone again, breaking bread, drinking wine, talking into the small hours. She wonders whether she might be able to persuade him to stay another night? There is pasta, and sausages from the butcher, and—

She feels a pang, a sharp jab to the stomach. She told him about the morphine. That was reckless. But he confided in her, too, didn't he? He told her about his marriage, about the trouble he was having at Fairburn. They've bonded, they are friends now. She can trust him. They can trust each other.

She checks the time—it is almost nine. She should wake him. In the shower, she plans their day: coffee, a quick breakfast, a walk through the wood, up to the rock. They can visit some of Vanessa's other favorite painting spots along the southern side of the island on the way back. Then perhaps more time in the studio? A walk on the beach? And an invitation to stay a bit longer. Like someone who doesn't realize how hungry they are until they have their first bite of food, Grace has not acknowledged how lonely she's been feeling, not until Becker turned up.

She allows herself to drift into reverie, to a time in the future when Becker comes to stay at the island for days, weeks even, sometimes bringing his wife and the baby, sometimes coming alone. They go for walks on the beach and Grace cooks and they sit up late, drinking wine, talking about Vanessa. She is invited back to Fairburn, Sebastian Lennox sees her differently now, as a person of value, an asset, someone with a contribution to make. She helps with the archiving of Vanessa's notes and correspondence; she has a role, a new purpose.

It's a daydream. She's not a fool. And yet there's no denying the bond between her and Becker. They are linked by Vanessa, and now by Eris Island, but their connection goes deeper than that. She's looked him up, she's read about him: he's not like the Fairburn people, he doesn't come from money. He's like her, he's a striver, he's had nothing handed to him. She suspects that she understands some things about James Becker in a way neither his moneyed wife nor his boss can.

Back in the bedroom, she pulls the curtains open. Glorious. A lively sea, tropical aquamarine in the sunshine and deep Atlantic blue where clouds throw shadows. The air is clear, the view so crisp Grace can make out the gannets roosting on the cliffs of Sheepshead. From the top of the rock, they'll be able to see forever.

She dresses in walking trousers and warm clothes—sunshine or no, it'll be chilly—and slips quietly out into the hall. As she walks through the living room she notices that her bedroom door—the spare room door—is already open. He's up! He's not in the kitchen, though; he must have gone for a walk. She is making coffee when she notices the scrap of paper weighted to the table by the pepper mill.

So sorry—had to go—emergency. Will email later to explain. Tks for everything. B

Her heart is gripped by a fist and it is squeezing, squeezing until there is no blood left in it at all. She starts to cry, like a disappointed child, and then anger strikes, vicious and backhanded, a slap to the face. She *hates* him. The coffeepot hits the wall with a crack like a gunshot.

TWENTY-SEVEN

Grace was in the queue at the university canteen when she heard, from just across the room, Paul's unmistakable public-school bray: "Mate, she's terrible. She just lies there. It's like doing it with an ironing board."

Jeers, laughter.

Grace bowed her head, tucking her chin to her chest, but from the corner of her eye she could see his straw blond mop of hair, his pudgy frame: Paul, the man with whom she had been sleeping for the past three weeks, the man to whom she lost her virginity.

"Seriously, it's a disappointment. I thought the ugly ones were supposed to try harder."

More laughter, uproarious. People were turning around, looking, listening.

"Like, they're supposed to be grateful."

Grace was rooted to the spot by terror: if she moved now, she might draw attention to herself. Someone might see her. *They* might see her; they would realize that she'd heard, that she'd been present for the verdict, for her humiliation—and how much sweeter would that taste to them?

"You're an arsehole, d'you know that?" Another voice, clear as a bell, cut through the noise. "Yes, I'm talking to you, Paul Connolly, you fat wanker. Do you seriously imagine anyone could be *grateful* to have *you* sweating away on top of them?"

Salvation! In the unlikely form of Nicholas Riley, a slight boy, pale as milk, with a sprinkling of freckles across his nose. Handsome in a quiet way, clever and funny with enough of a mean streak to make him interesting. Nicholas had been sitting alone at the next table over from Paul and his friends, and when he spoke up they turned on him, a few of them even getting to their feet, swaggering over toward him, spitting venom. Grace slipped silently from the queue, replaced her tray on the stack, and fled, hungry but relieved.

After that day, Grace tried to avoid Nicholas. She dreaded the embarrassment of having to acknowledge the incident at all, to concede that she had been present at the theater of her own public shaming. And yet she saw him everywhere—it was as though he sought her out: he was in the row in front of her in lectures, he was on the lawn in Russell Square at lunchtime, he was behind her in the ticket line for the cinema at the Brunswick Centre.

"It must be written in the stars," he said, tapping her on the shoulder. "We're meant to be." He winked. And in that moment she knew: they were going to be friends.

He made her laugh. "You're not like other girls," he used to say, which made her laugh more than anything: it was a stupid cliché, the sort of thing people said in idiotic romantic films, but it was actually true of Grace. She wasn't like other girls. She was different in a way that was difficult to pin down, but Nick didn't care. He never asked her to explain herself or to apologize for anything.

Nick had another friend, Audrey, and she wasn't like other girls either, but she was unlike other girls in a more conventional sense. She wasn't *weird*, just a bit quirky. Audrey was in the year above, studying psychiatry; she was tall and angular and intimidatingly clever. "Audrey doesn't like people," Nick said. "That's why she wants to be a shrink. To figure out why everyone's so fucking awful." But Audrey liked Nick. She liked Grace, too, and Grace liked her back, though sometimes she wished Audrey didn't exist, because whenever Audrey was in the room, Nick turned slightly away from Grace.

The three of them got a flat together, a squalid, mouse-infested place above a newsagent on Goodge Street, and for a time, they were inseparable. They studied tirelessly, holding themselves apart, drawing further away from the other students, from their own families. At last, Grace had found her people; she discarded the shame of loneliness like an old coat.

In the summer, they hopped into Nick's Vauxhall Astra and drove to France. They spent a week camping on a clifftop in St. Malo; they played cards and drank cheap red wine until they threw up. At Christmas, none of them went back to see their families; they stayed in the horrible flat instead, eating pizza or takeaway curry, watching films on VHS.

In early January, Grace fell ill. She had abdominal pain that grew increasingly severe, she developed a fever, she became delirious. Nick called a taxi and accompanied her, sobbing from the pain, to University College Hospital, where they diagnosed a ruptured cyst and an infection. She was admitted right away and remained there for eight days, receiving fluids and antibiotics through an IV drip.

It wasn't until around the fourth day that she was sufficiently alert to find it strange that neither Nick nor Audrey had come to visit. She wondered, in fact, whether they had come, whether in her delirium she had forgotten, but the nursing staff, who kept asking if she wouldn't like them to call someone, insisted that no one had been by.

There was no phone in the flat, so when the time came for her to be released from hospital, there was no one to take her home, so she left alone, shrugging off the nurses' pitying looks, walking out into a bitter wind.

When she arrived back at her building, she took a moment outside to compose herself, to practice her indifference. She climbed the stairs and unlocked the door.

The flat was cold in a way that suggested the heating hadn't been on for days, silent in a way that spoke to absence. Audrey's and Nick's things were gone; they had left no notes and no forwarding addresses. Grace didn't know where their parents lived; she had no contact numbers for them either. They had told no one at the university that they were dropping out, and they skipped out on the rent.

She couldn't understand it, and there was no one to explain it to her. She had begun to understand herself as part of their band of three, and now what was she? She was acutely aware that what she was feeling was *wrong*—it had been a friendship, after all, not a love affair; there was no call for heartbreak. No one had died, this was not cause for grief.

And yet, the return to classes was agonizing. She was sure everyone was talking about what had happened, certain that everyone knew: Grace had loved them, Nick and Audrey, and they had not loved her back.

She tried to throw herself into her studies, but she was exhausted. Whether from depression or illness, she could barely get out of bed in the mornings. She began to have worrying thoughts—persistent, intrusive. She imagined harming herself, all the time, she imagined taking her own life, she thought about how it would make Nick feel. She worried that he wouldn't find out about it, that he wouldn't even notice; she worried that she'd end her life for nothing.

She worried that one day he might come back and see what had become of her.

She was very frightened.

She did what she was supposed to do: she went to her doctor and asked for help, and he gave it to her. She was referred to a psychologist, a kind, patient woman from whom she always held something back. Still, she did as she was advised: rest, allow yourself to recuperate. She deferred her studies for a year, moved out of the flat and into a bedsit, got a secretarial job, volunteered at a care home, spoke to the psychologist once a week. She ate better, she exercised, she slept.

She went back to university, she worked hard, she finished her degree.

She did everything right.

The thing that stayed with her, afterward, was not so much the shock of the abandonment, or the hurt or the rejection; it was the excruciating shame of it all. The humiliation that came with realizing that there were rules she did not understand, that no matter how she tried, she never managed to feel the right things in the right way.

She moved away from London as soon as she could, up north to Edinburgh and from there out west. Small towns, rural places would be more forgiving, she thought; she'd be able to try again, to do good, to get things right, she'd escape her *wrongness*.

Only it followed her, it kept following her, all the way to Eris.

TWENTY-EIGHT

Down on the causeway, in the limbo between island and mainland, you can imagine yourself in another world; it feels uncharted, the seabed, never the same twice. Grace rarely crosses over on foot, as it always makes her feel a little afraid, even on days like today when the tide is low and the sun is warm on her face, oystercatchers piping and gulls calling, the sky reassuringly blue.

By the time she reaches the ramp at the end of the causeway, she is slightly out of breath. She slogs up the hill and, reaching the harbor car park, spies Marguerite, on her knees in front of her cottage, deadheading roses. Marguerite is singing to herself, softly and with perfect pitch. As Grace approaches, she starts. Getting quickly to her feet, she raises her hand to shield her eyes against the sun and then she smiles. "Ah! *Madame le médecin!* You are bringing my pills?"

More and more, as Marguerite's grip on the present loosens, she understands people in the context in which she first met them. So Grace is her doctor, Grace gives her medication.

"No pills today," Grace says. "I just thought I'd come and say hello."

Marguerite nods. "Come, come," she says, taking Grace's hand in her own. Her fingers are freezing, as cold as the earth. "You will have tea?"

Grace follows her through the front door to the kitchen at the rear of the house. While Marguerite fills the kettle, Grace fetches cups from the cupboard. They have been put away dirty and are now host to a flourishing green mold. "I'll just give these a quick rinse, shall I?" Grace asks. Marguerite nods, smiling shyly. When she reaches up to take the tea caddy from a shelf, Grace notices a bruise, its dark purple center bleeding away to greenish edges, on the underside of her forearm.

"Ouch," Grace says, wincing, indicating the arm. "That looks painful."

"Ouch, *oui*." Marguerite's expression is grave. "I fall, you see? Is not a lie. Really, really, *c'est vrai*."

This comes from the past, too, from the days when Marguerite would come to see Grace with an injury and a story to go with it—she slipped on a patch of ice, she banged her head on a cupboard door. And when Grace probed, gently, for the truth, Marguerite would dig her heels in, insistent. *Is not a lie,* c'est vrai. Now, though, it almost certainly *is* true. Grace believes her, she says so. Marguerite beams like a praised child.

But by the time they have moved from the kitchen to the living room, she has become agitated, bustling to the window every couple of minutes to look out over the car park toward the road. "I think he comes back soon," she says, clasping and unclasping her bony hands, misshapen by time and repeated breaks.

"No, Marguerite, you don't have to worry," Grace says firmly. "He's not coming back."

"No?" Marguerite smiles warily, hopefully: she wants to believe her.

"Come and sit down," Grace instructs her. "Sit down and drink your tea. Tell me, how did you hurt your arm? You fell here? In the house? Or outside?"

Marguerite thinks about this for a moment and then shakes her head slowly. She puts a crooked forefinger to her lips. "You do something for me, I do something for you," she says.

"All right," Grace says, though she is not sure *what* conversation they are having now. "What do you want me to do for you?" Marguerite claps her hands, giggling, and Grace glimpses the girl she must have been once, lively and coquettish. She was working as a chambermaid in a shabby hotel in Lille when she met Stuart, a giant truck driver with enormous hands and an irresistible grin; he persuaded her to pack it in and start a new life with him across the English Channel. Worst decision she ever made.

She arrived in Eris in 1992; Grace met her the following year, the year of the storms. The same year that Nick Riley turned up, surprising

Grace at work. Not surprising, no. *Surprise* doesn't begin to cover what she felt when Nick turned up unannounced, out of the blue. Shocked, yes, staggered. Floored.

Still, Grace has always reproached herself for the fact her attention was elsewhere that first time Marguerite came to see her at the surgery. She wanted something for the pain, she said. She'd had an accident, fallen off her bicycle. With hindsight, Grace knew she should have done more for her. Should have asked more questions, should have pushed harder, shouldn't have allowed Marguerite to persuade her that there was nothing amiss, no need to get anyone else involved. Why would there be, when she'd only had a fall? C'est vrai, *it's not a lie.*

Grace was distracted; she went along with Marguerite's story, all the while acknowledging to herself that a fall might account for a cracked rib, possibly even the fractured cheekbone and the knocked-out tooth, but it did not explain the livid, fingerprint-shaped bruises on Marguerite's neck and arms and thighs.

Now, Marguerite is on her feet again, looking out the window, across the water. "*L'isle ne se souvient pas,*" she says, turning to face Grace, who shrugs, shaking her head. *I don't understand.* "The island does not remember." Grace presses her lips together, suppressing a sigh. Her patience for this sort of meandering, riddling conversation is limited. Marguerite is looking at her expectantly, but Grace shakes her head again, and so Marguerite turns away. "I think he comes again soon," she says softly to herself.

The sad thing, Grace thinks, the *cruel* thing, is that while Marguerite remembers Stuart, she appears to have forgotten the other man, the one she fell in love with after her husband went to prison. He is dead now, but they shared years of happiness. But instead of reminiscing fondly about her mild and gentlemanly farmer, she stands at the window, anguished and fearful, eternally expecting the brute.

As Grace leaves, Marguerite follows her to the door, taking hold of her hand as she steps out into the sunlight. "Where did your friend go?" she asks, her eyes searching Grace's face. "What happened?"

"Nothing's happened, Marguerite," Grace replies, gently extricating herself. "There's nothing to worry about. Everything is all right."

The sun is bright and pale and low. Grace walks with one arm raised to shield her eyes from the glare. A headache is building at the back of her skull, she feels a tightness there as though someone has pulled her hair. Her tread is leaden; she is dog-tired, feeling the effects of last night's wine.

She told Marguerite that everything was all right, which is evidently not true. The old woman is becoming too ill to live alone, she isn't coping. She could have a serious fall, she could leave the gas on, burn the house down, give herself food poisoning eating off filthy plates. Grace ought to phone the surgery tomorrow, get them to send a social worker out to see her. Would that be the right thing to do? It wouldn't be the kind thing. They'd turf Marguerite out of her little cottage, take her to some awful institution. *No.* Grace would prefer to keep her there, on the harbor, where she can keep an eye on her.

Back down on the causeway in the lee of the island, the air is cold and damp. Over to her right, out on the sand, something moves and Grace starts, her heart rate spiking, but when she looks again, there's nothing there, just the flat light making beasts of shadows. She quickens her pace, looking up at the house as she does. From this angle, you can see only the narrower, kitchen end of the building. It looks small and undefended, as though a high tide or a fierce storm might carry it away.

The year Grace met Marguerite, there were two great storms. The house survived them both, though the roof from one of the barns was lost. The first storm felled the oldest pine in the wood, its roots ripping a vast, gaping hole in the earth. The second storm tore down three more trees and washed away a section of the causeway. Months later, the causeway was repaired, but in the wood, the fallen giants remained for years, ever so slowly returning to the earth.

Vanessa never knew the island before the storms, but Grace did. Grace remembers the island before the trees fell and afterward, before the causeway crumbled and after it was repaired; she can see the scars even if no one else can.

People have those, too, don't they? On the surface or beneath it, there is always some residue, some mark left when a path divides, when a life becomes a different one. For Marguerite, it was leaving home, coming here; and then later, Stuart's imprisonment, her release. For Vanessa, it was coming to Eris, it was Julian's disappearance, and everything that went with it.

Vanessa Chapman's diary

There is an emptiness to the house that feels wretched. I walk up to the studio in darkness and I return in darkness, I go round and round and round in my head, sketching and listening and looking and waiting. Nothing comes. No one comes.

The tide comes.

TWENTY-NINE

When Grace reaches the top of the steps, she pauses to catch her breath and then, instead of going into the house, she continues up the hill, past the studio, toward the tree line.

The light is failing, shadows gathering and thickening. Marguerite has a phrase for it: *l'heure entre loup et chien*, the hour between a wolf and a dog. The time at which one thing might appear to be another, when something benign might appear threatening, when an enemy might come calling in the shape of a friend.

When she was a child, very young, perhaps three or four, Grace got her hand caught in a slamming door (who slammed it? The wind? Her mother?) and the very tip of the third finger on her right hand was severed altogether. She and the severed fingertip were rushed to hospital, where a surgeon managed to reattach it.

Grace remembers almost nothing of all this; it was explained to her at some point, presumably when she asked why the third finger on her right hand was slightly misshapen and fractionally shorter than the third finger on her left.

What she does remember is that she stayed in the hospital overnight. Now, as an adult and a doctor, she can't imagine why she was kept in for such a minor thing, but she was. And the thing she remembers is this: when her parents came to get her the following morning, she was seized with an overwhelming terror; she did not want to leave with them, she clung to the ward nurse and howled. She was convinced they were not really her parents, she was sure that her real parents had abandoned her, that they no longer wanted her, and that these *impersonators* had come in their place. These enemies, in the shape of friends, these wolves in sheep's clothing.

The fear didn't last long, although it recurred from time to time in nightmares; Grace would wake and lie sweating into cold sheets, certain that some cosmic mistake had been made, that she was not where she was supposed to be. Grace couldn't figure out where this sense came from; she remembered her childhood as neither happy nor unhappy, her parents were not demonstrative, but they certainly weren't cruel. She was not neglected. She supposes she was loved. She just didn't seem to come from the same stock, that was all. By the time she was a teenager, she and her parents were strangers to each other.

Though they never mentioned it, Grace felt sure her parents never quite forgave her for that scene in the hospital. Why would a small child think such a thing? they must have wondered. With some justification: Why *would* a small child think such a thing? Why would a child imagine that her parents had abandoned her? What was *wrong* with her?

As an adult—and a doctor—Grace has returned to this question time and again. She's read the literature, she knows that attachment patterns are laid down in the first few years of life, that infants must have their needs met by some consistent presence that soothes and feeds and pays them the right sort of attention. Did she lack for that? Is that why she doesn't feel things the way other people seem to? Is that why she sometimes sees affection where only basic kindness is on offer, why she feels touch as caress or assault, nothing in between?

She walks on, into the wood. Here, it's all too easy to imagine figures between the trees, morphing in the gloaming into animals and back again, into men, into monsters. Somewhere in the heart of the wood a barn owl screeches; Grace's skin pimples, her pulse races, she can feel the pounding of blood in her head and in her chest. She walks on, into the dark, through the wood to the place where the trees fell.

The forks in Grace's road have usually been prompted by abandonment—starting, she supposes, with that first one, that imagined childhood desertion. And then there was Nick and Audrey, and after that Vanessa, too, in a way. Vanessa changed her life more than anyone else; meeting Vanessa changed her course irrevocably. Vanessa was the answer to a question she'd no idea she'd been asking.

After Vanessa died, Grace was required to hand back the equipment and the medicines she'd been using to care for her in her final weeks, but she was creative with her pharmaceutical accounting and so a single bottle of morphine remained at the back of the drawer in Vanessa's dressing table.

The day they came to take Vanessa's body away, Grace stood at the window in the kitchen, watching the ambulance head toward the mainland. She listened to the roaring silence in the house, dreading the darkness, willing the tide to come in so that she could be sure that she'd be safe and undisturbed.

She went for a walk: she walked through this wood right up to the rock and back; she heard the owl that night, too.

The following day, she went to Vanessa's room but hesitated outside the closed door. She realized that she did not want to die without once more swimming in the sea, she wanted to feel the shock and pain of the cold, and then the relief as her body responded, she wanted to taste salt on her lips, push her toes into the sand, submerge herself, listen to the breakers' roar.

One last time. So she turned back, went into the bathroom, and retrieved her swimming costume from the hook on the back of the door and went down to the sea.

The day after that, she stood outside the door again. Again, she did not go in. She walked on the beach that day, and on the next she went to the rock, and on she went, and on, and on, finding things to do, ways to keep herself occupied, every day finding some way to resist the call of the bottle in the drawer.

A few weeks later, she had a call from her old surgery in Carrachan; they were short-staffed, the administrator said, one of their two GPs had quit unexpectedly, they were desperate, was there any way they could persuade her to return, even if just on a part-time basis?

So, a new chapter began. Vanessa might have been gone, but people still needed Grace. The vial of morphine remained in the drawer.

It is dark by the time she leaves the wood. She walks slowly and carefully past the studio, keeping to the path, taking care not to lose her footing. The house is dark, but she allows herself to imagine that she is not alone, that someone is inside waiting for her, that all she needs to do is unlock the front door and turn on the light and the place will come to life; she will walk into a kitchen smelling of onions frying in butter, music on the radio, a bottle of wine open on the table.

She opens the front door. Turns on the lights. Silence rings out like a bell. She locks the door behind her and goes into the kitchen, where the shoebox sits, filled with letters. The one sitting topmost catches her eye. She didn't show him *this* letter, of that she's quite certain. There was something else on top of the pile.

This letter, she knows. This one, she loathes—it is Vanessa at her most pretentious, her most unkind. She doesn't want to look at it and barely needs to: she has read and reread the words on it so many times the most brutal phrases are etched, as if with a scalpel, into the walls of her heart.

Darling Fran,

Thank you so much for sending the Ted Chiang book of stories. I am loving it, its strange melancholy resonates so fiercely with me at the moment.

I am lost, still, unable to work. I move aimlessly, without purpose.

I try to void my mind and let my hands lead me, let the paint lead me, or the clay, but I cannot seem to let go of thought, and soon enough I find myself frozen, at once adrift and trapped.

Grace is ever-present. She is careful, solicitous. I cannot breathe when she is in the room. Her attention is smothering, she cannot know how I suffer. She is incapable of a certain depth of feeling. She does not know what it is to experience the sort of sexual love I had for Julian. I know it is not her fault, I know it is just the way she is made, and yet her lack of understanding infuriates me.

I love her, I pity her, too. And I wish she would not cling to me. I imagine her gone. I imagine the freedom and the fear of life without her.

I know you are upset with me for missing your Bristol show, I know I haven't been the best friend to you this past couple of years, I have been even more self-absorbed than usual.

Please forgive me. I miss you so.

Could I come and see you? If only I could just get away from this place for a while, I think I would start to feel more myself.

Love,
Vanessa

Frances never replied. Vanessa was deeply hurt, and even when—a year or so later—they talked and Frances explained that she'd never received the letter, their friendship did not recover, not fully.

Grace's vision blurs; she blinks away her tears. Even now, all these years later, Vanessa's words cut deep. She is not *incapable of a certain depth of feeling*! If anything, she feels too much, she feels disproportionately.

And sometimes she acts accordingly.

The reason Frances never replied to Vanessa's letter was because Frances never received it. Grace, on one of her periodic checks of Vanessa's state of mind in the weeks and months following Julian's disappearance, opened the letter she had promised to run across to the postbox in the village. Wounded by Vanessa's words, she enacted a cruelty of her own: she held the letter back and allowed Vanessa to imagine that her oldest friend had forsaken her.

All is fair in love and war, and friendship is love, too, isn't it? And a kind of war sometimes as well.

THIRTY

When he walks into the hospital ward and sees them—Helena in the bed and Sebastian at her side, holding one of her hands in his—Becker feels as though he has traveled to an alternative dimension. In this new reality, everything is just as it should be: beautiful, blue-blooded Helena Fitzgerald is married to rich, handsome, and aristocratic Sebastian Lennox; she spends her days and nights in the splendor of Fairburn House, not shacked up with the help in the cramped confines of the Gamekeeper's Lodge. In this new reality, James Becker has not insinuated himself into a world in which he does not belong; he has not taken Helena from the life she deserved and broken Sebastian's heart in the bargain. He is alone and unloved, watching from the outside, nose pressed to the glass.

Just as he should be.

Becker feels cold, his insides contorted; it's as though a chasm has opened beneath him into which he is tumbling. And it's his fault. For not being there when she needed him. For entertaining, even for a fraction of a second, the idea that he might choose Vanessa over Helena. It's his fault for not listening to that voice in his head, that wordless, soundless voice, the one that's been telling him something bad is going to happen.

Just as he is thinking this, Helena turns her head toward him and her eyes meet his. "Beck!" she calls out, voice breaking, taking her hand from Sebastian's and reaching out to Becker. He's at her side in a second, kissing her. "Thank God you're here," she says. "I thought you'd never get here." He pulls her tighter to him as a sob builds in his chest. "Don't cry, you big girl," Helena whispers into his hair. "I'm OK. *We're* OK. We're fine."

When finally they break apart, Becker realizes that they're alone. Sebastian has gone. And everything is fine. Helena is fine, the baby is fine. It was just normal bleeding. All right, a bit more than normal, but nothing is wrong. They can't find anything wrong.

"Which is it?" Becker snarls at the doctor. "Nothing's wrong or you can't *find* anything wrong?"

"Leave him alone, Beck," Helena says. "I'm *fine*." She looks fine: a little pale, though, and a little pained, with spots of color high in her cheeks, her eyes dark and wet and her lips bitten. She clings to Becker's hand so tightly that his fingers begin to ache.

FIVE DAYS HAVE passed since Becker left Eris, and Helena has been back home for three. Becker has taken the week off work and the pair of them have retreated into their very own lockdown: they have barely ventured from the house except for short, leisurely walks; they have lit fires and read books, watched television, made love *carefully*. They have eaten well, eschewed alcohol. Becker has not had a cigarette in seventy-two hours.

And he is climbing the walls.

This morning, a technician at a private laboratory in London broke open the glass case of *Division II* and detached the bone from the gold filament holding it in place. Becker was not there to see it. He chose to stay at Fairburn with his wife and so has had to wait, pacing the narrow hallway between sitting room and kitchen, until the technician rings to say that, yes, a visual inspection confirmed the bone is human and that they will now extract a small sample to send for testing. They will be able to determine roughly how old the bone is as well as the sex and age of the person it came from. They expect to have answers within a week, two at the most.

By midafternoon, when Becker has finished speaking to the technician, Sebastian, and the curator at Tate Modern, Helena—who has spent much of the day on the sofa, trying to read—has had enough.

"For the love of Christ, Beck, please go and watch them setting things on fire, you're driving me *insane*." It's the fifth of November,

Bonfire Night, there's a party at the main house for the neighbors and the estate workers and their kids.

"Are you sure you'll be all right?"

Helena grimaces. "I'll be fine, but I can't vouch for your well-being if you keep bloody fidgeting and pacing and hovering over me. Go!"

He goes.

From the bridge, he can see a crowd gathering on the west side of the main house where the bonfire has been built; he can hear laughter and the shrieks of children tearing around the lawn. He can smoke, he realizes, because if he has one now, the smoke from the fire will cover the smell of cigarette.

He leans against the guardrail, looking over the edge. Even in the half-light he can see that the water is frozen solid. He takes a deep breath, feeling the scrape in his lungs, the twitch of a muscle in his chest; it's the feeling of fate, tempted. He pushes his hands into his pocket to feel for his cigarette papers, but his fingers come upon something else. The letter he took from Grace's kitchen. He'd forgotten all about it.

There is just about enough light left for him to read it.

February 2003

Dear Grace,

Sorry I have not replied to your last few letters, but between legal matters and the leaking roof, I've not had a lot of time to spare. I think the lawyers may finally have reached an agreement with Douglas—it will be a great relief to have that settled, it's been a strain and a distraction. Money will be even tighter, but I go nowhere these days, and I spend nothing, so I should be all right.

I had a message from Isobel—she is still very angry with me. Despite the letter I sent, she clings to the fiction I have offered no words of sympathy. She is in France now—apparently a man matching Julian's description was seen somewhere on the Riviera. Somehow I doubt she'd be following the lead up if the sighting had been in Riyadh or Rhyl. It is a waste of time, of course.

I have found a way to work. Being alone has helped. I am more creative when left to my own devices, I always have been. I can keep my own hours and not worry about anything or anyone else. I have not been painting much but I have started work on a new sculpture series—I call it <u>Division</u>—working with found objects as well as ceramics. It's a new direction and I think it has promise.

I don't know how to respond to your letter, only to say that I <u>don't</u> want you to come back to Eris. You know things you shouldn't, and I'm not sure how to be around you again. I hope you understand what I mean.

We need to be free of each other now.

Love,
Vanessa

A gust of wind catches the paper, almost snatching it from Becker's fingers. His heart rate skitters upward. A cheer goes up behind him; he hears the crackle and pop of sap in the wood as the fire takes hold, the children's excitable voices reaching a fever pitch.

We need to be free of each other—almost exactly the same words Vanessa used in her note to Julian Chapman. She writes about freedom all the time in the diaries; it comes up in interviews, too. It's the thing she seemed to cherish above everything else, above love or friendship or companionship even. How far would she have gone, Becker wonders, to set herself free? What does she mean when she writes that Grace *knows things that she shouldn't?* What does Grace know? The feeling of dread Becker thought he'd left at the hospital returns; it wraps itself around his shoulders like a cloak.

ON THE FAR side of the bonfire, a group of children clamors excitedly around Sebastian, who appears to be doling out treats. The lord of the manor, Becker thinks, dispensing largesse. When Sebastian spots him, he waves and smiles so warmly Becker is skewered on his own lack of charity. "There you are! How *are* you? How's our girl?"

Becker feels his smile falter for a fraction of a second. "She's good," he says. "She's much better. She's thrown me out of the house, actually— apparently I've been hovering."

"Ah well, I might be able to help with that—I've a mission that might take you away for a day or two. Can you get out to Eris again within the next week?"

Becker pulls a face. "I'd really rather not go away right now. Why do you want me to go back?"

Sebastian is about to reply when an elderly man approaches, a child at his side. It's Graham Bryant, the gamekeeper. The *patsy*, as Becker has come to think of him. Bryant greets Sebastian, introduces his grandson, asks after Emmeline. "I expect she'll be out shortly," Sebastian says, beaming at him, ruffling the child's hair. "Don't go anywhere, I know she'll want to say hello."

The smile slides from his face as he turns back to face Becker. "I'm concerned," he says, "about what happens if it turns out there is a DNA match between the bone and Julian Chapman. We're not going to be able to control the story, because the first person to be notified will be Chapman's sister. She might not go to the press—"

"But given what I've read about Isobel," Becker interrupts, "there's a good chance she will."

Sebastian nods. "And then there will be a *frenzy* of press interest in Eris—the island, the house, the place the bone was found . . ."

Becker sees where he is going. "Grace will panic," he says. Who knows what she might do? She might even start to get rid of anything she thinks is private or sensitive.

Sebastian puts a friendly arm around his shoulder. "I know you don't want to leave Hels right now, I understand that. But she's doing better—you said so yourself. And I can keep an eye on her."

BECKER LEAVES SEBASTIAN at the bonfire. In his darkened office, he sits at his desk and composes a brief email to Grace, explaining why he left Eris in a hurry and asking whether it will be all right if he comes to Eris within the next few days to pick up the rest of the papers. Then he thinks better of it: better if he speaks to her on the phone, surely? *Friendlier.* He'll call her instead. He deletes the message, shuts his computer, and leaves the room, noticing as he does a shaft of light spilling into the corridor from the open door to the Great Hall.

EXCEPT FOR THE spotlights on the paintings, the gallery is dark. Becker enters, walking slowly into the gloom, coming to a halt in front of *Black I—Darkness Causes Us Not Discomfort,* Vanessa's first painting of the sea. Its seaweed greens and oily splashes of crimson absorb the glare from the spotlight, making the image on the canvas seem to roil and churn.

"Ghastly, isn't it?"

Becker jumps. Somehow, Emmeline has snuck up on him. In the dim light she looks small and pale, as insubstantial as a ghost.

"If it were up to me," she says, peering up at the painting, "I'd take it outside and put it on the fire with the Guy.

"Just *ghastly,*" Emmeline repeats, turning her back on the canvas and on him. She begins to walk slowly around the gallery in an anticlockwise direction, toward the north wall, where more of the seascapes hang. "You know she only left them to him to spite me," she says.

Becker laughs, and she turns sharply. She's wearing flats, that's what it is! That's why she's so small and silent—she's dispensed with her usual heels. Still feeling that fall, perhaps? He's on the point of pitying her when she fixes him with a look of such intense loathing that he can almost feel himself wither.

"Is . . . is that really what you believe?" he manages to stammer. "That when Vanessa was dying, she was thinking of *you?*"

He follows her past *Monotone,* a moonlit view of the sands, past *Wreck* and *Arrival* and *To Me She Is a Wolf,* all the way around the gallery until finally she comes to a halt in front of *Hope Is Violent.*

"*This* one I like," Emmeline says. "The brushwork, it's different, stilted somehow. You can almost feel her pain. And the sky, that dark line on the horizon, the color of blood. You can tell she was looking at the end." She smiles coldly at him. "That nonsense Douglas talked when he was asked about her legacy, do you remember? All that tripe about intimacy, about their *connection* . . ." She laughs bitterly. "He could be such a fool."

Emmeline walks on. A cheer goes up outside; they're burning the Guy. The light from the flames dances on the windowpanes, making their shadows—his and Emmeline's—leap disturbingly across the walls.

They have almost finished their tour of the gallery when Emmeline pauses again, in front of *Black V—The Wood for the Trees*. She sucks her teeth, tutting disapprovingly.

"Sometimes you have to take a step back," Becker says, "to tell what you're really looking at. If you stand right here, you see, you can tell that—"

"Do you honestly think I need lessons in art appreciation, Mr. Becker?" Emmeline cuts in. "From *you*?" Her lip curls. "I doubt you have much to teach me about anything, most of all about recognizing what's going on right in front of me."

This time, when she walks on, Becker does not follow but lets her go on ahead. He stands there in the middle of the hall, allowing himself a moment to imagine that the little stooped figure in front of him is just some benign old lady taking a stroll around an art gallery, that she's taken a wrong turn in search of the still lifes.

It takes an age for Emmeline to reach the end of the hall. When she does, she turns around. "I need you to do something for me," she calls out.

Now lit from one side, her face is a death mask. Suffused with dread but determined not to show weakness, Becker walks briskly to join her and asks as politely as he can, "What's that, Lady Emmeline?"

"I need you to settle this thing with that caretaker person on Eris Island and, that done, I want you to hand in your resignation, take your wife, and leave."

Becker shakes his head. "I'm not going to do that, you know I'm not going to do that."

She sighs wearily, raising her eyes to the ceiling while rubbing a gnarled forefinger across her bloodless lips. "Mr. Becker, this is in your interest as well as mine. Without you, the Chapman expert, Sebastian will lose interest in all *this*"—she waves her hand vaguely in the air— "and move on to something else. He just needs a push. He has such trouble moving on, don't you agree?"

"No, I don't actually," Becker replies stiffly.

"Well." Emmeline's smile fails to reach her eyes. "We were just talking about how sometimes you need to take a step back to realize what it is you're looking at, were we not? I'm sure that if *you* did that, if you took a step back, you would see—"

"Look." Becker cuts her off, and her mouth drops open—she's so astonished at his effrontery he almost wants to laugh. "I understand," he says instead, "why Vanessa Chapman is not your favorite artist, but I'm not about to resign just because you ask me to—"

"Then *don't*," she says sharply. "Resign because it's in *your* best interest. Resign because every time you leave this estate, my son goes running over to see your wife. Doesn't it bother you? Your car is barely out of the gates and he's over there, checking on her. Tending to her every need." Emmeline's laugh is low and gravelly. "Does that not give you pause, Mr. Becker? After all, you know what kind of woman she is. You know just how easily she can be—"

"I *do* know what kind of woman Helena is," Becker interrupts again, "and the thing I think you fail to understand is that *so does Sebastian*. Your son might still love her, but he also accepts her choice, because he respects her. And he respects me, too, so while he might enjoy spending time with Hels—someone he's known since he was a teenager, someone he was friends with long before they went out—I don't think that's something I need to worry about. Because, as you said, I know her."

Emmeline laughs again, an unforgiving sound. "You're a fool," she says. "You're just like Douglas was, you're blind."

Becker's had enough. He starts walking toward the door, glancing up at *Black II* as he goes, the light catching the smile at its center, that flash of sharp white teeth sending a prickle all the way up his spine.

"Eight months now, isn't she?" Emmeline calls after him. "So that would make it . . . what? Late February? Early March? The end of that first lockdown, around the time you went to Hamburg to look at those Hockneys. Everyone was so keyed up, weren't they, after being cooped up for so long, everyone just looking for some sort of *release* . . ."

Becker wheels around. He thinks for a moment that he will strike her, for a second he can see it in his mind's eye, this small, frail, elderly woman cowering beneath his fist. He takes a deep breath. "I ought to feel sorry for you," he says. "I really should. You're old and bitter, and I imagine you're very lonely, you might even be grieving. I ought to feel sorry for you, but I don't, because I can't help thinking that you made your bed. And you can carry on, if you like, dripping poison, casting your petty insinuations, but the fact is this: I'll outlast you. When you're gone, I'll still be here, and so will Helena, and so will our child."

As he walks away, he glances once more at *Hope Is Violent* and he thinks of his mother, so tiny in her bed at the hospice, looking at the little landscape on the wall, and he can't help himself, he turns back to look at Emmeline. She hasn't moved, she's standing there, hunched and miserable, her hands at her sides, clenched tightly into fists. "My mother left behind a son who loved her," he says quietly. "What do you imagine your legacy will be?" She says nothing, but as she turns away from him he thinks, or perhaps imagines, that he can see her hands start to shake.

THIRTY-ONE

Someone is choking, and she can't save them. It's a boy, usually, a young man or a teenager, they're choking, and Grace is not strong enough or quick enough, she cannot get to them in time, and when she does, her efforts fail. It's not a dream, it's a thought she keeps having, a scenario she imagines, despite herself.

This started a few days ago, after Becker's visit, this thought, occurring and reoccurring. It first came when she woke: definitely not a dream, though, not so easily dismissed. It occurred on waking and now it comes to her more and more frequently: when she is walking or making coffee, reading or listening to the radio. Without wanting to, she finds herself picturing this man, his desperation.

Grace has been here before: she knows what this is. It's an intrusive thought, no more than that. Not a memory, not a premonition, just something unpleasant her subconscious keeps offering up to her conscious mind like a cat coughing up a hairball. She needs to dismiss it, but *casually*, she needs to ignore it without seeming to try. She needs to take better care of herself. Go for walks, eat well, don't overdo the caffeine, sleep.

She needs to break out of the bad habits she's allowed herself to slip into, her tidal-ness, her lunacy. She drives up to Carrachan to see her doctor, gets a prescription for sleeping pills, establishes a strict bedtime regimen. She sets her alarm for six, forces herself to get up and go out for a walk, she eats porridge for breakfast, she drinks her one and only coffee of the day. She starts to feel a little better.

But the doctor would only give her enough pills for ten days. Now they have run out, and she finds herself lying awake for hours. Last night, she was awake until three and so when her alarm goes off at six she reaches out and knocks it to the floor.

When she wakes again, she sees him. Not the boy, this time, but a man. And not an intrusive thought but an actual intruder: a man at the window, hands cupped around his face as he looks in on her. Grace cries out; she jerks upright, the bedclothes falling away from her to reveal her naked torso. The man outside jumps, rearing backward like a shying horse; she can hear him calling out, *sorry, sorry.*

She grabs a robe, pulls it around her, and rushes out into the hall. She picks up the shotgun, unlocks the door, and barrels out, squinting into bright sunshine.

The man is backing away with his hands in the air: he's a hiker, wearing walking trousers, carrying a backpack. His companions—two other men, probably in their twenties—are standing a little way behind him.

"What do you think you're doing?" Grace barks.

"I'm *sorry,*" he says again, lowering his hands to his side. "I was just . . . I thought the place was empty, I wanted to see—"

"Empty? There's a car outside. This is private land."

The man raises his eyebrows, spreads his arms wide. "Well, there's a footpath just there"—he points over his shoulder—"and there's right to roam here, so—"

"Not up to my bedroom window there isn't. What is wrong with you?" The man turns away, apologizing again, but his friends are smirking. "Keep away from here!" Grace snaps, turning back toward the house, gathering her robe around her. She can hear them laughing as they head off up the hill toward the rock.

She feels a fool. There was no need to shout, no need to go running out here at all. She imagines them mocking her, imagines what they will say about her nakedness, the sort of jokes they will make about her repulsive body, her loose skin and sagging breasts, her desperate solitude.

She returns the gun to its position in the hallway and locks the front door. It is almost the middle of the day; she's overslept by hours and now she knows for certain she will not sleep tonight, that this will set her back, right back to square one. And sure enough, almost as she thinks this, there he is: the boy, one hand clutching frantically at the base of his throat.

She forces herself to do practical things: sweep the kitchen floor, clean the shower cubicle, take the food waste to the compost heap. There are bills to pay, but the internet is down—it failed four days ago and since she has no phone signal, she had to go across into the village to call someone about it. Which she duly did, and yet despite the call center employee's reassurances, it is still down. She has no way of knowing why or for how long—the only way she can make any progress at all is to drive across to the village again, and phone again, and be put on hold again. She's exhausted just thinking about it, but what choice does she have? Becker might be trying to contact her. He said he would email, after all, to explain his disappearing act.

She showers and dresses, locks up the house, and drives down the track, trundling out across the causeway under a cerulean sky. Two seal pups, fat and pale and vulnerable, sun themselves on the sands beneath the house. They raise their little heads, doglike, to watch her pass. *Look, Vee*, she wants to say. *Look.*

On days like today, Vanessa's absence is a knife in her side.

The village seems unusually quiet. It isn't until she parks her car outside the shop and sees that it is closed that she realizes it's a Sunday. No coffee, then, no fresh bread. Her disappointment is so acute she thinks she might burst into tears.

Do the internet people even work on a Sunday? Turns out they do. Grace spends half an hour on hold but, in the end, someone answers. Yes, the person says, there is a fault. *I know that*, Grace replies. *I know there's a fault. I know that because the internet is not working today and has not been working for four days.* The person at the internet company is very sorry about that. They will investigate the fault and ring her back in a couple of hours. What time would be convenient?

If she waits for her phone call, she will miss the tide, so no time is convenient. But she cannot explain that to a person who works in a call center in Gateshead or possibly even Bangalore, so she just laughs helplessly and says, *As soon as you can. Call me as soon as you can.*

As she is driving back down the hill to the harbor, she glimpses, out of the corner of her eye, a flash of yellow at the end of the car park; she pulls over and parks next to the harbor wall.

On the bench directly in front of her cottage sits Marguerite. She is wearing her high-vis jacket and smoking a cigarette. Grace walks over to say hello and raises a hand in greeting.

"I see you," Marguerite says quickly, "*à l'heure bleue*, before the sunrise."

Grace shakes her head. "I don't think so, Marguerite. I slept very late today."

Marguerite pouts, aggrieved by the contradiction. Grace smiles at her. "How are you feeling? How's your arm?" Marguerite knits her tiny features into a frown. "Your arm, Marguerite. You hurt it?"

"Ah, *ça va*," she says, dismissing Grace's concern with a wave of her cigarette. Grace points at it and shakes her head. Marguerite scowls in reply. Slowly and deliberately, she brings the cigarette to her lips and takes a long drag. Her face breaks into a wicked grin and she starts to laugh. Then, something dawns on her, and her face changes. "Is your friend coming back?"

Grace's smile grows stiff. "Maybe," she says, turning to go. She doesn't have the energy for this today. "Look after yourself, Marguerite," she calls out over her shoulder. "Don't smoke too many of those, OK?"

She wonders as she walks away why she's even bothering, because Marguerite is obviously not going to listen to her, and why should she? She cannot have that much time left—why shouldn't she enjoy her remaining pleasures?

BY THE TIME Grace gets home, the internet has miraculously been restored. Grace's delight is quickly dampened by the discovery that she has no new WhatsApp messages and no emails, except for junk and a Google Alert she set up years ago to search for Vanessa's name.

The alert links to an interview with Sebastian Lennox that appeared in one of the weekend papers. *An Artistic Legacy*, the headline proclaims. Beneath it is a photograph of Lennox, who is fine-boned and elegant-looking—he favors his mother. His father looked like a Glasgow gangster. He is pictured standing on the lawn of his home next to a Barbara Hepworth bronze; the article is illustrated with other works of art, too: a Francis Cadell of Iona, a rather beautiful Samuel Peploe still life, and Vanessa's *Hope Is Violent*.

The piece itself is rather dull, a by-the-numbers Saturday feature crammed with clichés: Sebastian Lennox's "ancestral home" has been "lovingly restored"; his father, Douglas, was a "fearsome patriarch" whose life was cut short in a "tragic shooting accident," his mother was a "society beauty" whose health is "fragile." Then there is the inevitable run-through of the dispute between Vanessa and Douglas and the surprising revelations of Vanessa's will.

"Of course we were shocked," Lennox says of the Chapman bequest. "Although my father and Vanessa had once been close, their falling-out was spectacular and pretty bitter."

Lennox believes, however, that despite the bad blood between Chapman and Douglas Lennox, she knew Fairburn would be a fitting home for her work. "I like to think that Vanessa would have known that we would cherish her pieces and honour her legacy," he says. There may, of course, be a more prosaic reason for the bequest: Chapman died childless, with no close family—she had no one else to whom she could bequeath her work.

Grace blinks. She reads the last bit again, and then she scrolls down, down, down to the mention of James Becker, the curator Lennox brought to Fairburn specifically because of his knowledge of Vanessa Chapman's work. *"To find myself the guardian of this collection is a dream come true,"* Becker says.

Despite herself, Grace finds herself smiling at the description of Becker as boyish, earnest, a *"state-school boy who excelled at Oxford."* She reads on, one hand pressed against her chest, filled with a facsimile of maternal pride.

Becker gives a quote about the exhibition they are hoping to mount the following year, bringing together for the first time over sixty of Chapman's paintings, drawings, sculptures, and ceramics, the majority of which have never been exhibited before.

"It's my view that this collection could go some way to reassessing Chapman's importance and establishing her as a major figure in British abstract expressionism," Becker says. "Until now, her output has been largely overlooked, in part because she's a woman, and in part because, in the early part of her career, she was out of step with the more fashionable, conceptual artists of the YBA movement."

Another expert, a man Grace has never heard of, says that if Vanessa's work has been ignored it is Vanessa's own fault: she is the one who chose to withdraw from the art scene, to withhold her work from the world. This observation is—predictably enough—a cue for the usual muckraking, the allegations about the "troubled beauty," her "many lovers," her "tempestuous marriage," and above all the mystery of Julian's disappearance from Eris Island.

"I've been out to Eris," Becker is quoted as saying. Grace's heart lifts, her eye scanning eagerly on. *"I've seen Vanessa's home and her studio, the places she lived and worked, the island she loved, the landscape that inspired her. I've had the pleasure of reading some of her notebooks and letters, and I can't wait to share them with the world, to introduce her work to a whole new audience."*

Grace wants to turn a page. She wants to scroll further down, to the part where Becker mentions how the two of them have sat together at the kitchen table, reading Vanessa's words and talking about Vanessa's life; she wants to read the part where Becker talks about Grace's importance to Vanessa, her devotion to her. But there is no page to turn and nowhere further to scroll. There is no mention of Grace anywhere at all.

The blade in her side slips deeper still.

Marguerite has her cigarettes, what pleasures are left to Grace? She can swim in the cold sea and walk on the island, but she is lonely on the beach now, and fearful in the wood. She thinks of the men from this morning, how they laughed at her; now she pictures their faces and one of them begins to change, laughter to panic, he becomes the choking boy. She closes her eyes. Have they left, those men? Or are they still here, on the island? The tide is in, and she has not seen them leave. Are they waiting for darkness? And what will they do to her then?

Her hands tremble a little as she walks back through the hallway to the front door. She places her hand on the deadbolt, but before she draws it back, she hesitates. If she opens the door now, if she goes out there, she will see the hillside, the pathway leading up toward the studio and the wood and it won't help. She won't *know* if the men are still on the island or not. She will have to stand in the cold and wait, she will have to wait until they walk down the hill and back over the causeway, and if they don't? If they don't, will she wait there all night?

Better by far to leave the door locked and turn her back, to tell herself that they are gone and let that be an end to it. Don't give in to madness. Be rational, keep busy: cook, eat, read a book, go to bed.

But she finds she cannot move. She cannot bring herself to go through the motions, knowing that tomorrow she will have to do it all again, and again the day after that—that this is how it will always be.

This is hardly a *revelation*, and yet as she stands at the door with her hand on the bolt, it feels like one. There was her work, and there was Vanessa, and then there was the pandemic, which meant more work—punishing, brutal work—but though it was grueling, at times unbearable, Grace came to see it almost as a blessing. She was not just needed, she was *essential*. What purpose is left to her now? Her daydream is not going to come true: Becker is not going to visit with his family, he is not going to make her part of the Fairburn project, she will be forgotten. She has already been forgotten.

Eventually, after what seems like hours, she prizes her cold fingers from the deadbolt and turns away from the front door. From the hidden storage space behind the screen in the living room, she retrieves three paintings one by one: the small portrait first, and then *Totem*, and finally the largest of the three, the one that has been in there since before Vanessa died, her final black painting.

She takes all three canvases to Vanessa's room and arranges them along the wall facing the bed so that they are looking at her. Only herself for company.

She returns to the kitchen, riffling through the box of papers she has kept for herself. For quite a vain woman, Vanessa was oddly camera shy; there are very few pictures of her, and none at all of her with Grace. At the bottom of the box Grace finds a couple of photos of Vanessa with Frances in Cornwall, on the beach at Porthmeor, along with the picture of herself and poor Nick Riley, his beautiful face scratched out. She takes them back to the bedroom and arranges them on the chair next to the bed, folding them over so that Frances and Nick are no longer visible, there is only Vanessa and Grace.

Better.

She opens the window. It is very cold, but there is no wind. The sea is placid, night falling quickly, and the air is blue and still, the gulls quietening as they drift like phantoms over the shore.

Shivering a little, she pads over to Vanessa's dressing table and pulls open the drawer. She reaches in to retrieve a syringe and a 300ml bottle of morphine sulphate, 10g/5ml, which she places on the bedside table. Then, almost as an afterthought, she fetches a glass tumbler and a bottle of Lagavulin from the kitchen and brings them back to Vanessa's room.

She locks the door.

She longs for a storm. The night Vanessa died, the waves thundered against the rocks, rain and spray battered the windows, but they were safe from it all, from the gales and the hungry sea, they were together, sheltered and dry, unreachable. Grace would like to slip away on a night like that, too.

She pours herself an inch of whisky and raises the glass to her own image. She wraps herself in a blanket, leans back against the headboard, and allows herself to give in: to the warmth of whisky, to the image of the young man choking, to the tears that have been building like a storm front behind her eyes.

THIRTY-TWO

Staying sane is a trick.

It's a technique: sanity is something you hold on to—loosen your grip for too long, allow your mind to go to the places it fears or the places it craves, and you risk letting it slip away. There are things that, for the sake of your sanity, you do not allow yourself to recall.

Grace remembers that afternoon in the studio, the terror and the thrill of it. The excitement she felt when she slipped the clay cutter around that man's neck and pulled. The sounds he made, so stirring: his cry of surprise, the roar of anger that followed, the choking sound he made as she drew her hands together, cinching the wire tight. She remembers the wave of exhilaration washing over her as his knees buckled, the ecstasy of control she felt as she pulled, tighter and tighter, the wire cutting into his throat, blood dripping onto the collar of his coveralls. She remembers the desire—oh, it was almost overwhelming—to draw the noose tighter still when Vanessa left her alone, when she ran to the house to call the police. Grace longed to punish him as he deserved to be punished. She resisted: not out of mercy but out of fear, the fear of what Vanessa might think of her, the fear that Vanessa might truly see her for who she was.

GRACE REMEMBERS THE days and weeks and months after Julian went missing, how difficult Vanessa became: irrational, secretive, strange. Silent. She lied to the police, she would not explain to Douglas or the newspapers why she'd withdrawn from the show, she didn't work, didn't walk, didn't swim in the sea. She sat in the kitchen, hunched over an ashtray, smoking, listening to the phone ring and ring until

eventually one day she ripped it out of the wall and hurled it out the
window.

Grace brought food. She cooked meals that went uneaten, she
cleaned and tidied and sorted through the mail. She lied, as required,
to the police, to anyone who asked: she stuck to Vanessa's version of
events.

In the first week of the new year, six months after Julian's visit,
Grace drove to Carrachan to buy a new phone. She was plugging it in
in the kitchen when Vanessa turned from the window and looked at
her, looked at her as she hadn't done for months. "Why are you *always*
here?" she asked. "Every time I turn around, there you are, with your
soup and platitudes. I don't want you here." Grace felt a shriveling
inside her, a chill, bone-deep. "I never wanted you here."

"That's not true," Grace said. She stood up straight, her voice and
her gaze level. "Vanessa, you know that's not true."

Vanessa put out her cigarette and immediately lit another. "No,
you're right," she said, sighing, picking at the dry skin on the palms of
her hands. "It's not true. I did want you here." She blinked slowly. Her
eyes, when they met Grace's, were as cold as the January sea. "And now
I don't."

GRACE REMEMBERS SITTING on the faded orange chair next to
Vanessa's bed. It was noon, but the room was dim, the curtains drawn
against the light. Vanessa was cursing the sound of the sea. "I can't
stand it, I can't stand it," she kept saying. "It's driving me mad, I can't
shut it out." Grace had barely slept in two days; she was frazzled, at the
end of her rope. "I can't stop the tide, Vanessa. Use the earplugs I gave
you, here, come on—"

"Leave me alone!" Vanessa hissed, slapping her hand away. She was
mean and feral, half mad with pain, poison spilling from her lips. "Let
me go, you ugly old bitch, why won't you let me go? *Boule de suif,
boule de suif,* he was right! He was right about you. You're dragging me
down, keeping me here against my will, imprisoning me. You won't let
me go! Why won't you let me go?"

———————

STAYING SANE IS a trick.

If Grace allows herself to think about it, she wonders whether in the end she gave Vanessa the extra dose of morphine to ease her pain or just to shut her up.

THIRTY-THREE

When she wakes, freezing, the window is still open and the bottle of whisky is half empty on the nightstand, but the seal on the vial of morphine is unbroken.

There is a voicemail on her phone from Mr. Becker. "I need to talk to you. I'd rather do it in person than on the phone. Would it be OK if I came up this week?"

Grace goes online, she looks at the weather forecast, she checks the tide timetable.

Next weekend is best, she writes back to him. *Storm due to hit the following week. Saturday—any time after 10:30 a.m. Low tide is 1:30.*

She gets up and closes the window and crawls back into Vanessa's bed. She falls asleep quickly, picturing Becker and Nick Riley and Vanessa and her—all of them here, inside this house, while outside the sky empties itself into the sea. A fire in the wood burner and food on the table and all of them together, safe from the storm.

Vanessa Chapman's diary

Women aren't supposed to look, are they? They're supposed to be looked at.

And if they see something violent or ugly or frightening, they're supposed to cover their eyes and swoon, they're supposed to flinch. They're supposed to look away.

They're not supposed to move closer, to narrow their eyes and peer, to examine and observe and appraise.

They're not supposed to make of horror something of their own.

THIRTY-FOUR

The sky ahead is slate-gray, the pines along the roadside bristling in the wind. A storm is coming—it's due to hit the west coast on Sunday night, according to Grace, which gives Becker forty-eight hours, though he's hoping to be in and out by the end of the day or by tomorrow morning at the latest.

On the radio, they're talking about *Don't Look Now*. Du Maurier again! The film adaptation is coming up for its fiftieth anniversary, there's talk of a rerelease. The man on the radio is talking about mesmeric horror, about the tricks played by a tortured mind, about recurring patterns and motifs that remind the viewer that some griefs are inescapable, some destinies inevitable.

Becker turns the radio off.

Just before he gets to the coast road, he stops for petrol. He fills up the car and goes into the little shop to pay the cashier, holding his phone against the card reader to feel its reassuring haptic buzz. On his way back to the car, he feels the buzz a second time: checking his phone, he sees he has a message, from Helena.

Hey, can you come over? We need to talk x

He stops in the middle of the forecourt, staring at the screen. *Come over?*

The driver of the Volvo station wagon attempting to leave the garage toots his horn and Becker jumps out of the way. He looks at his phone screen again.

This message has been deleted.

Fumbling for the key in his pocket, Becker unlocks the car and climbs into the driver's seat. *Every time you leave this estate, my son goes running over to see your wife.* His hands are trembling a little as he presses the ignition button and puts the car into drive. *Don't worry about Hels, I can keep an eye on her.* He pulls away from the petrol pump. *You could go and talk to Grace Haswell, go on, I know you've been itching to get out there.*

It was Helena who suggested he go to Eris in the first place. They were in his office, the three of them, that first day when they found out about the bone—it was Helena who told him to go. His heart is thumping fit to burst, he feels a little lightheaded. He checks the rearview—there's no one behind him. He picks up his phone again. He could call her. And say what? He could turn left into the road ahead, drive all the way back to Fairburn, arrive home unannounced. He pictures himself, opening the front door of the lodge, quietly making his way up the stairs.

He turns the phone off and turns right, toward Eris.

GRACE IS WAITING for him at the end of the track, in front of the chain, arms folded across her chest.

"Shall I bring the car up?" he asks as he climbs out, and she shakes her head.

"No, I don't think so." She looks at him, unsmiling. "You had something you wanted to talk to me about?"

He exhales loudly. *Jesus Christ.* "Yes, Grace, I have things I need to speak to you about. I've been running back and forth up here to try to finalize Vanessa's estate and we really need to get this done now, we—"

"Oh, I see." She cuts him off. "And there I was thinking that maybe you'd come to apologize. Or perhaps to return the letter you stole?"

Wrong-footed, he starts to mumble an apology, but she is already walking away from him, not back up toward the house but on to the beach.

Becker follows her over the sands, his hands thrust deep into his coat pockets and his eyes narrowed against glare and grit. A couple of paces behind her, he has to strain to catch the words snatched from her mouth by the wind.

"It was a betrayal of trust," she shouts. "You promised me that we would work together and then you took that letter, you left without a word, you—"

"You're right," he says, annoyed with himself for ceding the moral high ground. "I shouldn't have done that. I saw the word *Division*, and I couldn't resist . . . I was in such a state, I wasn't thinking—"

"Of me? Of my wishes? Of how I would feel about you taking a letter I'd told you was private? You certainly were not. I saw that article in the newspaper. Anyone reading that wouldn't know I existed at all. I'm just an obstacle to you, aren't I? An *inconvenience*."

"That's not true," Becker says, breaking into a jog to keep up with her, feeling ridiculous and wretched at the same time. "Please don't think that. I've never wanted to make you feel that way, I've never wanted to make the loss of Vanessa's work harder for you."

"It's not a *loss*," Grace retorts, wheeling around to face him. Her face is blotchy, her cheeks wet with tears. "I didn't *lose* anything, she gave it all away. As you said in the newspaper, she had no one else to leave it to, did she? She had no one in her life."

Becker shakes his head vehemently. "I did not say that, the journalist did, and he was wrong. Had he put it to me like that, I would have set the record straight." Even as he's saying this, though, he's remembering what Sebastian said: How was it that Grace was left with so little when she and Vanessa had been so close? *Why was that, do you think?*

THIS FAR OUT, Becker can see that the sea is wild, the wind-whipped waves crested with poisonous-looking yellow foam. "You left Eris, didn't you?" he says to her. "At the time of that letter, you were living somewhere else, somewhere in England—"

"Carlisle."

"That's it, and Vanessa wrote to you, she said—" He is interrupted by a cacophony of screeches—gulls overhead banking into the wind, diving and whirling like fighter planes in a dogfight.

Grace folds her arms and starts to walk, more slowly now, toward the sea. "Vanessa didn't want me around any longer," she says. "After

Julian . . . she changed." Becker lets her lead the way; he walks at her shoulder, careful not to crowd her but desperate to hear every word. "She became difficult. Secretive, watchful . . . she was like someone with post-traumatic stress." She glances quickly at him. "Do you know what that's like? She was hypervigilant, fearful, she lost her temper easily . . . When I suggested she get help—*proper* help, you know, from a psychologist—she became enraged."

Becker is struck by the similarity with Emmeline's situation—also suspected of having PTSD, also infuriated by the idea that she needs professional help. Discomforted by the thought of similarities between Vanessa and Emmeline, he bats the thought away. "Did anyone help her?" he asks. "Did anyone help *you* with her? In the later notebooks, she doesn't talk about people much, there's barely a mention of Frances or—"

"She cut everyone off," Grace says. "She wouldn't see a soul. I walked about on eggshells for months. Then, just after Christmas, about six months after it all happened, she asked me to leave. She was"—Grace exhales forcefully through puffed-out cheeks—"rather cruel about it."

She turns toward him, face stretched into a strained smile. "I was terribly upset, but I did as I was asked. I got myself a locum job in England and off I went. I thought . . . I assumed that she needed to grieve, to be alone, to deal with . . . whatever guilt she was feeling." Their eyes lock, and Becker startles at the implication. "I wrote to her often, but for months she didn't reply. Eventually I got that letter, the one you took."

"When you say she had to deal with her guilt," Becker says, "do you mean . . . ? What *do* you mean?"

Grace lifts her hand to shade her eyes; she squints at the sea. "We should go back," she says, ignoring his question. "The tide is turning. We don't want to get caught out." To Becker, the water still looks to be a safe distance away, and he says so. "You'd be surprised," Grace says, "by how quickly it comes in, how quickly you can lose your footing, even in shallow water."

————————

THEY TURN THEIR back to the water. Scraps of sea-foam skitter like birds across the sand in front of them, and the sky ahead threatens rain, but with the wind at their backs, it's easier to talk.

"You said Vanessa felt guilty?"

Grace nods, glancing behind her, toward the sea. "About Julian," she says.

"About Julian?"

She nods again, impatient. "*Yes*, about Julian. I suppose she thought she could have done more for him."

"More? How do you mean?"

"Given him more time, or more money, I suppose, which is what he always wanted." She shakes her head. "We never really spoke about it. After I left, we didn't really talk about him again."

"But you came back?" She gives him a look. "I mean, *obviously* you came back."

"She found a lump," Grace says. "She was frightened, so she asked me to come back. She begged me to come."

They walk toward the island quickly and in silence, Becker's eyes trained on the damp gray sand beneath his feet.

AT THE BOTTOM of the steps, Grace stumbles, falling heavily onto her left knee. Becker tries to help her up, but she waves him away furiously, struggling back to her feet, pink-faced and breathless.

"What else is it you've done?" she snarls at him.

"I'm sorry?"

"You've been skulking like a kicked dog since you arrived. You owned up about the letter, we've talked about that interview. What else do you have to tell me?"

For someone with so few social skills, Becker thinks, Grace can be remarkably astute. All the time they've been talking, he's had in the back of his mind Helena's disappearing phone message and all the scenarios, all of them painful, it conjures up. But he's certainly not about to confide in Grace about that.

Instead, he tells her about the sculpture. "They opened the case to *Division II*," he says flatly. Before she has time to react, he gets it all out. "They haven't done any tests yet, but there's no question the bone is human."

Grace turns away from him. Dusting sand from her knees and thighs, she starts to climb, her knuckles whitening as she grips the rusted handrail. "Did I ever tell you about the wolves?" she asks.

"The wolves?"

"They used to bury the dead out here. For hundreds of years, the people who lived on this coast brought their dead to the islands to bury them, to keep the bodies from being dug up. To keep them safe from wolves."

Vanessa Chapman's diary

Who am I writing all this for? Not for myself, presumably, not to remember, because if I were writing to remember, wouldn't I write <u>everything</u> down, leave nothing out?

I've been thinking a lot about Douglas. Since I got ill again I find myself wanting to write to him, to explain everything, but it feels too late. Why didn't I tell the truth right away? I couldn't remember, and so I went to my notebooks for the answer and found nothing—they were no help at all. If I knew the answer back then, if I ever knew the answer, I kept it to myself.

(but aren't these books myself?)

My memory isn't all that good. I don't think that's new. I don't think it's ever been good, or at least, not in the way I need it to be now. I don't remember the exact way things happened, the sequence of events, who said what to who and when.

I remember images, snapshots. I see my bloody hands, white porcelain all over the studio floor. The ruined pictures. I see the faces of the policemen, how they looked at me, their mouths turned down, doubtful, dubious. Like they knew I was lying to them.

This is what I think now: it was too late to tell the truth, even before I began to lie.

It was already too late: the blood had been washed away, the evidence destroyed. How then could I have said to them (to the police, to anyone?), look what he did! He tried to kill me! (Because I have to believe that's what Julian tried to do, that he must have known that when I saw the wreckage I would have wanted to lie down in its midst and die.)

By the time I saw the whole picture, it was already too late. I was at war: with Douglas, with myself, with Grace, too, though she didn't seem to know it.

I can't remember when I started to put the pieces together, when it was that I stood back and allowed the whole image to come into focus, when the trees became the wood and the sheepskin fell away to show me the wolf. Maybe I did glimpse it right away, maybe I was too frightened to acknowledge it. Too frightened or too loving. I don't think I knew then how murderous love can be.

I only know it was already too late.

And now it's too late to tell.

How can I write to Douglas now? I can barely make sense of it all for myself.

I took horror and I made something of it: I painted and I created and now I have something to give. I can be kind, I can be generous. I can make amends to Douglas. I can't give him the work I promised him, but I can give him everything I've made since. And to Grace, I can show mercy.

THIRTY-FIVE

They hear the sound as soon as Grace opens the front door. Something slamming or falling, and then a cry of pain.

Someone is in the house.

"The door was locked!" Grace cries out; she turns back, pressing her body against Becker's as she tries to escape. Repulsed by the feeling of her soft belly and breasts pushing into him, he shrinks back, flattening himself against the wall.

Grace is panicking, she pushes past him, she runs back out of the house onto the lawn, she seems terrified. Becker picks up the rifle and, wielding it like a bat, creeps into the kitchen. Empty. He stands very still, listening. Laughter bubbles up inside him—he is ridiculous. He lowers the gun and rests it against a chair, pulls off his jacket, and slings it onto the table and—*there*! Wait. Someone *is* in the house. He can hear a muffled sound now, quite definitely, too gentle for footprints, a sort of rustling, as though something is being dragged along the floor.

"Hello?" Becker cries out, picking up the gun once more. "Is someone here?"

He walks back through the hall into the living room, ducking quickly into the back bedroom. It's empty. He comes out again, pauses in the hallway, holding his breath, listening once more. The silence expands, pressing into him. He hears something behind him and jumps: it's just Grace, closing the front door behind her. He wants to giggle again; he's like a child watching a horror movie, waiting for the next jump scare, caught somewhere in that strange limbo between terror and delight.

Grace peers around the door into the living room, her eyes wide and her face white. Becker shrugs at her and shakes his head and then, suddenly, there is a terrible shriek from Vanessa's room, and the two of them start. Grace cries out, and Becker runs toward the sound, heart pounding, the rifle raised.

In Vanessa's room a herring gull is sidling back and forth against the wall beneath the window. It's a juvenile, its feathers still dappled, its cry forlorn.

"A bird, Grace," Becker calls out, setting the gun down on the floor. "It's just a trapped bird."

Grace edges into the room. Seeing the bird, her shoulders drop in relief, her equanimity quickly restored. At once, she is practical and reasonable, fetching an old sheet from the linen closet, which she unfolds and casts like a net, flinging it over the gull. Becker steps in, trying gingerly to pick up the creature, but the force of its frantically beating wings takes him by surprise and he drops it.

Grace is not so tentative. She scoops up the bundle, crushing it to her chest. Furiously the bird fights her, its screeches bloodcurdling, but Grace is undeterred; she steps quickly to the window and, leaning out as far as she can, flings her arms wide, gripping tightly to the edge of the sheet as she releases the struggling, shrieking bundle into the air.

For a few seconds the gull tumbles, screaming, scrabbling desperately until instinct takes over and it banks hard, soaring upward into the wind, over the house, out of sight.

Becker helps draw the sheet back through the window. His eyes meet Grace's, and they start to laugh with relief, enjoying at last the break in tension between them.

Grace reaches out, catches Becker's hand, and squeezes it; he's taken aback, has to make a conscious effort to allow her to hold on to it, but he does so, until he turns toward the bedroom door and notices a canvas leaning against the wall.

He pulls his hand away, inhaling sharply—with surprise and with pleasure, the delight of seeing something beautiful for the first time, something familiar in style and yet, to his eyes, completely fresh. He is so struck by the picture—a portrait of a woman holding a wooden carving of a bird—that it takes a few moments before he processes what it is that he is looking at.

Grace, with bird.

"*Totem*," he says at last.

"That's right," Grace replies.

She rolls the sheet into a bundle and walks from the room. He watches her go, taking in as he does so a smaller portrait, also of Grace, leaning against the wall next to the larger one, and beyond that, half hidden behind the bedroom door, a third canvas, something larger and darker. He walks slowly toward it, his heart pounding painfully, and pushes the door aside.

It is a black painting, one he's never seen before. Black paint overlaid with grays and damsons, with deep bloody reds and flashes of gold, is applied in wide gestural strokes with a palette knife. A pool of light holds the center of the painting, as though a searchlight has been turned directly onto the figures at the heart of the scene, catching them in the act. The first lies prostrate, head thrown back; the second person kneels, touching the prone figure around the neck or the face. Behind them stands a third person, a watcher, and on the voyeur's face is a hint of white at the mouth, a flash of teeth, the suggestion of a grimace or a smile.

Becker hears Grace's footsteps in the corridor and takes a step back from the door. As she pushes it open, she glances to her left, looking at the canvas and then back at him. Her lips are a firm line. Becker stands back, his arms crossed, viewing the three pictures as in a gallery. "So," he says, indicating the first painting, "that's *Totem*. And the smaller portrait?"

"*Grace*," she replies. "It's just called *Grace*. It was the first one she did of me, it's dated on the back, 1998."

"Are there more like this?" Becker asks.

"No," Grace says, standing beside him to look at the pictures. "This is everything."

Becker nods, biting his lower lip. "You told me that Julian destroyed *Totem*."

"Well," Grace says, turning to face him, her chin tilted upward, her expression defiant, "I lied." She exhales. "Vanessa gave me the portraits. Years ago, she gave these to me. I've no proof of that, there's nothing in writing. I knew the Fairburn people would contest my claim, so I just kept quiet about them."

Becker nods. "Portraits?" he repeats, indicating the largest painting. "That's not a portrait."

Grace shrugs. "It's me," she says. "Me, with Stuart on the ground."

"Stuart?"

"Marguerite's husband," Grace says. "The man who attacked Vanessa. It's me, with Stuart on the ground, and Vanessa behind us. It's not a formal portrait, I'll grant you, but it's still a picture of me."

THIRTY-SIX

"You're painting again?"

When Grace arrived at the house that evening, Vanessa was in the kitchen, standing at the Aga, dressed in jeans and a man's shirt, spattered with paint. The shirt, one of five or six Vanessa worked in, had always been oversized, but now it drowned her. Grace's heart twitched in her chest: Vanessa looked like a child playing dress-up.

"Yes!" Vanessa said, turning to her with a smile. "I am." She looked ghastly, her eyes sunken, lips drawing back from her teeth, her skin pallid, green-tinged. She was only back on Eris a few days after six weeks in Glasgow for her latest course of chemotherapy.

"I hope you're not tiring yourself out," Grace said.

Vanessa shrugged. "I feel fine, Gracie," she said, opening her arms. Grace accepted the lie and the embrace, though she winced as she felt the sharp wings of Vanessa's scapulae protruding through her shirt. Vanessa placed her head gently on Grace's shoulder. "I've missed you," she murmured. Then she pulled away. "I don't have the strength to work with clay, but I can draw and I can paint. I want to paint."

"Just so long as you're allowing yourself enough rest."

Vanessa nodded vigorously. "It's good for me—you know how uncivilized I become if I don't work." She winked. "I've actually made a start on something big, something quite ambitious." She gave a sly little grin, and Grace raised her eyebrows. "No, you can't see it," she said. She stepped forward, brushing her chapped lips quickly against Grace's cheek. "It'll be a while yet, at least a few weeks."

Eighteen months later, she took Grace up to the studio to see it. Painting had been delayed by a bout of flu that became pneumonia, by a sprained ankle that prevented her from getting up to the studio, and mostly by her mood, which swung wildly between reckless optimism and abject despair.

It was morning. They walked up the hill from the house together, taking their time, Grace enjoying Vanessa's mood, the excitement that vibrated off her at times like this, when something was completed and ready to show.

As they arrived at the crest of the hill, Vanessa reached for Grace's hand. She was breathing heavily, a faint whistle in her chest.

"Are you all right, Vee?" Grace asked. Vanessa nodded and smiled, and as one they walked into the studio.

When Grace saw the canvas on the easel, she inhaled sharply, dropping Vanessa's hand as though scalded; she saw at once what it was. In the archway in the center, she saw herself, kneeling on the ground, the cutter between her hands, intent on the task at hand. And she saw him, fighting her, his arm reaching up as he tried to fend her off. And she saw the figure behind her, standing in the doorway, watching.

"It's you," Vanessa said. Grace looked at her, aghast, shame burning through her, but Vanessa was smiling. "It's *us*. You and me and him. Don't you like it?" Her voice was light and thin, like the mewling of a kitten. She was nervous.

Grace took a step closer to the canvas, tears stinging her eyes, the image blurring in front of her. She realized in that moment that Vanessa *had* seen her that day, she had seen her for what she was, and more than that, she had understood. She loved her still. All this time, she'd been so afraid that Vanessa might see the scales beneath her skin and reject her as a monster, but instead, Vanessa saw the scales and loved her more.

"We could have killed him," Vanessa said languorously, "couldn't we? I think about that now, I think about it often. We could have killed him, we could have cut him into pieces and put him into the kiln, we could have fired him, and no one would have known."

She reached for Grace's hand again, and Grace understood now that not only did Vanessa love her, but that as different as they were, as essentially opposed in so many ways, in this they were kindred. "Sometimes," Vanessa said, "I dream about raking through ashes, raking through ashes and finding bones."

At last, Grace spoke. "If you're having nightmares," she said, her voice husky with tears, "we can get you something for that. To help you sleep."

Vanessa laughed softly. "Always so practical," she said, "my Grace. My Grace." She lifted Grace's hand to her lips and kissed the tips of her fingers, one by one. "Do you want to know what I called it?" she asked, pulling Grace toward her. Together they walked around to the back of the canvas so that Grace could see, written on the back of the frame, *Love*.

THIRTY-SEVEN

When he looks at the black painting, at *Love*, a second time, Becker sees *Judith Slaying Holofernes*. The reds are those of Holofernes's cloak, of his arterial blood. The gold is Judith's dress. One woman working, the other watching on, the brute dying. Only *this* brute didn't die. Did he?

"I won't give it up," Grace says. Her face, usually so soft, has in this dusky light taken on an obdurate cast. "I won't give any of them up. These are all that remains to me of our life together."

Becker turns away from her, hands on hips, and sighs in frustration. He looks at the painting, at the figures on the floor, locked in mortal combat and swathed in darkness, and he feels exhausted, exhausted and sad. The past couple of weeks have been draining: Helena in the hospital, that horrible scene with Emmeline, the long drive, Helena's missent message, the walk on the beach against the wind, the screaming gull, and this—Grace's lies, her obfuscation, her desperation—all of it has worn his nerves gossamer thin.

"It wasn't perfect," Grace says quietly, looking at the picture, "but it *was* a life. What Vanessa and I shared was as rich and textured as any love affair, and you can try all you like to reduce it to nothing—"

"I have been trying to help you!" Becker shouts. Grace starts, but only slightly. She holds her ground. "If you had told me about these *gifts* when I first came here, we might have been able to avoid a serious conflict, I might have been able to talk Sebastian out of getting the lawyers involved, but *now*?" He shakes his head. "You've made your bed, Grace. He will come after you for these, and for all of Vanessa's papers, even the private ones, and there will be nothing I can do to stop him."

Grace juts out her chin. "Fine," she says. "But you can tell him from me, I'll do what I can to make it unpleasant for him, for his mother, too. I could make life difficult for that family if I put my mind to it."

Becker shakes his head again; he starts to walk away from her, into the hallway, toward the living room. "Is there anything else I need to know about," he asks wearily, "before I go back to Fairburn? Any other *gifts*?"

"Are you accusing me of lying?" Grace snarls, and Becker laughs. He starts to move away again but has barely taken a step when he feels her hand on his forearm, gripping it painfully. "Don't you dare!" she exclaims, tightening her grip further still, quivering with rage. "Don't you dare mock me!"

"*Grace.*" Sometimes talking to her is like dealing with a child. "I'm not mocking you. But you admitted lying to me just a moment ago, so you can't be angry when I don't take you at your word."

Reluctantly, she releases her grasp. "I *was* her totem," she says, her voice faltering, filling with tears. "Without me, everything went wrong. That man, Stuart Cummins, he would have killed her. Julian would have wrecked her life; he would have dragged her into his mire of debts and debauchery. He did his best! And when he went missing, who was here for her? Frances? Douglas? Not a chance! It was *me*. I saved her, protected her, cared for her, risked everything for her—my license, my *freedom*! You can try to write me out of her story, but you won't succeed. I will always be a part of it. There are things I know about Vanessa that you will never understand. You have no claim over her! She was mine."

THIRTY-EIGHT

The storm has hit early; Grace said it wasn't due until Sunday night or the early hours of Monday morning, and yet here he is on Saturday evening and rain is stinging the windowpanes like pebbles flung against glass. The wind is savage; it screams in the trees. All the way across the bay Becker can hear the waves smashing against the harbor wall; it sounds like a bombardment.

Grace has locked herself in Vanessa's bedroom with the paintings. Becker tries, briefly, to reason with her, but she refuses to engage, and after a few minutes he can hear her talking to someone else on the phone. A lawyer, perhaps?

He slinks off, back to the kitchen, where he fills a glass with water and checks the tide timetable on the wall. He should be able to cross by around 10:30, although if the weather gets any worse, who knows? Could he be trapped here all night? The idea fills him with dread.

He sips his water; it tastes faintly brackish. Perhaps it is just the salt on his lips, but he suddenly craves something sweet. He makes tea, spooning a generous mound of crumbly brown sugar into the cup. He finds biscuits in a jar on the counter and helps himself to one of those, too, and walks over to the window. The darkness is complete—he cannot make out any light across the bay—but the sea sounds wild; even at this distance he can hear the ferocious boom of waves hitting the harbor wall.

You can't always see what's right in front of you.

Or who is right in front of you. He's thinking of Sebastian, of his disarming smile. *How's our girl?* Our girl. Could Emmeline be right? Has he been so blinded by love, or by guilt over the way that he and Helena got together, that he didn't see what was playing out in front of him? Perhaps he's been reading Sebastian wrong all along. When he looked at him, he saw stoicism, that stiff upper lip, but maybe what he was really seeing was a smooth operator playing a long game?

But what about Helena? Surely he couldn't have misread *her*? He feels his heart rate pitch up again and he checks his phone; he has no missed calls and no messages. For a few moments, he argues with himself, and then he calls her; he listens to the phone ring, the knot in his gut tightening with each beep. He tortures himself for a full minute before ending the call.

He is gasping for a cigarette. He rolls one and then a second—just in case—and makes his way through the kitchen, noticing as he does the key to the padlock on the studio door hanging on the hook next to the kitchen door. He slips it into his pocket with his lighter. Outside, he huddles in the corner of the courtyard to light his cigarette, but even in what is probably the most protected spot on the island, the wind proves too strong and he gives up. He crosses the courtyard, head down and shoulders raised against the wind, and walks up the hill to the studio.

Almost everything has been cleared, though there remain a couple of small boxes on the trestle table and, right at the back of the room, a little whittling knife on a shelf. He slips the knife into his pocket and picks up the boxes to take down to the house. He's rather hoping Grace will see him, that she'll come out to remonstrate with him—right now, he'd relish a confrontation. And it's not like she could prevent him taking anything, she couldn't physically stop him, could she? Although his forearm is still smarting where she grabbed hold of him earlier—for a woman clearly not in peak physical condition, she has a surprisingly strong grip.

Back in the house, he places the boxes on the kitchen table and pauses a moment, listening for any activity. He hears nothing over the sound of the wind and the gulls, and the ominous rumble-and-crash of waves hitting the rocks below the house. He takes out his phone and tries Helena again, but the Wi-Fi no longer seems to be working—perhaps the storm has knocked it out? It hardly matters, he tells himself, he'll be on the road within a few hours. An optimistic forecast, given the state of the weather, but what can he do now but act? He must be decisive. He will pack up the car so he's ready to leave as soon as it's safe to cross. It's still parked down at the bottom of the track, so he'll need to bring it up—he doesn't want to be negotiating the stairs while carrying heavy boxes in this weather. He thrusts his hands deep into his coat pockets.

Where did he leave the car key?

THIRTY-NINE

The storm has hit exactly on schedule.

Grace fudged the timings a bit, because she knew he wouldn't want to be stuck here in bad weather, but she wanted him here for the storm, she wanted him to see Eris Island at its most elemental, its most exhilarating: gales hurling rain and sea spray at the windows, wind tearing at the trees, the whole house moaning as it clings to its rock.

She'd imagined them seeing it through together—bonds are forged when you spend the night with someone during a storm. Unfortunately, it isn't to be.

It was a mistake to let him see the paintings. She has wanted to show them to him for a while, because they demonstrate so clearly the depth of her connection to Vanessa. They are evidence—indisputable evidence—that she is no minor character, no bit part in Vanessa's story, that it is only through her that it is truly possible to understand who Vanessa was.

But she should have laid the groundwork better; she ought to have prepared him for the fact that she'd held some pieces back. In the end, she was overtaken by events—she couldn't have foreseen the bird, she couldn't have imagined Becker would go rushing into Vanessa's bedroom like that.

Now, she moves to the bedroom door and presses her cheek against it. The house is moving, creaking and groaning as it resists the wind, but she can hear him, too, moving around in the next room. She glances over to the bedside table where his car key is in the drawer: she took it from his jacket pocket when she took the gull-sullied sheet through to the kitchen to put it into the washing machine. She realized at once there would be a chance of a row once he'd seen the paintings, and she didn't want to give him the option of leaving with things unresolved. Now, having made the phone call she needed to make, she disconnects the router.

She turns off the light and climbs into Vanessa's bed; she crawls under the cover and pulls it up to her chin. She luxuriates in the thrilling sound of the coming storm, in the comfort of knowing that she is safe and warm and dry and *not alone.*

In the darkness, she can make out the pale lines of her own body in *Totem,* she can see the shape of her shoulders, her cradling hand. Whatever happened to that little bird? She hasn't seen it in such a long time. In the storeroom, perhaps?

When Vanessa painted *Totem,* she had been going through a carving phase: whittling wood, trying her hand at stone, too. You could hear it from the house, the noise of the hammer singing as it struck the chisel, regular as a bell.

It's possible the little bird is in the living room somewhere, in one of the cupboards—they're full of all sorts of things, maquettes and shells and stones from the beach, whittled spoons and trinkets Vanessa collected from all over the place.

A bird in the hand is a good thing, a bird in the house not so much. It foretells a death, doesn't it? Isn't that what they say? Whoever *they* are, the weak-minded, those gripped by superstition.

It's unsettling, though, that's for sure, a wild thing trapped in a domestic space. Impressive, too, the ferocity with which an animal will struggle, the violence of the urge to escape, to *live.* When they are desperate, people are like that, too.

FORTY

It had been raining for weeks, but that morning, the sun shone.

Grace was sitting in the kitchen, reading the newspaper over breakfast, when Vanessa appeared, shyly smiling. Her face was flushed, and her fingers trembled a little as she took Grace's hand. "I have something to show you," she said.

Up at the studio, leaning against the wall, was the picture, the portrait of Grace holding the wooden bird. Vanessa had been working on it ever since the rain started.

"I call it *Totem*," Vanessa said. She paused for a moment, then inhaled quickly. "Well, what do you think? Do you like it?"

Grace swallowed. She was embarrassed to find herself moved to tears. "I do," she said. She coughed to clear the lump in her throat. "I really do." She was not beautiful in the portrait—she could never be that—but she was majestic. Sitting at their kitchen table, she had pushed her chair back a little so that you could see that she was holding, in her lap, a carving. The wall behind her was the yellow of old paper, the afternoon light soft and warm. In her faded blue shirt, Grace looked a nobler and more relaxed figure than she ever could have imagined herself. Vanessa slipped her arms around Grace's waist and squeezed. "I'm so pleased. I'm so happy with how it's turned out, but I know what it's like to sit for a portrait and expect one thing and then to be confronted with it . . . it's never an uncomplicated sensation." She squeezed again. "Grace . . . are you crying? You are! Oh, *Grace*."

There had been something between them lately, an awkwardness, unspoken; they both knew where it came from, but both had been ignoring it. "You don't mind, do you," Vanessa said, "not coming to opening night? I *would* like to have you there, it's just . . . we belong to different worlds, you and I, don't we? And those things are always so stressful, I never feel myself, I'm so nervous, and I'll have to be pressing flesh and . . . *selling*, and you won't know anyone, and I won't be able to look after you. I worry you won't enjoy yourself—"

"I don't mind," Grace said quickly, though she did. She'd not told Vanessa that, although she'd grown to suspect she might not be invited, she had already picked out an outfit to wear; she'd been pricing rooms at three-star hotels, thinking about where they might eat before the show. "I understand completely. I'll come the week after the opening, and then we can relax and enjoy ourselves, have dinner somewhere nice." She fell silent a moment, swallowing her disappointment, tamping it down, determined that it would not ruin this moment between them. "It's so *odd*," she said finally, "to think that this will be hanging there in a fancy gallery, and people will be looking at it, and then someone will buy it and take it home. Me! On the wall!"

"Very fine you'll look, too," Vanessa said, beaming. She let go of Grace and took a step back to admire the painting from slightly further away. "I mean, I would *love* to keep it, I'd love to hang it in the house. I'd love to give it to you, but I'm afraid we need the money." She laughed. "You know what? Although I can't give you the portrait, I can give you . . . this." She reached behind her and from the trestle table seized the little wooden bird, holding it out in front of her like an offering.

"Oh, *well*," Grace said, her smile teasing. "I am honored." She took the bird in her hands and held it to her breast. "All this makes me feel *very* important." Her face flushed. "It connects us, doesn't it? You and I? We're linked by it."

"We are," Vanessa said, taking Grace's hand again. "No matter what happens, there will always be this, the moment I put the brush to the canvas and painted you. Always."

The next day, Julian arrived.

———————

THE FOLLOWING WEEK, on the Thursday, after Vanessa's argument with Julian, after she drove drunk through the village and argued with Grace, too, Vanessa left Grace's home in the village early to get back to Eris, to pick up the smaller paintings and drive down to Glasgow. That same day, Grace arrived to a full waiting room at the surgery. There was a bug going around, and half the kids in the village seemed to be off school with it, so it wasn't until around 2:30 that she finally managed to take her lunch break. She escaped, as usual, to her bench overlooking the harbor and it was from there that she saw Julian Chapman's little red sports car come haring over the causeway, throwing spray high into the air. The car came racing up the hill and accelerated through the village, and Grace thought, *Oh, thank God, he's gone.*

As soon as she finished work that evening, she drove across to the island.

She took a pair of dishwashing gloves and some cleaning products from beneath the kitchen sink and set about scouring the place, removing all traces of him. She worked methodically through the house, from the kitchen, which was in a foul state—dirty plates and glasses everywhere, ashtrays overflowing on to the counter, pans encrusted with dried-on food—to the living room and the bathroom, and finally into Vanessa's room. She stripped the bed, shuddering with disgust as she retrieved a used condom from between the sheets. She loaded the washing machine and was remaking the bed with fresh linens when she spotted Vanessa's note, which had fallen down between the bed and the nightstand.

J, we can't keep going round and round and round!

I'm going to be back on the weekend and you <u>must</u> be gone. There's no more money in the pot.

We have loved each other and we have hated each other and now we can be free of each other.

Isn't that wonderful?

You must find your own way.

Love,

Nessa

Grace could feel herself beaming as she read it. *Now we can be free of each other.* Hallelujah! She wanted to punch the air. He was banished. Gone! Out of Vanessa's life, out of her own. Out of their life together.

On the little stool in front of Vanessa's dressing table, Grace spotted a black wallet. She picked it up and looked through it: four credit cards (no wonder the man was in debt), fifty pounds in cash, and a photograph of Julian with a woman who was not Vanessa. Celia Gray, perhaps? Julian looked very happy in the picture. Grace slipped the wallet into the drawer, making a note to herself to tell Vanessa to send it back to him on her return, but then she changed her mind. *Sod him,* she thought. She retrieved the wallet from the drawer, pocketed the cash, walked across the room, and flung the wallet clean out of the window, into the sea.

It must have been around eight o'clock when she finally finished cleaning the house. She took the padlock key from the hook in the kitchen and strolled up the hill to the studio. It was a glorious evening, peach clouds scudding over a pale sky, the coconutty scent of gorse in the air. When she got to the door, she saw that there was a note there, too, tucked into the arch of the padlock. She extracted it, slipping it into her pocket with the cash while she unlocked and rolled back the door to allow the soft evening light into the studio.

Everything was in order here. Against the south wall stood a number of large canvases while the ceramic pieces destined for the show were ranged on the trestle table in the center of the room, along with a giant roll of Bubble Wrap and two rolls of tape, ready for packing.

Grace took the note from her pocket.

OK, Nessa, you win. I'll leave you be.

But I worry about you, locking yourself away up here. The work you are doing is beautiful, but so are you.

Eris is a wonderful retreat—don't make it your whole world. Come back to the land of the living! You can't hide away here forever, knocking around with dreary old butterball—you'll go mad.

I meant what I said about Morocco. Izzy is taking a riad in Marrakech in October/November—there will be loads of room and I won't bother you (unless you ask nicely).

No one will bother you! You can work, play, go out into the desert, look at the stars.

Paint the stars.

Think about it.

See you on opening night!

All my love, always,

J

Before she even knew what she was doing, Grace's hand had closed around the sinuous, flared-lip vase closest to her right hip, and an instant later it was flying through the air, hitting the wall with a satisfying crash. The sound of fine porcelain tinkling to the floor was like music.

Opening night? *Julian* was going to *opening night*? While she was told to stay at home, because she wouldn't enjoy herself, because Vanessa couldn't *look after* her?

And *Morocco*? With *Izzy*? That would happen over Grace's dead body. A shallow bowl, perfectly weighted and glazed in icy blue, went flying.

"What the fuck are you doing?"

Grace yelped in fright and spun around, knocking her hip against the table as she did, sending another piece crashing to the ground.

Julian was standing in the doorway, arms folded across his chest, lip curling. "Butterball? What *are* you up to?"

GRACE FELT THE earth tilt beneath her feet. "What are you doing here?" She took a couple of steps toward him. "Vanessa told you to leave."

"I know, and I did. Got all the way down to Fort Augustus, popped into the petrol station, and realized I'd left my wallet behind. I had enough cash to fill up the car, but my phone was out of juice and I worked out that by the time I got back, the tide would be in. This fucking place!" He grinned at her. "I don't know how you stand it. I had a snooze in the car and then I drove all the way back up here. Have you seen it?" He walked toward her, squatting down to retrieve a saucer-size disc of porcelain from the floor. "My wallet?"

"No," Grace said, "and I've cleaned the house, so you must have left it somewhere else."

Julian placed the piece of porcelain on the table. "I don't think so," he said softly. He took another step closer and reached out, taking hold of Grace's arm, looping his fingers around her right wrist. She tried to pull away, but he tightened his grasp. "So, what's going on, Butterball? Why are you up here smashing Nessa's things?"

Grace's heart beat painfully hard. She struggled to pull away from him, but he held on. "I wasn't smashing anything, it was an accident, you *saw* that, you startled me and I knocked against the table—"

"*That* might have been an accident," Julian said, wrapping his whole hand around her wrist now, squeezing tightly, "but the first time wasn't. Or"—he looked around, at the shards on the floor—"or was that actually the *second* time? Christ, how many pieces have you broken?"

Grace was starting to panic; she could feel darkness closing in at the edge of her vision, as though she were entering a tunnel. "I didn't mean to . . ." She thought she might cry, and the thought appalled her. She would not be able to bear the humiliation of breaking down in front of him.

"What's happening?" Julian's voice was like treacle. "What's caused this little tantrum?" He looked around quizzically until finally his gaze came to rest on the note clutched in Grace's hand. "Oh," he said, "*that*. Poor Grace. Are you feeling left out?" He mocked a pout. "Upset about our holiday plans? Did she tell you she's coming to Venice with me for her birthday? We thought we'd stay at the Cipriani like we did when we were on honeymoon. We might actually try to see a bit of Venice this time. Or we might just stay in the room and fuck."

"She's not going to go away with you," Grace said. "She'd never do that, she . . . Let go of me!"

But still he held on, his grip tight and painful. "Ah, but you see, that's the thing about Nessa. No matter how she tries, she can't deny herself that." He licked his lips, looking at Grace from beneath lowered lids. "She always opens up for me." He laughed, a soft chuckle. "I've got a room for us on opening night, too. So we can celebrate. It's a shame you won't be there. I think she genuinely feels bad about it, but she just couldn't bear it, the thought of you there in some hideous trouser suit, lowering the tone."

Tears ran down Grace's face unchecked. She couldn't stomach it— the heavy scent of his aftershave she'd smelled on Vanessa's sheets, the stink of tobacco on his breath, the mocking twist of his lip—not for a second longer. She wrenched her arm free of his grasp and tried to flee, but her trembling knees buckled and she stumbled against one of the canvases leaning against the wall.

"Careful," Julian said, "don't want to do any more damage." He grinned. "Do you know," he said, "that I sold a painting of hers once without her permission? Has she told you about that? I was short of cash and in a bit of a fix and so I flogged one of her pieces. I got a good price for it, too—but she didn't talk to me for *months*." He turned away, walking slowly toward the studio door. "I can't even begin to think what she's going to do when she finds out what you've been up to. I suspect you might find yourself banished from paradise."

There was a moment, then, when everything stilled. The gulls fell silent and the wind dropped, and Julian stood silhouetted in the door-way, looking out toward a shimmering sea. And then the sun dipped behind a cloud, and the world went into black and white; Grace must have made a sound, a shivering gasp, perhaps, or maybe she trod on a shard of broken pottery as she approached, because Julian turned his head a little, just enough for Grace to see the shock register on his face as she swung the mason's hammer, smashing it into his temple and shattering his skull.

FORTY-ONE

Becker rises before the sun is up. He makes himself a cup of coffee and slips out the front door into a world scrubbed clean. The storm has blown itself out, the air is cold and fresh and tangy with salt. He makes his way over to the wooden bench on the hillside that overlooks the channel and there, for a quiet half hour, he watches the sky above the hills to the east turn from fiery orange to a rich, yolky yellow. When he glances over his shoulder he sees that the sunrise has set the house alight, its glow reflecting in the kitchen windows. Ahead, the tide is high, the channel molten gold. Then slowly, gradually, the color begins to leach away, the clouds mellowing, now pale orange, now primrose, the sky finally settling on a clear and hopeful blue.

His mug is not long empty when he hears the front door open. A few moments later, Grace appears, holding a steaming pot of coffee. She walks across, refills his cup, and sits at his side. "Quite a storm," she says, glancing quickly at him before looking back at the sea. "Did you manage to get much sleep?"

"I slept fine, thank you," he says tersely. Without looking at her, he asks, "I don't suppose you've seen my car key? I couldn't find it last night."

She frowns at him. "No, I don't recall seeing it . . . Might you have dropped it in Vanessa's room during the kerfuffle with the gull? I'll have a look in a minute; perhaps it's under the bed?" He can feel her stealing glances at him as she asks, "I was wondering whether you'd like to walk up to the rock today?"

"There won't be time," Becker says. "I need to pack up the car, I need—"

"Oh." She cuts him off. "Pity. We've a good day for it at last." Becker says nothing and glances at his watch. "It'll be a few hours before you're able to cross," Grace says, "and I'm afraid we've still no internet, but if you wanted to call anyone, you might get a signal up beyond the wood, you usually can . . ."

Becker grits his teeth. He's loath to admit it, but she's right—he can't leave right away, and this might be the last time he comes to Eris for a while. He would really like to be able to take some photographs from a few of the places Vanessa loved to paint. And he would also like to be able to talk to Helena.

He looks at Grace, who is smiling up at him, anxious but hopeful, and for a moment he sees her as he did when he first arrived here—a lonely, frightened old woman. He softens, thinks of the lengths he went to to find that little landscape his mother loved so much—what has Grace really done, in the end, other than cling to all that remains of someone she adored?

"All right," he says. "I would really love to see the view from the rock."

"Wonderful!" Grace says, relief written all over her face. "We can take a bit of a tour, if you like, we can visit the vantage point for *South* and *Darkness* on the way—that's just up on the bluff there." She indicates a point on the southern coast of the island, a little way west of the house. "The views are quite extraordinary."

After more coffee and a couple of slices of toast each, they set off. Their pace is leisurely, as Grace has plenty to point out: here was Vanessa's favorite sunbathing spot, over there Douglas Lennox got into a drunken fistfight with one of Vanessa's old boyfriends, just here you can see in the ground the imprint of some ancient habitation.

It's a steady climb up to the bluff. Beyond a thick bank of gorse is a clearing which looks almost as though it were designed as a painting platform: flat-topped and protected from the wind by the gorse bushes, it gives a near 180-degree view of the sea and the islands to the south of Eris.

Becker reaches the clearing first. Grace is still laboring up the path behind him, so for a couple of minutes he has this hallowed place to himself. He is alone with the screech of the gulls and the waves breaking on the rocks hundreds of feet below, and he feels much as he did when he was surprised by the sight of *Totem* in Vanessa's bedroom the night before: delighted, exhilarated, he is seeing something for the very first time and yet it is so deeply familiar to him it is as though he is returning to a place of childhood. He has never stood here before and yet he has seen the view a hundred times, at sunrise and sunset, in summer and winter, in bright sunshine like today and when the sky lowers over the sea like a threat.

"Don't go too close to the edge," Grace says sharply, as finally she joins him. She is breathing heavily, her face pink with exertion, sweat gleaming on her upper lip. She watches while he takes photographs, saying nothing, though Becker can feel tension radiating from her, her eyes following his every move.

When he has taken photographs from every conceivable angle, they move on, making their way back down from the bluff and to the left, following a path that leads through a shallow culvert flanked on one side by a steep bank and on the other by the wood. "Some of the pines are more than two hundred years old," Grace tells him. "One or two might be three hundred years old, although the very oldest were lost to storms in the nineties."

They have been on this steadily ascending path for ten or fifteen minutes when Becker's phone picks up a signal and starts to buzz, over and over and over—he's missed calls, has messages. He stops and turns, looking back down the hill; Grace has fallen a few hundred yards behind. He takes a deep breath and calls Helena's number, swearing softly in frustration as he connects immediately with her voicemail. He ends the call and dials in to listen to his messages.

The first was left last night. "Beck, darling." Helena sounds anxious, her voice a little shaky. "I really need to talk to you. Can you call me as soon as you get this?"

Blood thudding in his ears, he tries her again, but once again he gets her voicemail—either she's on another call or her phone is switched off.

He listens to the next message, which was left in the early hours of this morning. "Hi." Her voice is small now, and gentle—he's heard her talk to her sister like this, when she's trying to soften a blow or deliver bad news. "I've been trying to get you on WhatsApp but I can't get through and it doesn't look like the message I sent was delivered either, so . . . Look, something happened." Becker's heart seizes. "It's not me or the baby, we're fine. It's Emmeline."

Becker's heart starts beating again. *Emmeline?* "She collapsed, they're not sure what happened, it might have been a stroke or perhaps her heart . . ." He almost feels like cheering. "Sebastian wasn't there when it happened, he was . . . he came over here to talk to me . . ." Not so cheerful now. "We're at the hospital, in Berwick. The whole thing seems to have been caused by a visit from the police. Apparently they just turned up tonight, or last night I suppose it is now, wanting to talk to her about Douglas. They said someone has been making allegations, saying it wasn't Graham Bryant who fired the shot that killed him . . . Seb doesn't think they're taking it seriously but still. Look, please just call, OK? As soon as you can?"

A handful of people at Fairburn know the truth about the day Douglas died, but to Becker's mind there is only one person who would have made the call to the police and she is laboring up the path right in front of him.

I could make life difficult for that family.

"You spoke to the police!" he calls out as she approaches. Grace comes to a halt; she bends at the waist, hands on thighs, trying to catch her breath. "Yesterday," he says. "You called them, didn't you? You said something to them about Emmeline Lennox?"

Grace stands up straight. Her face is flushed, but only from exertion; her expression is pure insolence. "I told you I didn't believe his death was accidental."

"Christ!" Becker yells, hands clenching into fists. "Do you have any idea what you've done?"

Grace squares her shoulders, raises her chin. "I've done what you should have had the guts to," she snaps. "So Douglas was a snake. Does that mean he doesn't deserve justice?"

Becker turns away from her and starts off up the hill, too angry to respond.

"I did you a favor," Grace says, as she follows behind him. "You told me that Emmeline was making life difficult for you and your wife. *Beck*," she pleads, plaintive. His flesh crawls. "We're on the same side, you and I. We want the same things."

He wheels around and, with all the self-control he can muster, says, "I don't think we do. If it's all right with you, I'd really like to carry on alone from here."

HE STOMPS OFF up the hill, fuming, furious at himself more than anyone else. *He* is the one who let slip that Emmeline took that fatal shot, *he* is the one who has taken so much time to realize that Grace's neediness is pathological, that her loneliness has warped the way she sees him, the way she sees them. As if there were a *them*, he thinks queasily, as if they have some sort of relationship.

THE PATH CLIMBS gently at first, and then more steeply, and finally becomes a scramble, so that by the time he clambers on hands and knees onto Eris Rock, he is sweating and out of breath. In front of him is a level expanse of granite that extends just a few yards before shearing away in a dead drop to the Irish Sea. He stands, inhaling a lungful of salty air, and takes a few cautious steps toward the cliff edge. The wind is cold and the sky is perfectly clear; in the middle distance he can make out the shapes of small islands, familiar as old friends, and in the distance the horizon is resolutely defined, as though in ink. He feels his face stretch into a smile and his heart lifts in pure elation, everything forgotten but this, this dizzying view, this glorious place, the place that shaped Vanessa's painting, the place in which she confronted her impossible sea, where she embraced her expressionist self! Stand here and you understand why so many of her sea paintings are so small—a slight woman couldn't carry a large canvas and easel up here, and even if she could, the wind would have taken them, and her with them. So she painted glimpses, moments, dense and vibrant, filled with love and desire and terror.

Becker edges closer to the precipice. Very carefully, he lowers himself so that he is sitting with his feet dangling over the rock. He slips his phone out of his pocket and dials Helena's number again. She answers on the second ring.

"Sorry," she mumbles, her voice full of sleep. "Sorry, have you been calling?"

"It's all right," he says gently. He feels calm now, immediately soothed by the sound of her voice. "Are you OK?"

"I'm fine," she says. "It was just such a shock. I only got back here at four, I've been sleeping. Where are you? Are you on your way back?"

"Not yet," he says with a smile. "I'm sitting on the edge of a cliff, actually, on Eris Rock. Looking out across the sea."

"Oh, wonderful." He can hear the smile in her voice, too. "Don't fall in, will you?"

He laughs. There's a little pause. "So . . . what happened with Emmeline, then? You said she was alone in the house when she was taken ill?"

Another pause. He hears her take a deep breath. "I asked Seb to come over." And another. "I think you know that, don't you?" Becker doesn't reply. "I asked him to come round because I thought it was time I talked to him about our situation."

"What do you mean?"

"It isn't working, Beck."

"*Helena.*" He wants to pitch himself forward, into the sea. "Don't . . . please don't say that—"

"Us living at Fairburn, Beck, *that's* not working. Not you and me. And you see, this is exactly what I mean," she says, rushing on. "You're not sure of me! I want you to be sure of me. I need you to be. And you should be. But you're not, and it's not all that surprising, because he's around all the time, and Emmeline's doing her best to make us all miserable. It was a nice idea, the three of us being all civilized and grown up and *French* about everything, but it's just too hard . . ."

Becker lies back on the rock, squinting up at the sky. The sun is warm on his face; he can taste salt on his lips. "All right," he says. "We'll go."

"We don't have to cut all ties, you can still work at Fairburn. Seb and I agreed that—"

"Seb and you?"

"I wanted us to be able to present you with a united front," she says.

Becker laughs again. "You're such a schemer," he says. He listens to her breath and to the sea, and for a while neither of them speaks.

"Please come home," she says at last. "I need you here. We need you."

HE FEELS LIGHT when he crawls away from the edge of the rock. He feels as though if he jumped up into the air the wind rushing up the cliff would catch him, blow him clean away. A gull swoops overhead, he ducks and laughs, he wishes Helena were here, to see this, to see him, on Vanessa's island, on her sacred rock. He starts to take photographs again, knowing as he does that they won't come close to conveying the majesty of the place, but he persists anyway, taking dozens of pictures before it occurs to him that he never finished listening to all his messages.

He dials into his voicemail again. "Becker? Are you there?" It's Sebastian this time, calling early this morning. He sounds distracted and slightly out of breath. "Yeah, listen . . . I assume Hels has filled you in on all this, but we've had quite the weekend here. Lady Em's in hospital—on the mend, I think, but . . . we had quite a scare. I'm just waiting for the doc now . . . but I thought I'd give you a call, because the lab doing the testing sent an email on Friday—with all the drama yesterday I missed it—I'm going to forward it on to you in a minute, but the headline is that this bone, this rib, it comes from a man, they estimate his age to be late twenties, though there's apparently a window of error on that—seven or eight years or something, so . . . yeah . . ."

There's a pause. Becker can hear Sebastian speaking to someone else in the background, and then he hears something else, something close, and he turns to see Grace, grim-faced, hauling herself up onto the rock. He takes a step back.

On the phone, Sebastian is still talking. "Uh . . . yeah, sorry . . . they can also tell that it isn't an old bone—they haven't done the full range of tests yet, but they can tell from *mineralization*, I think? Something like that anyway, they can tell that the bone hasn't been in the ground for hundreds of years, it's much less than that, possibly less than a decade . . . They're going to do carbon dating, which will give us a more accurate picture of when the person died, and they're also going to extract DNA so they can do a comparison with the sample they have from Chapman's sister. So that's where we are. Look, all in all I would say there's a strong chance we've found Julian Chapman. Things could move pretty quickly from here on in, and if I'm right, this is going to be a very big story. We need to get ready, and we need to do it soon. Give me a call when you can, yeah?"

BECKER PUTS HIS phone back into his pocket. He is standing in the middle of the rock, around three feet from the cliff, five feet from its opposite edge, where Grace now stands, red-faced, panting like a dog. "I couldn't leave you to come up here alone," she says, wiping the sweat from her face with the palms of her hands. "I'd never forgive myself if something happened." What, Becker wonders, could happen? He could slip and fall, he supposes, but what on earth would Grace do about that?

Now, far from being helpful, she is in his way, blocking the only safe route down from the rock. She peers at him intently. "Is everything all right?" she asks. "You're not still angry about Emmeline, are you? I was only thinking of you, you and Helena."

Becker says nothing, but she must read something in his eyes, or perhaps the color has leached from his face, because he sees it dawn on her. She *knows*. "Oh," she says, "the bone, then?"

He nods. "Yes."

"It's not Julian," Grace says right away.

Becker exhales slowly through pursed lips. "It *is*, Grace. They haven't done the DNA testing yet, but they've established that the rib comes from a man, a man who died young, in his twenties or thirties." Just then, he sees something, or thinks he sees something—a flicker of fear crosses her face. "And he didn't die hundreds of years ago; he died in the past few decades." Grace covers her mouth with her hand. "So, it seems pretty likely that it is Julian Chapman."

He steps to one side, gesturing with one arm, miming *excuse me*. "I need to get going," he says. "I need to get back—there's going to be a lot to sort out. As soon as they get a DNA match, the lab will have to tell the police, and the police will inform Chapman's sister, and once that happens . . ." He spreads his palms wide. Who knows?

"It's not Julian," Grace says again. She no longer looks afraid, she looks sad—*resigned* almost. Defeated. "They won't get a match," she says softly. She takes a step toward him, and then another.

Becker shuffles backward. "You can't say that for sure," he says, glancing quickly over his shoulder and taking another step back. She's too close to him, much too close, and she keeps coming.

"I can," she says, and she raises her hands, palms facing toward him. Becker shrinks back—*what is she doing?* He thinks for a moment that she is going to push him, but instead she brings her hands to her lips, pressing her palms together in front of her mouth as though she were praying. "I can say that," she says. "I can say that, you see, because I know where Julian is, and he's not in the wood."

FORTY-TWO

On her hands and knees on the grass outside the studio, Grace leaned toward Julian's body, trying not to look at him as she placed her forefinger and middle finger on the side of his throat to feel for a pulse. His head was completely caved in on the other side, so a pulse wasn't *likely*, but you never knew. You couldn't be too careful.

There was no pulse, and yet, as she crouched there on the grass, she thought she could feel his heartbeat through the earth, feel the blood throbbing out of him, soaking into the soil. She closed her eyes and breathed in the rich ferric smell of it, in and out, in and out, in and out, she breathed, waiting for her own heartbeat to slow.

When she opened her eyes again, when she felt strong enough to get to her feet, she saw that the tide was coming in. It was almost too late to cross over. She allowed herself a moment of relief. No one was coming. No one would catch her with blood on her hands. She had time now, a full six hours, and by that time it would be the middle of the night.

She touched him. She slid her hand down the side of his body and into his trouser pocket. Then she leaned over him and searched the other pocket, her hand closing around his car key. He'd left the sports car at the bottom of the track. She needed to move it as soon as possible.

As she walked down the hill, she felt a moment of elation: the hills opposite were velveted in lush, dark greens, the gorse had been burnished by the sun to a faded gold, the sea was glittering and glorious, and Julian was dead. She wanted to sing, to proclaim her victory to someone, to say, *Look! Look what I have done!*

Just a moment, and then the giddy feeling passed, and she came down to earth, to face the practicality of her situation. She opened his car, recoiling from the heat and cigarette stink, and drove it up the track, parking it on the blind side of the house.

She went inside and washed her hands, splashed cold water on her face, poured herself a glass to drink. She considered her options. The sensible thing would be to wait in the house until nightfall in order to avoid being seen, but she found herself suddenly seized by an irrational fear that the next time she looked up the hill he would be gone, or the next time she looked up at the window, there he would be, his head stoved in and that terrible smile on his face.

So she went back up the hill and sat at his side, where she could keep an eye on him. Where she could watch the clouds turn pink and orange and red until finally all dusk's color bled away, like Julian's blood into the ground beneath her, until the sky was as cool as his skin. In that blue hour, with night encroaching, the sky beginning slowly to fill with stars, Grace wept a little, fearful of what she had done and of what she had still to do.

But once it was properly dark, she shrugged off self-pity and set to work. She intended to drag him down the path and across the hillside, over to the south side of the island, to the bluff. From there, it was a sheer drop to the sea. When they found him—*if* they found him—it would be impossible to tell, she reasoned, that his head injury came from a blow rather than a fall or from being dashed against the rocks by the waves.

But almost as soon as she took hold of his wrists and started pulling his body along the ground, she knew that if she had all night and all of the next day and possibly the day after that, she would never get him up to the bluff. He was a tall man, around six feet, and not slight. After twenty or thirty minutes, she was pouring with sweat and had barely moved him more than a few feet—and that was going *downhill*. She let go of his wrists and collapsed heavily to the ground, crying out in pain as she landed on something hard.

The septic tank.

It took her a while to get it open. For several desperate minutes, she thought she wouldn't be able to shift the lid, a piece of concrete twenty inches square and very heavy. But eventually, after minutes of struggling and swearing, of gagging as she inhaled the fetid stench of the tank's contents, of jamming chisels beneath the lid in order to give her leverage, she managed to tip it upright, resting it against a stone. Under the moonless sky, she walked back up the hill, selected another large stone from the side of the path, and brought it back to wedge beneath the waistband of Julian's trousers to help weigh him down. And then, with an undeniable surge of pleasure, she began maneuvering him, headfirst, into the stinking, filthy mire.

As she moved the concrete lid back into place, she managed to catch her forefinger between the lid and the lip of the opening. Crying out in agony as she tore it free, she staggered to her feet, tears filling her eyes, gripped by the sort of all-consuming rage that came with stress and pain, gripped by the feeling that *she* shouldn't be the one suffering. This was Vanessa's fault, all of it. If she hadn't welcomed him to their island, to their home, into her bed, if she hadn't colluded with him, hadn't promised to go away with him, none of this would have happened.

Blinded by fury, she ran up to the studio, where she grabbed hold of the edge of the table and wrenched it upward, sending the remaining ceramics crashing to the floor. She grabbed a shard of porcelain and sliced through the nearest canvas, through *North*, through *Eris Rock*, through *Winter*; in a frenzy of violence she slashed and ripped and did not stop until she was confronted by her own solemn gaze, by *Totem*.

FORTY-THREE

Becker can feel the wind on his back; he can hear the waves crashing against the rocks at the bottom of the cliff, unnervingly clear. "What do you mean," he asks Grace, "he's not in the wood? Are you saying you know where Julian's body is?" He feels as though Eris Rock is tilting, as though it's about to tip them both into the sea. He steps to one side, but Grace comes with him, mirroring him; she reaches toward him, beseeching. He shifts his weight back again, adrenaline surging through him; he feels dangerously close to the edge, his legs starting to tremble. A blast of wind catches him, throwing him off-balance, and Grace lunges, grabbing hold of his arms, pulling his body toward hers in an awkward embrace. Despite himself, he leans into her, away from danger. "Self-defense," she says, her breath hot against the base of his throat. "It was self-defense."

Still clutching his arms, she starts to tell him what happened: that Vanessa returned from Glasgow to find Julian still on the island. He'd left, just as Grace told the police, but then he came back, there was some story about a wallet. Vanessa and Julian argued, they were up in the studio when it happened, and he lost his temper. The argument became violent, he started smashing things up. "She was just trying to stop him," Grace says. "It wasn't her fault . . ."

This isn't true, Becker thinks. *It doesn't sound true.* In reality, he can barely process what she is saying because all he can think is that he wants to get away from here, off the rock, away from *her*. He pulls his arms from her grasp and takes hold of her shoulders, pushing against her, *hard*. She stumbles backward, mouth open in shock. "What are you doing?" she gasps. Relief courses through him as, at last, he maneuvers his way around her bulk and onto safer ground. "You need to hear this," Grace says sharply, "before you go running back to Fairburn, before you pass judgment on us. You have to understand . . . she was almost catatonic when I found her. Covered in blood, beyond reason. She wouldn't let me call the police. I had to clear up after her. I had to clear up her mess."

SOME OF WHAT she says has the ring of truth, some of it sounds like lies; Becker is having trouble telling one from the other. He hesitates at the top of the path, feeling exhausted, bereft: with every new revelation Vanessa slips away from him, she becomes something different, someone violent, destructive.

"How," he asks, turning back to look at Grace, "how did she—"

"I had to wait," Grace interrupts him, "until the early hours of the morning before I could drive his car across the causeway. There was no moon, and I didn't want to turn the lights on . . . I was terrified I was going to veer off the track onto the sand and get stuck." She looks up at him, animated now, like a child telling a ghost story. "I put my bike in the boot of his car and I drove north—there's a quarry about ten miles from here. The pool is terribly deep, it's very dangerous, you hear all kinds of stories, about children falling in, about suicides. There was a padlock on the gate, but I was expecting that, so I took bolt cutters from the storeroom. I drove off the road, up a bank to the north side of the pool . . . it wasn't difficult, I just had to give the car a push, start it rolling . . ." She blinks slowly. "I was very frightened cycling back. I didn't want to use a light, you see, I didn't want to attract attention to myself . . . Those roads are deathly quiet, especially at night, but still . . . it would only have taken one van, one car going too fast . . . but I made it, eventually, though it was just getting light as I crossed the causeway." She leans closer to him. "By the time the police came asking questions," she says, her voice almost a whisper, "I had an alibi. Marguerite. French onion soup with Marguerite! I knew that if I told her what he was—that he was a bad man, like her husband, like Stuart— she'd understand. I knew she wouldn't betray me."

Becker hugs himself; between the story she's telling and the rising wind, he feels the cold creep into him. "He's in the quarry?" he says. "Is that what you're telling me? Julian's body is in the quarry?"

"Oh, no." Grace shakes her head, frowning at him as though he's an idiot, as though he hasn't been listening to a word she's said. "I couldn't get him all the way down to the car, not on my own, he was much too heavy."

Becker exhales, a short huff. "So then . . . ?"

"I put him in the septic tank."

Sadder and sadder. Vanessa's idyll, her sanctuary, this hallowed place—it is nothing like; it is a place of unhappiness, of horror.

"You . . ." Becker's teeth are starting to chatter. "You—" He breaks off—he can't bring himself to repeat it. *Jesus Christ.* "And Vanessa? Where was Vanessa when this was happening?"

She ignores his question again. "You mustn't tell anyone," she insists, taking hold of his forearm. "Please, promise me you won't tell anyone."

He stares at her, mouth open in disbelief. "All right," he says at last, because what else is there to say? "I promise."

Grace's eyes search his face; he doesn't for a second imagine he's convinced her, but she nods. "Thank you," she says, shuffling past him. "It's cold, isn't it?" She climbs carefully down on to the steepest part of the path, using her hands to steady herself. "I think we should go down now."

BECKER SITS AT the top of the path for a while, waiting for Grace to descend. He watches her walking away toward the wood—back straight, head high—as though nothing terrible, nothing seismic, has just happened. His hands thrust deep into his jacket pockets; he grazes the pad of his thumb back and forth over the blade of Vanessa's whittling knife.

What to do? If he tells the police what Grace has told him, they will send detectives and forensics people, they will drain the tank. Grace will be charged, presumably, with being an accessory, possibly with other crimes, too. And Vanessa will become a killer, will be *known* as a killer.

And if he doesn't tell them? What then?

He calls Helena again, but the phone rings out. She's turned the sound down, probably, gone back to sleep. He leaves her a message. "I'll be leaving soon," he says, checking his watch. "I should be back . . . late afternoon, I think. I'll see you in a few hours. I love you."

He scrambles quickly down and follows the path that Grace took, the most direct route back to the house, through the wood. The wood where Vanessa found that bone, picked clean.

If it isn't Julian's body in the wood, who is it?

Who is the man in the wood?

FORTY-FOUR

Grace's tread is leaden as she descends from the rock. As soon as she arrives on safer ground, she does her best to straighten up, shoulders back, head held high, but she gathers pace, scurrying along the path until gratefully she steps from sunshine into shade.

She has gambled, and she has lost.

She walks through the trees, pulse beating at the base of her throat, her blood dangerously close to the surface of her skin. So fragile, she thinks, it's absurd how fragile we are, how ill-suited to a world as perilous as this one. We should be like wolves, we should be able to hide in the shadows, to run for miles, to tear our prey with our teeth.

We should be able to see in the dark.

Looking back, she realizes that Becker isn't following. Perhaps he took the long way around the wood, perhaps he is still on the rock. Making a phone call? She hoped that his devotion to Vanessa would be enough to keep him quiet, but she fears his sense of civic duty will prevail. He's a good man, after all.

She's a little unsteady on her feet, her legs trembling after all that climbing. She needs to rest. Stepping off the path, she crouches down, leaning against the trunk of one of the trees, allowing her mind to empty. She inhales the earthy green scent of leaf mold, listens to the slow creak of old pines resisting the wind, to birdsong and the quick, frantic rustle of tiny animals in the undergrowth.

There is life here, more life than anywhere else in the wood: this is where the trees were ripped, root and branch, where their trunks lay rotting, feeding the earth. This is where the light gets in. Grace knows this place better than any in the wood, it's the place she returns to, over and over, when trying to make sense of all the things that confound her, when trying to make sense of herself.

At this moment, she would like this cold black earth to split open, to swallow her. How easily she laid all the blame at Vanessa's door! She would never have imagined herself so disloyal, but something about the way Becker was looking at her made it impossible to tell the truth. She couldn't find the words. She's never had to before, she never needed to: she and Vanessa understood each other.

Vanessa knew Grace was responsible for Julian's death, she made that clear in her letter: *You know things you shouldn't*, she wrote, and though it took a while, Grace figured out what she meant—she meant *Morocco*, she meant *Venice*. How could Grace know about those plans? They were made after Grace left the island, when Vanessa and Julian were alone. So it followed: Grace must have spoken to Julian sometime after Vanessa went to Glasgow. In itself, no smoking gun, but enough to make Vanessa wonder or perhaps to confirm a suspicion that had already formed.

This understanding remained, an unspoken thing between them, for the rest of their time together—ugly at first, and painful. But when Vanessa painted *Love*, Grace came to understand that she wasn't angry—or at least she wasn't angry any longer. When Grace looked at *Love*, she knew that Vanessa had forgiven her, because *Love* showed her that Vanessa understood that an act of violence could be an act of devotion, too.

Would Becker understand that, if she told him what really happened? She doubts it. Confession would be cathartic, but Grace knows the feeling of relief wouldn't last. Saying the words out loud is one thing, but then you have to live with them. You leave the house as one person and you return as another; you have to walk through the wood and past the studio where Julian died and over the tank where his body rotted, and you cannot be the person you were before.

SHE HEARS THE sharp crack of a branch snapping, and when she looks around, there he is, walking slowly but steadily toward her.

"How did it happen?" he asks, as soon as he reaches her. "How did Julian die?"

Grace hesitates. Part of her would like so much to tell him, but now's not the time, and try as she might to imagine how Vanessa would have killed him, she can't picture it. "You mustn't think about that," she says. "It's terrible, of course it was terrible, but you mustn't feel sorry for Julian, he wasn't a good man, he wasn't at all like you." She reaches out to place a hand on his arm, but he recoils extravagantly. Déjà vu hits her like a fist to the solar plexus, breathtaking.

Becker forces his way past her. He walks briskly away, through the wood, toward the light, his desire to put physical space between them almost palpable. A wave of disappointment as powerful as grief crashes over her. Her mind is no longer blank, she sees what lies before her.

Grace has gambled, and Becker has lost.

FORTY-FIVE

Where the fuck is his car key? The tide has turned, the water is receding fast, and within the next half hour he will be able to cross, or *would* be able to cross, if only he could find his car key. He has searched the kitchen and the living room; now he is checking behind the paintings in Vanessa's room for the third time.

The front door slams. Grace is back.

Didn't he throw it down on the kitchen table when he came into the house, when they heard that noise? Could she have moved it? He looks around Vanessa's room, his eyes falling on the bedside table. He's about to open the drawer when Grace appears in the doorway.

"It isn't in there," she says sharply. "Is it possible you dropped it on the beach?"

Becker yanks the drawer open, eyeballing her all the while. The drawer is empty. Grace holds his gaze and then turns away; he listens to her footfall as she stomps back to the kitchen. *Christ's sake.* He sits down heavily on Vanessa's bed, head in hands. Maybe he did drop it on the beach? If so, it's long gone, it'll be halfway to Northern Ireland by now. He'll have to walk across the causeway and call someone when he gets to the other side. Maybe Sebastian can send one of the staff with his other key?

He climbs wearily to his feet, crouches down, and checks, *again*, underneath the bed. No key. Definitely no key, but right underneath the bedside table, pushed back against the skirting board, is the Wi-Fi router, and its light is off. It's unplugged.

Someone has unplugged it.

In the pit of his stomach, something flips. On hands and knees he crawls closer and pushes the plug back into the socket, watching as the light flashes orange, orange, orange . . .

"Have you found it?"

He scrabbles quickly to stand and hurries from the room, almost colliding with Grace in the hallway. "Well?"

"No," he says. "No, you must be right, I must have dropped it on the beach."

She nods. "I'll make us a cup of tea," she says, turning back toward the kitchen, "and then we can go and look."

Heart battering his ribs, he waits a moment before following her. "I doubt there's much point," he says, "not after that storm." Grace has her back to him and is filling the kettle. "I don't want tea," he says curtly, and she turns to look at him, expression almost wounded. "I'm going to walk across and call Fairburn," he says. "They can send someone with the spare." Grace nods again. She takes two glasses from the cupboard, filling them from the tap; she takes a sip from one glass and hands him the other. The water is brackish again, brackish and bitter.

Becker's phone, tucked snugly into his inside jacket pocket, vibrates gently, and he allows himself a small smile of victory as he moves toward the door. A crease appears between Grace's brows. "You're not going right now?" she says. "There's still water over the causeway in the middle, you'll get wet."

He turns his back on her. "All right," he says. "I'm going outside to smoke a cigarette."

He retrieves one of the cigarettes he'd made earlier and lights it while walking over toward the bench he sat on that morning. Checking his phone to see if he still has Wi-Fi, he sees that Sebastian has messaged: CALL ME.

The phone rings just once before Sebastian answers. "It's not Julian Chapman."

"Oh-kay," Becker says. His heart is beating oddly fast; he feels lightheaded, as dizzy as he did on the rock. He drops his barely smoked cigarette and puts his boot on it.

"You don't sound very surprised," Sebastian says.

Becker hesitates, perplexed. She was telling the truth. "I . . . I *am* surprised." Grace was telling the truth. "I suppose this is good news," he says.

"Yes," Sebastian says, although he sounds disappointed, his hopes of front-page stories about the museum crushed. "They've found a familial match on the DNA database, some guy who went missing in the nineties, he'd had mental health issues, drug problems. He was last seen in the Lake District." There's a pause. "Did Vanessa ever spend time in the Lake District?"

"I . . . Not that I know of," Becker says. He hears a noise and turns to see Grace coming out of the house, carrying something in her hand. She sees him and stops, raising her other hand to shield her eyes from the sun. He cannot see her expression, but dread courses through him, ice cold. "Is Emmeline all right, Seb? Is she going to be OK?"

"Yeah, I think so. She's stable, in any case. Thank you for asking. I can fill you in on all the details when you get back, but the immediate takeaway from this bone business is that we can no longer display *Division II*. Not as it is, not until we've spoken to the Rileys, but I can't really see them giving us permission."

Becker takes a couple of steps toward the bench; he wants to sit down, he is feeling quite unwell. "Sorry, who? *Who* do we need to speak to?"

"The family," Sebastian says. "The Rileys. The man who went missing, the chap whose rib ended up in this sculpture, his name was Nicholas Riley."

Becker vomits all over his shoes.

FORTY-SIX

CARRACHAN, 1993

Grace was at the surgery in Carrachan—it had been a busy day, there had been a cold snap, it was the start of the flu season. At the end of a grinding shift, just as she was shutting down her computer, getting ready to leave, the practice nurse popped her head around the door. "Dr. Haswell, there's a young man in the waiting room, says he knows you. He says he's not ill, though if you ask me he doesn't look too clever. Nick, from London." *London*, said as though it were an especially virulent STD.

Walking down the hallway from her office to the waiting room, Grace was trying to think whether there could be a different Nick from London, because it couldn't be *her* Nick, could it? How could he be here?

And yet there, sitting in one of the bright yellow molded plastic chairs against the opposite wall, he was. He looked up, but she couldn't meet his eyes; instead she looked down at her feet. Her face was burning; she felt as though she might fall if she took another step.

When she raised her eyes at last, he was on his feet, holding out his arms. "Hi, Grace."

He *did* look ill—scrawny and whey-faced, his pretty face pimpled with spots—but there was still plenty of the Nick she knew a decade earlier: the light in his soft hazel eyes, the deep dimple just to the left side of his mouth. She didn't hug him, but she smiled, and his own grin widened in response, and she felt . . . not *elation*, because that would be less complicated, that would be purer. What she felt was pride, the absence of shame.

That is what the end of loneliness felt like, she thought. It felt like the end of hostilities: with the world, with herself. It felt like the beginning of possibility. The hard edges of her world began to soften, the boundary dividing her from everyone else began to break.

NICK STAYED. HE slept on her couch. He'd be there when she left for work and when she returned, the duvet pulled up to his chin. He rarely ventured out. He was cold, always cold, he couldn't warm up though he'd had her heating turned up high all day long. She made him soup, persuaded him to eat, to wash; eventually to talk.

He was sorry, he said, just showing up like this; he didn't deserve her kindness. He'd been going through a bad patch. He and Audrey had got themselves into trouble—with drugs, then with money. He'd nowhere else to go.

"Where is Audrey now?" Grace asked. "Do you know?"

He shook his head. They'd lived for a time with Audrey's sister in Manchester, but they argued constantly and the sister threw them out. Nick crashed with friends, sleeping on sofas until they tired of him, too. When Audrey got a job at a pub in Kendal, in the Lakes, he followed, but there was someone else on the scene by then, some other guy, so that didn't work out either.

"I think she's probably back in Manchester. But . . ." He sighed heavily. "I think she's lost to me. I only dabbled with the gear, but Audrey really *invested*. I love her," he said sadly, "but I knew in the end I'd have to make a choice: I could be with her, or I could get clean, and I chose to get clean."

"You always were canny," Grace said.

He shook his head, looked up at her from his nest on the couch. He was so sorry, he said, so sorry for leaving the way they had. It was unfair. It was cruel. He hadn't meant to be cruel at the time, hadn't meant anything at all. Audrey had wanted to go, and he'd just followed her out the door.

"It was a long time ago," Grace said, though when she thought about it, the hurt was just as fresh as if it had happened the day before. "Bygones," she lied, smiling. "Water under the bridge."

She told him he could stay for as long as he liked. It would be just like the old days.

Nick laughed. Oh yeah. Just like that.

Being around Nick awakened in Grace an old longing, though for what exactly she wasn't sure. Friendship, certainly, but more than that, she wanted attention, she wanted *comfort*. She kept thinking about the trip to St. Malo, watching Nick comb tangles out of Audrey's long dark hair after they'd been for a swim. She wanted something like that, but she didn't know how to ask for it; just the thought of asking for it made her cringe with her whole body.

So instead, she took care of him. She worked and cooked and cajoled; Nick barely moved from the couch. She noticed quite early on that if she left money lying around it disappeared; she noticed that the leather jewelry case containing an ancient string of pearls she'd been left by her grandmother was gone, too. And yet he wasn't *using*, she felt sure. She could tell. Surely she'd be able to tell?

He was depressed, though, anyone could see that. He needed to get out more. At the time, Grace was still living in Carrachan, in an ugly little house with a view of the distillery, the air thick with the smell of yeast and vinegar. Nick needed light. He needed fresh air and exercise.

"This weekend," Grace said to him one day, "if the weather holds, we could go out to Eris. It's a tidal island, a bit further south. It's very beautiful. We could take the bus down, go for a walk? You used to love a good hike. It'll be like that time we went to France, do you remember? Just like the old days."

THE WEATHER DIDN'T hold. By Wednesday, the Met Office was predicting storms, an amber warning, winds forecast to reach ninety miles an hour. When the storm hit in the early hours of Friday, it was even worse than feared and Grace thought the gale would rip the roof off. Train services were halted, roads closed. Hundreds of trees were felled along the coast.

But on Sunday, the sun shone. The advice was still not to travel unless necessary, but Grace was desperate to get Nick off the couch and out of the house, so they put on their coats and took the bus to Eris.

As they walked through the harbor car park they saw someone sitting on one of the benches, sobbing as though her heart might break. She was so small they thought at first she was a lost child, but as they started to approach, she looked up and they saw it was a woman, beautiful and bruised. She spat out a word that sounded like a curse.

"Bit *Wicker Man* out here, isn't it?" Nick muttered. He was wearing a matching red scarf and hat he'd borrowed from Grace, and the ensemble made him look childlike, too.

It was cold, the wind brisk, the waves choppy, higher than they would usually have been half an hour after low tide. Eris Island was deserted—no one else fool enough to cross—and miraculously beautiful. The world washed clean, the sea wild, the bracken golden, still sparkling with rain.

They made their way up the track past the derelict farmhouse, slogged up the hill, skirting the wood. "It might be dangerous," Grace said. "Some of the trees might be ready to come down."

Nick was quiet but biddable, shivering in his too-thin coat, pulling the sleeves down over his hands and retracting his head into the collar like a tortoise. "Who owns the house?" he asked as they paused for a moment on the shoulder of the hill, looking back down the slope toward the mainland, their breath clouding the air.

"It's a matter of some dispute," Grace said. "At least that's what the nurse at the surgery told me. The owner died intestate a couple of years back, his kids are arguing over what to do with the place, and all the while the house is left to crumble into ruins."

"Wonder how much they'd take for it?" Nick said, plunging his hands deep into the pockets of his coat. "Be a pretty good place to lie low, wouldn't it?"

"Is that what you're doing?" Grace asked.

Nick shrugged. "It's what I'd like to do. Just . . . live quietly, get my shit together. Somewhere like this?" He smiled at her, and Grace's heart lifted.

At the top, they ate their sandwiches with their legs dangling over the edge of the rock, watching the gulls do battle with the wind, watching the sea hurl itself against the cliff face. When they had finished eating, Nick climbed carefully to his feet and reached for Grace's hand, pulling her up.

"This has been a good day," he said, his hand still holding hers. "Thank you."

It had been a good day, but they'd lingered too long. By the time they started their descent, the sky was already taking on the inky blue of night, and so they took the most direct route, through the wood, hurrying, Grace glancing anxiously at her watch, cursing herself beneath her breath. Bloody idiot.

"Could you give me a lift to the station tomorrow?" Nick asked as they maneuvered their way around a deep pit left where a tree had been uprooted.

Grace stopped abruptly. "To the station?"

"Yeah," Nick said, "if the trains are running, that is. I need to get down to Manchester. I saw . . ." He paused. It was almost dark in the wood, but even in the low light, Grace could see his gaze shift, his eyes sliding from her face, focusing on some point beyond her. "I was thinking I might try to track Audrey down . . . I'd like to try again, just one last time, to sort things out. And I need money, I need to start looking for work."

"But . . ." Grace felt her breath coming suddenly very fast; she dug her nails into the palms of her hands. "What about . . . what you said, about making a choice between being with her and getting clean? What about—"

"I am clean now," Nick said. "I don't need to choose any longer."

"But what about everything you said, about lying low, about the old days—"

"*You* talked about the old days, Grace." Nick sounded exasperated. "And I mean, *lying low*? I was just talking, I was daydreaming, I'm not going to buy a fucking house on an island, am I? I barely have enough money to keep me in milk and bread." He craned his neck to look further over her shoulder. "We should go, we don't want to get stuck here—"

"You could look for work here," Grace said, standing her ground.

Nick laughed grimly. "Here? What the fuck would I do *here*?"

"You could get a job at the hotel," Grace suggested weakly, "or maybe the pub?"

"I know I didn't finish my degree, Grace," Nick muttered, rolling his eyes, "but I was studying medicine. I think I'm probably capable of a *bit* more than bar work."

"Of course you are, I just meant—" She broke off. "You don't really need to work at all, not right away. I'll look after us for a while. We'll hang out, keep each other company. It'll be like the old days."

"Oh, for fuck's sake, Grace," Nick snapped, "we're not students any longer. It's not going to be like the *old days*." He moved to his left to get past her, but she stepped out to block his way and so he pivoted to the right instead, pushing her to one side, but as he strode forward, he trod right on the lip of the hole the tree roots had left and his ankle turned and he fell, yelping in pain, into the pit.

If Grace hadn't been so upset, she might have laughed at him, flailing around in the mud, in the semidarkness, cursing at the top of his voice.

"Are you all right?" she asked when eventually he stopped yelling. She gathered he'd twisted his ankle. "Is it bad?"

"Yes it's fucking bad," he snarled up at her. "Help me, for God's sake, don't just stand there, give me your hand."

He held out a hand to her. Grace looked at it and took a small step backward.

"Oh, *now* you won't help me?" He started scrabbling up the side of the bank, but his old trainers were not suited to the terrain; he kept slipping back, sliding down into the mud. "After weeks of hovering over me, treating me like a child . . . no, a *pet*, something you can *keep* . . . now because I won't stay here playing . . . *happy families* or whatever it is you want, I never could understand, what do you want? A friend? A brother? Do you want me to fuck you?"

Grace put her hands up to her ears, she couldn't bear it, to hear him talk to her like that, but he wouldn't stop, on and on he went; as he dragged himself onto level ground he insulted Grace, her *miserable* little house, this *godforsaken* place, her pathetic, lonely life. She couldn't bear it, she just wanted it to stop, she would do anything to make him stop and so while he knelt at her feet spitting venom, she raised her walking boot and brought it down heavily on his hand. His cry of pain was like a melody.

Shaking with rage, he struggled to his feet. "That was assault, what you just did," he hissed. "Are doctors allowed to go around assaulting people? Or do you think that would get them into trouble?" He cradled his hand, his face twisted in pain, tears streaking through the mud on his face. "You'll pay for that, you ugly bitch, you'll—"

"No, please, please don't say that—I'm *sorry*—" She was horrified by what had happened, by what he had said and what she had done. In her mortification, she reached for him, her mouth open and her eyes wet.

He recoiled in disgust.

Without Grace really understanding what was happening, without *intention*, her gesture of supplication became something else. Her left hand rose up to join her right, and both closed around his neck, her thumbs pressing against the front of his throat.

Grace was smaller than Nick, but he was slight, and he was injured, and she had a butcher's hands.

FORTY-SEVEN

Grace helps Becker onto the sofa. He is confused and embarrassed—he has been sick all over himself. Gently, she coaxes his arms up over his head so that she can remove his jumper and T-shirt to put into the wash.

"There you go," she says, as she lays him back on the couch, propping his head up with a pillow. She pops some cushions behind him and rolls him onto his side, just in case it happens again, and then she covers him with a blanket.

"Wh-wh-wh—" He is shivering; his eyes are wide, their whites luminous in the windowless room.

"I'll get you some water," she says.

Standing at the sink, running the water to get it properly cold, she catches sight of her reflection in the window, disconcertingly doubled, and she flinches.

Grace thinks of herself in a lot of different ways. Like anyone, she could describe herself with any number of adjectives: conscientious, hardworking, loyal, strange, lonely, unhappy, good. She is a doctor, a friend, a carer. She is a killer. She says the word quietly to herself, sounding it out. It sounds absurd, melodramatic. Protector, she thinks. Mercy killer. But kill three, she has heard, and that makes you a serial killer. She almost wants to laugh. It's ridiculous, it's like saying you're a unicorn. Three strikes and you're in.

She picks up a mixing bowl and carries it, with the glass of water, back to the living room, arriving just as Becker retches again. She kneels, placing the mixing bowl on the floor in front of him.

"Don't worry," she says, "it's quite normal. Nausea is a common side effect of morphine." Tears are running down his cheeks.

"I am sorry," she says, touching the side of his face. "I honestly didn't think it would be Nick. I knew he was in the wood, but I was so sure he was safe."

He was buried deep, down in the pit the fallen tree had made. Grace covered him with dirt and branches, with as much debris as she could find. She had no plan, she was sure he'd be found by a dog walker within days, but she was lucky. It was a brutal winter, and the next week there was another storm, worse even than the first. It washed away a section of the causeway and, for a time, Eris became a real island, not just a tidal one. When eventually Grace was able to return to the island in spring, she found that more trees had fallen, completely covering the place where Nick's body lay, and so felt certain that nothing would get to him.

Becker struggles to a sitting position. His head is hanging, his chin almost touching his chest. His breathing is fast and shallow. He wipes tears from his face, wipes a bubble of vomit from his lower lip. He raises his head, looks at Grace, bewildered. He looks like a child with a fever, helpless.

She places her hand on his leg. "When you first came here, when you told me about the bone, I was *convinced* it would be an old one, I was so certain I had nothing to fear. The silly thing is that you're the only person who would make a connection between me and Nick. All because of that photograph! I wasn't sure you'd even remember the name, but you do, don't you?" She looks into his eyes and sees that she is right. She's done the right thing. "It's just bad luck. His parents never knew me, and we are forty years and hundreds of miles removed from our student days."

She sighs, reaching out and pressing the back of her hand against Becker's forehead. He's clammy and cool, his breathing is slow. "Marguerite knows. Marguerite has always known. She was at her window, like always, waiting for her brute, she saw me out there, on the causeway. She asked me about it, that first time I met her in the surgery. *Where did your friend go?* I got such a fright. *You go to the island*, she said, *and you come back alone. Alone, before the sunrise.*" Grace shakes her head. "I was young and so afraid, but in fact it wasn't difficult to persuade her that she was mistaken. She was completely isolated and far from home and very frightened, too—all I needed to do was talk about calling the police, about getting them involved in her own domestic situation, and she would do or say whatever I wanted."

Becker shakes his head; he opens his mouth but no sound comes out. He closes his mouth, closes his eyes, and then he leans forward. With great effort and concentration, he tries to get to his feet. Halfway up, he topples, collapsing backward onto the sofa.

"Come now." Grace places her hands on his shoulders and presses him down. "You're only making yourself feel worse. Here." She adjusts the angle of his body, scooping his legs back up onto the sofa so that he is lying down again. He struggles against her, but weakly, and only for a few moments. "Don't think badly of me," Grace says. "You mustn't think badly of me. I never meant to do it."

"It was an accident?" he asks. His voice is touchingly hopeful.

"Well," Grace says, "no. I don't think I could say *that*."

It's difficult for her to explain, because for so long the moment of the killing has existed outside words, the memory of it elusive as smoke, all but irretrievable. If she did try to recall it—something she rarely allowed herself to do—it seemed dreamlike in its absurdity. It made no sense at all: they were walking, it was a beautiful day, they stood on a hill, they looked at a house, they ate sandwiches, held hands, talked about lying low, starting over. Then it was dark, the wind tearing at the trees, the sea raging, and she was freezing, filthy, frightened. Alone. In between those two states of being there seemed to be nothing at all, no bridge, no causeway.

The tide was out and they were together, the tide came in and he was dead.

Connections between these two situations came to her only rarely and in brief snatches: the sound of his voice, mocking and relentless, the sensation of soft, tender fingers crunched beneath her boot. Such a small thing, that stamp: petulant, ludicrous, *deserved*. Small and momentous at the same time: once done, there was no taking it back; once done, the story wrote itself, the ending was clear: there was no possibility Nick could ever leave the island.

She only understood this much later, when she realized that what she had done had been self-defense. He was threatening her, wasn't he? Didn't he say that he would make her pay? And there was a physical threat, too, wasn't there? He was down the hole and she was on the edge of it, but surely there was menace when he said, *Do you want me to fuck you?*

What choice did she have?

And once it was over, what else could she do but cover him up and leave him there and never speak of it? What good would it have done to turn herself in? No one would have understood. It would have given no comfort to his parents to learn of their son's final moments, though it would have given them closure, and for denying them that, Grace has always been sorry.

But what good does *sorry* do? Who does *sorry* help?

"You have to think of all the good I have done," she says quietly to Becker. "There is so much more on *that* side of the scale."

Becker coughs, shaking his head. "That's not how it works; you can't weigh one life against another."

"You can," Grace insists. "I've helped countless people, I've saved lives. I saved Vanessa's life, Marguerite's, too." She slips the belt from the top of her trousers and loops it around his upper arm; she slips one end through the buckle and pulls it taut. "I killed Julian for her," she says. "I did it to keep her safe." She would like to tell him about the art, too, not because she is proud but because she wants to confess to *some-one*. After all, Vanessa's forgiveness was granted without knowing the enormity of what Grace had done, and so if she's honest with herself, it wasn't really forgiveness at all.

Becker starts to struggle again, so she places her forearm across his throat to subdue him. "I'm sorry," she says. "Please don't struggle. Please don't make this harder than it already is." She can see that he doesn't forgive her, he hates her. She presses harder. "It's all right now," she says. "It's all right." He looks so frightened. She doesn't want him to be frightened. She removes her arm, kisses him on the forehead, and slips the needle under his skin. "Rest now. You can stay here with me."

FORTY-EIGHT

The old lady has put arsenic in his tea. Is she going to stuff him?

Becker has stopped crying. He feels so much better. Everything is going to be fine. He'll just sleep for a while, right here, on the sofa.

No, not on the sofa. He's not on the sofa, is he? He's sitting up. The car. He's in the car. His car. Did he walk out to his car? He can't remember walking to the car. He's not sure he's OK to drive. Oh, that's OK, he's not driving. She is. Grace is driving. They're going down the hill, down they go, down down down.

We've missed the tide.

The tide is too high. Grace, the tide is too high.

It's dark now. Or did he just have his eyes shut? No, it's dark.

Where is Grace?

He can't drive, he's in no state to drive. Where is Grace?

Grace is gone.

Grace. Amazing grace, the grace of God. Good graces, bad graces. Grace killed Julian, Grace destroyed Vanessa's work. How did it take him so long to see the light?

He can see a light.

The light at the end of the tunnel?

That's gone now, too.

Oh, there it is.

The lighthouse. It's the lighthouse.

It's cold, his feet are very cold.

His feet are wet.

There is water coming into the car.

There is water coming into the car!

It's OK, it's all right. It's just a nightmare, he remembers now. It's just a nightmare.

It's not a nightmare.

He's been sick again.

He needs to get out of the car. He must get out of the car, he needs to do it now, it's not too deep yet. He'll wade across, it's not that far. It's not too deep. It's not too far.

The water is freezing, it is already up to his thighs. It buffets him one way and then *tears* him the other. He loses his footing almost instantly, he gasps in terror, he struggles to stand, he cries out. Help me. Help me. There is no way he can get to the other side, he has to go back, he has to turn back.

Oh, he's so tired.

The cold is torture, it's like ice, he cannot stand it, he cannot stand it another moment, it is agony.

And then it's not so bad. It's not so bad. It's not so cold now.

He thinks of the black paintings.

No, not those, not Vanessa's black paintings, the originals, Goya's black paintings, hanging in the Prado in Madrid. He visited when he was younger, he was with a girl, he can't remember her name now. Not Helena.

He is the dog, the Drowning Dog, trying to keep his head above water.

Helena. Oh, Helena.

The baby.

He sees the light again, water splashes against his face. If he could get back to the car, if he could just get back to the car, then maybe he'll be all right. His phone! Where is his phone? If he could hear her voice again, just once.

He hears her voice.

She is calling him, a voice is calling his name.

It's the gulls. The gulls are saying his name.

He sees the light again, from the lighthouse, it is strobing, flashing faster now, faster, it is no longer white, now it's blue.

Now it's blue.

Now it's blue.

Vanessa Chapman's diary

I didn't think to stay so long.

I thought it would be a few years, a decade at most. Back then, I thought I had all the time in the world, I thought I had a lifetime. I did, I suppose—it just turns out to be rather a short one.

The Glasgow doc had nothing good to say.

In the car on the way back, I thought about the first time I ever crossed over, the first time I saw the house, the house I'd bought sight unseen. I was so brave then! And so young. For the first time in forever I thought about that clipping that arrived, the one I was sure had been sent by a friend, but which no one ever owned up to. It suddenly came to me— Julian! Of course it was Julian, trying to get rid of me, giving me a gentle shove. He of all people would have known what it was I'd be unable to resist.

Poor Julian, he sealed his own fate.

Grace was out somewhere when I got back to the island, so I went up to the studio and cried and raged alone. I feel so cheated—I wanted to burn the place to the ground.

I never could, of course.

So, a short life. Not always a happy one. But free! I've been free here on my island. I escaped the drudgery of domesticity, the violence of men. I worked with my hands, loved fiercely with my body.

Thank god! Thank god I realized, in the nick of time, that I didn't want to live the life I was expected to, thank god I bolted, thank god I ran.

Thank god for my island, for Eris.

Now that my hope, once violent, is a small and pitiful thing, I need to be practical. I need to consider what happens after I'm gone. Part of me bridles—what does it matter? A life is not a collection of things, after all. What does it matter what we leave behind, since the waves crash on, relentless, oblivious? What does it matter, when one day—probably not too long from now—this island will be under the sea, and the house, too, and the rock and all the bones beneath it?

Somehow, it does. It matters what you leave behind.

The art you made, or the people. The friends you loved. The good you did, the bad.

It matters.

ACKNOWLEDGMENTS

My thanks go to Dr. Tim Clayton, Professor Dame Sue Black, Professor Derek Hamilton, and Professor Turi King for their advice on matters forensic, including the identification and dating of bones. Any errors made on this subject are my own.

I would also like to thank Heather Wilson and Nick Stenhouse at Redbraes Pottery, and Annabel Wightman at Marchmont Creative Spaces, for allowing me to observe them at work.

Thank you to Stuart Cummins, winner of the 2023 Young Lives vs Cancer Good Books auction, for the use of your name.

To my editors, Sarah Adams and Kate Nintzel, thank you for helping me to see the wood for the trees and to sort the bones from the driftwood; to my agents, Lizzy Kremer and Simon Lipskar, thank you both for being the perfect combination of supportive and scheming.

To Ben Jefferies, thank you. (I can't say what for, but IYKYK.)

And thank you to Simon, for your patience, your sense of humor, your great cooking, and your willingness to wear headphones when I'm writing.

ABOUT THE AUTHOR

Paula Hawkins worked as a journalist for fifteen years before she wrote her first novel. Born and brought up in Zimbabwe, Paula moved to London in 1989. She now splits her time between London and Edinburgh.